"I don't need a bodyguard."

"Dammit, Tasha." David held her by the shoulders, peering into her face, trying to force her to believe him. "Somebody is out to get you. I don't know who. I don't know why. But this attack on your car proves it."

She shook free from his grasp. She'd done nothing wrong. She didn't need protection. "I don't need you, David. I don't need anybody."

She dived behind the steering wheel of her car. It took three tries to finally slam her damaged door, and she had the feeling that it wouldn't open ever again. But she didn't care. She just wanted to be gone, to run away and hide from this strange confusion that had settled upon her when she first laid eyes on this sexy, mysterious bodyguard who had appeared out of the blue....

Dear Reader,

Sometime, somewhere, any woman might need protection. And who could be more sexy—or dangerous—than her bodyguard? You're about to meet some of the bodyguards at Protection Enterprises Incorporated. Over the next three months, in three tales by three proven authors, you'll meet women in jeopardy and the strong men who are ready to lay down their lives for them.

This month Cassie Miles brings you *Guarded Moments*, the first book in the MY BODYGUARD series. Sexy bodyguard David Marquis is to die for...but can he protect a woman who doesn't want his help?

I know you'll enjoy *Guarded Moments* and hope you'll look for the upcoming titles: #394 *Shadow Lover* by Carly Bishop and #398 *Protect Me, Love* by Alice Orr. Don't miss the MY BODYGUARD series!

Sincerely,

Debra Matteucci
Senior Editor & Editorial Coordinator
Harlequin Books
300 East 42nd Street
New York, New York 10017

Guarded Moments
Cassie Miles

Harlequin Books

TORONTO • NEW YORK • LONDON
AMSTERDAM • PARIS • SYDNEY • HAMBURG
STOCKHOLM • ATHENS • TOKYO • MILAN
MADRID • WARSAW • BUDAPEST • AUCKLAND

To Lesly Terrance, a woman with the good taste to love beautiful things and the strength to face that which is painful.

ISBN 0-373-22391-9

GUARDED MOMENTS

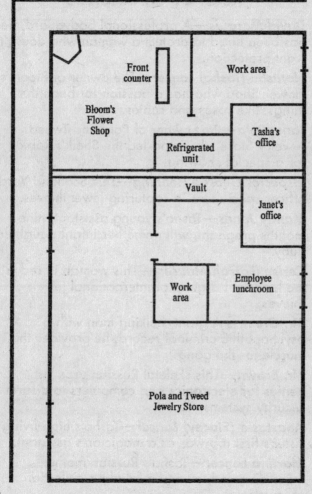

Third Avenue

Bloom's
Flower
Shop

Front
counter

Work area

Refrigerated
unit

Tasha's
office

Vault

Janet's
office

Work
area

Employee
lunchroom

Pola and Tweed
Jewelry Store

CAST OF CHARACTERS

David Marquis—A professional bodyguard, he has been hired to protect a woman who doesn't want protection.

Natasha (Tasha) Lancer—The owner of Bloom's Flower Shop who has a passion for beautiful things, like roses and rubies.

Janet Pola—Part owner of Pola and Tweed Jewelry Store, she imported the Sheik's Rubies for a special showing.

Inspector George Henning—This Scotland Yard officer specializes in capturing jewel thieves.

Mandy Jones—Tasha's young assistant, nine months pregnant, will name her infant daughter Ruby.

Cerise (Farrah Mauser)—This woman in red is the leader of a gang of international jewel thieves.

Mr. Green—A giant, hulking man with a psychopathic criminal record, he provides the muscle for the gang.

Mr. Brown—This skeletal Russian uses his genius for electronics and computers to disarm security systems.

Anastasia (Stacey) Lancer—Tasha's high-living sister's first job was as a magician's assistant.

Martina Lancer—Tasha's Russian mother, twice divorced, owned a fabulous collection of jewels.

Chapter One

Morose and tense, Mr. Green sat outdoors at a corner coffee boutique. He wasn't supposed to hurt Miss Lancer. Those had been his instructions. His job was to frighten her, to threaten her enough that she wouldn't go to the police. He was supposed to bring her to a meeting, and it wasn't the type of appointment that could be arranged with an engraved invitation.

Green sipped at his mid-afternoon dose of French Roast in a cardboard cup and kept a watchful eye on Bloom's of Cherry Creek. The florist shop was in a block of retail stores on the opposite corner from where he sat with the sports section of the *Denver Post* spread out on the wrought-iron table in front of him. The traffic on Third Avenue was steady, halting at every other corner for a four-way stop. The wide sidewalks were busy with a regular flow of pedestrians who patronized this trendy square mile of shops that ranged from a bead store to an herbery to a fine jewelry boutique to the largest bookstore west of the Mississippi, the Tattered Cover.

Too many people. Too much traffic. Everywhere Green looked there were witnesses. The setup couldn't be worse. However, after two days' surveillance, he finally had an idea about how he could abduct his prey.

She'd be hurt, but he didn't see any other way to do it. Besides, he'd always found pain to be useful. If Miss Lancer knew he was serious, she'd be more willing to cooperate.

Green checked his watch when she appeared in the doorway of Bloom's. It was half past three o'clock. Usually at this time of day, she raced down the street to Bagel Bonanza where she grabbed a snack. Today, however, she paused at the intersection. The hairdo seemed messy to him, but he supposed the tendrils that framed her face and clung to her long, slender neck were supposed to be chic. Her overly large brown eyes peered across the street. Was she looking at him?

He pretended to concentrate on the newspaper. Out of the corner of his eye, he watched as she darted across the intersection. She was a small woman, delicate. He could tell by her style and manner that she had a stubborn attitude. In her yellow vinyl miniskirt, black tights and black turtleneck, she looked like a bumblebee. She buzzed right past him and went into the coffee store.

As soon as she was inside, he slid out of the chair, dumped the newspaper in the trash basket and moved around the corner. Green was a huge man. He stood out in a crowd, and he didn't want her to notice him. Not yet, anyway.

Later, Miss Lancer would learn to know him. And to fear his presence.

TASHA LANCER HURRIED back inside Bloom's with two tall, iced herbal teas and honey croissants for herself and her assistant, Mandy. For once, Tasha was glad there were no customers in the store. She had a very important project that needed to be finished in the next hour, and she wasn't entirely pleased with the progress of this dramatic floral arrangement.

Frowning, she set the iced teas on the front counter and stepped back to critically assess her work. "Mandy, take a break, and tell me what's wrong with this thing."

Mandy heaved a long-suffering sigh. Her feet dragged as she maneuvered her protruding belly around the counter. The seventeen-year-old blonde, who always dressed in black, was really much too glum and grumpy to be working in a flower shop. Her sullen expression and black lipstick were suitable only for discussing funeral arrangements.

But Tasha appreciated the spark of artistic talent in this young woman who was unmarried, eight months' pregnant and obviously needed a job. Tasha was willing to take up the slack.

"What do you think?" she asked.

Mandy pounced on the croissants. Lately, her only real enthusiasm centered on food. Mumbling through a mouthful of sweet dough, she said, "It's okay, I guess. I like those waxy red flowers with the yellow spikes that stick up."

"Anthurium," Tasha said. "Hawaiian heart."

"Whatever. They're pretty."

Tasha fretted. Tonight, her arrangements would decorate the shop next door, Pola and Tweed Jewelry. Janet Pola, the owner of the shop, had specially invited her very ritzy clientele to a premier showing of the Sheikh's Rubies, a fabulous necklace and two bracelets that were worth a fortune in gems alone, not to mention the intricate goldwork and the mythic history. There would be an impressive cadre of the local wealthy and elite in attendance, and Tasha wanted to impress these people. She wanted them to realize that her little corner shop that had only been open for six months was capable of providing flowers for high-tone events.

Three of the five designs had been tall but simple. Since the theme was a sheikh's desert tent, Tasha had used papyrus and palm fronds mixed with tall branches of exotic red orchids that would exude a lovely fragrance. Those displays had already been placed in Pola and Tweed amid scarlet draperies to reflect an opulent desert tent motif.

Tasha's other two arrangements also used scarlet ginger and protea. "I love the smaller one," she said to Mandy. "I was so lucky to find that brass Aladdin's lamp at the secondhand store."

"And I was so lucky to have to polish the dumb thing," Mandy muttered.

"Too bad a genie didn't pop out and grant you three wishes."

"Yeah." Mandy polished off her second croissant. "First thing I'd wish for is a million dollars. Then I'd wish this baby was here. Then, for my third wish, I'd want to take a trip to San Francisco."

Tasha didn't bother to point out that the arrival of the baby pretty much canceled out traveling. Though Tasha had dragged the girl to a series of infant care classes, Mandy's approach to pregnancy was not grounded in the reality of dirty diapers and day-care.

"What about you, Tasha? If you had a genie, what would you wish for?"

"I'm really not sure." Her major goals had been fulfilled. After struggling for most of her twenty-seven years, she'd finally set up shop. Because she worked with flowers, she was always surrounded by beauty and fragrance. Her apartment could have been larger, but she was content with two bedrooms and was gradually furnishing the place with objects she loved.

"Come on," Mandy urged. "If you could have anything in the word, Tasha, what would it be?"

"The Sheikh's Rubies."

As soon as the words were spoken, Tasha regretted them. There was absolutely no point in lusting after those gems. They were worth at least two and a half million, far beyond her grasp. But that fabulous necklace and those bracelets had occupied a corner of her imagination from the moment she first heard they were going to be on display next door.

"Strange," Mandy drawled, making the word into two syllables. "You have great jewelry. Why would you want those things? From the photos, they look really old-fashioned."

"The rubies are real." Just thinking about the legendary necklace caused her heart to beat faster. "I can't wait to see them tonight. The center jewel in the necklace is twenty-eight carats. A pigeon's blood ruby with a fire inside. Oh, Mandy, you can't imagine what it's like to hold real gems in your hand. It's mesmerizing. They're almost warm, hot."

Tasha shook her head and cleared her mind. This was a dangerous fantasy. She turned her attention back to the flower arrangement that stood on the countertop before her. The upper section stood more than three feet tall at the tip of the feathery white plumes that contrasted with the fan of spiky fronds painted black as a background for the waxy red anthurium. When this piece was anchored into the container, it would be nearly seven feet tall.

In designing this piece, Tasha had drawn upon the Japanese techniques of *ikebana*, using emptiness and the elegance of space to delight the eye and stir the senses. But she still wasn't satisfied. "What else does this need?"

"I don't know."

"I'll assemble it in the vase so we can get the whole picture." Before handling the arrangement, she pulled on a pair of yellow nylon gloves that matched her mini-skirt. Working with prickles and thorns taught her to be careful, and she tried to protect her hands as much as possible. Though most designers preferred using their bare hands, gloves had become her trademark. In the drawer behind the front counter, she had dozens of gloves in different fabrics and styles.

She glanced at her wristwatch. "It's almost time to take this next door, and it's got to be perfect."

"Are you going to eat your croissant?"

"Help yourself."

Tasha lifted the towering upper piece of the arrangement. The feathery plumes wafted gently as she settled it into the three-foot-tall black lacquered vase. Just as she stepped back to study the effect, the tinkling bell above the door announced the arrival of a customer.

Tasha pivoted. A ready smile touched her lips. It was vitally important to create goodwill with her customers, even when she was preoccupied with creative concerns.

She found herself standing too close to a serious-looking man in a navy sports jacket. They were nearly touching. Yet he didn't back away. Nor did she. His nearness was a challenge, daring her to retreat or to lean closer into an embrace.

Her automatic smile faded. This was not a man who would be easily appeased with a standard offering of politeness. Who was he? A definite presence, she thought, very sexy and compelling. He warmed the air like steam heat, exuding a devastating animal magnetism that attracted her instinctively. If she hadn't been a civilized businesswoman whose life was filled with responsibility, she might have leapt into his arms and whispered, "Take me. I'm yours."

But Tasha had worked hard to cultivate a sophisticated demeanor appropriate to the upscale Cherry Creek area. And she knew better than to fling herself at any man. Forcing herself to speak, she squeaked, "May I help you?"

"I'm here to help you."

Okay, she thought. This had to be a fantastic dream. It was crazy to believe this Adonis had strolled into her shop and was offering to take care of her. "I beg your pardon?"

This guy was *somebody*. He was perfectly groomed, straight out of *GQ*. His dark brown hair fell neatly into place. The cleft in his chin was clean shaven. His gray eyes were steady and cool. His gaze fastened to her face with an unusually intense concentration. Still, he was diffident, neutral and uninvolved. Something in his attitude warned her back—which was probably why she contrarily yearned to be close to him.

He queried, "Are you Natasha Lancer?"

Her voice was breathy. "I'm Tasha Lancer."

"My name is David Marquis. I've been hired to act as your bodyguard for the next two weeks."

"Bodyguard?" She took a step back, giving herself breathing room. This had to be a misunderstanding. "I'm afraid you've come to the wrong place. You're probably wanted next door at Pola and Tweed Jewelry. They've hired several guards to protect the Sheikh's Rubies."

"No," he said. "I'm here for you."

"I don't think so." What was going on here? Was this some kind of practical joke? She didn't need a body-guard!

Tasha tried to convey lack of amusement with a hard-edged glare, but the view of David Marquis was even better from a slight distance. He was average height, but his shoulders were broad. He had the kind of shoulders that begged to be leaned upon, the kind of long, sensi-tive fingers that were made for soothing caresses. Oh, good grief, what was wrong with her? He was just a man. "I don't have time for this."

Mandy teased, "Uh-oh, Tasha, what kind of trouble are you in?"

"I'm not in trouble," she said crisply. She straight-ened her spine, planting her feet firmly. "Obviously, this is a prank. Right, David?"

"No, Tasha." His gray eyes remained cool and calm, as if he were in complete control of the situation.

Who would pull something like this? Tasha didn't have all that many friends outside work. "Somebody put you up to this, didn't they? I know. It was Mrs. McQuaid from the Lutheran Church. She's always trying to fix me up with blind dates."

"I'm a bodyguard," he repeated. "I work for PEI."

"But there's no reason on earth that I would need a bodyguard."

When he reached inside his jacket to retrieve a slim leather wallet, she caught a glimpse of his shoulder hol-ster. Whoever was playing this prank had gone to a lot of trouble to make it look realistic.

He consulted a slim notebook. "You're Natasha Lancer. Nicknamed Tasha. You're the owner of Bloom's Flowers of Cherry Creek. You live at 1266 Columbine, Apartment Eight."

"Yes, but—"

"For the next two weeks, I'll be accompanying you everywhere, twenty-four hours a day. I would appreciate if you could provide me with a schedule, highlighting any unusual travel or events. Where are you parked?"

"Hold it right there." This had gone too far. No matter how gorgeous he was, she wouldn't allow herself to be ordered around by anyone. "This isn't funny. Now, who really sent you?"

"As I said, I work for Protection Enterprises, Incorporated. PEI. Out of New York City." He withdrew a business card from his wallet and held it out to her.

She peeled off her gloves, took the card and studied the engraved script. It looked official. "This doesn't prove a thing. Anybody can print up a business card."

He flipped open his wallet, displaying his New York driver's license. "How about this?" He showed his license to carry a concealed weapon. "And this?"

"I don't get it." She threw up her hands. "I can't believe that you came all the way out to Denver from New York City to act as my bodyguard."

"Believe it or not," he said with a casual shrug that emphasized his strong, masculine shoulders. "You're my assignment for the next two weeks."

His cool gray-eyed gaze scanned the large picture windows that encircled the corner store, allowing natural light to splash through and drench the greenery. "Security in here is going to be tough. It's like living in a glass house."

"You learn not to throw stones...at least, not usually." She confronted him again. "If you really are a bodyguard, who hired you?"

"That information is confidential."

"How very convenient!" Her sarcasm lashed out. "Listen, David, if you're here to watch over me, don't I at least deserve to know who hired you?"

"PEI built its reputation on confidentiality. Most of our clients include names that everyone would recognize. Celebrities. High-ranking politicians. Visiting royalty. Possibly, the person who hired me to protect you is—"

"Impossible!" Now Tasha was sure somebody was pulling her leg. "I don't know anybody famous."

"Sure you do," Mandy put in. "There was that actress from Aspen who came in and bought all those orchids. She's famous."

But she would hardly think of hiring a bodyguard as payment for flowers. The closest that Tasha got to celebrities was accepting their credit cards. She flipped the business card between her fingers. "Who's your boss?"

"Joseph Singleton owns the agency."

Tasha went behind the counter and picked up the telephone. Though it was after four o'clock in Denver, which meant it was after six in New York City, there must be somebody at this number she could talk with. She kept an eye on David as Mandy sidled up to him with her hugely pregnant body and offered him the tail end of the last croissant.

Instead of brushing her off, which was the way most men reacted to poor Mandy, David accepted the crumbling piece of bread. "Thank you very much," he said.

Mandy giggled. Actually giggled! The girl was flirting, and she looked happier than she had in months.

A Brooklyn-accented voice answered the phone. "PEI."

"Yes, I'd like to speak with Joseph Singleton, please."

"He's not available. I'll take a message."

"No," Tasha said firmly. She wanted this matter settled. "Let me talk to someone else, someone in authority."

"It's after business hours. Can I take a message?"

"This is an emergency."

"Please hold."

The "hold" music was a radio station playing rock 'n' roll from the 1960s, an era that Tasha considered as ancient as classical. She stared at the floral sculpture near the door. Golden oldies. The arrangement was almost right. Golden . . . gold.

In a flash, Tasha knew what was missing from her work. Glitter. Sparkle. She envisioned a single strand, a golden thread, weaving amid the stems and spilling across the base in a shimmer of pyrite.

Anxious to complete the work, now that she knew what was missing, she almost hung up the phone.

A cool, deep, female voice came on the line. "This is Delia Marie Barry."

"Natasha Lancer. I'm in Denver, and there's a man here who claims to be my bodyguard. Is this on the level?"

"Yes, it is."

"Who hired him?"

"I can't divulge that information."

Her voice rang with a firm, authoritative note that made Tasha realize argument was futile. "There must be some kind of mistake. I run a flower shop. I'm not rich, not famous, and I don't need a bodyguard."

"Apparently, someone thinks that you do."

"That's nuts! I don't know anybody in New York, and nobody there knows me."

"Actually, we have a great deal of information on you."

"Such as?"

"Your father was Mortimer Lancer. He's deceased. Your mother is Martina Petrosky Lancer, who immigrated to the United States from Mother Russia in 1959. You were born in Denver, spent your early years in a fashionable southeast suburb before your parents divorced. When you were fifteen you ran away from home with—"

"That's enough," Tasha said. Her teen years were too painful to recount, especially when funneled through a disembodied voice from New York City. "If you can't tell me who, at least tell me why? Why would I need a bodyguard?"

"I should think it's obvious, Tasha. You're in danger. Extreme danger. Please accept David's assistance. He's very competent at his job."

Tasha didn't doubt his abilities. She had the distinct impression that David was good at anything he put his hand to. As she watched him with Mandy, she couldn't help being impressed with how quickly he had charmed the moody pregnant girl. "But I don't want somebody following me around."

"Have a pleasant evening, Tasha."

"I'm not paying for this."

"The expense has already been covered."

"What kind of danger?"

"Allow David to do his job, and you may never need to find out."

The phone went dead in her hand, and a chill chased up and down her spine. It was as if the cold hand of fate had grabbed her by the nape of the neck and was shaking her. *Pay attention, Tasha! You're in danger.* But why? There had been times in her life, foolish times, when she'd been threatened. But there was always a reason, not an unnamed peril that intruded on her hard-won security.

She looked over at David again. He was listening to Mandy who bubbled with excitement as she explained the varying species of potted plants, dried flowers and terrariums that decorated the front area of the shop. Though he seemed to be giving her his complete attention, his eyes flicked here and there, seeking out threats.

From what? A vicious philodendron? A homicidal fern? She didn't need a bodyguard, and she intended to send him packing. Just because some woman in New York thought there was danger didn't mean it was true.

Tasha pulled on her gloves and found a roll of shimmering golden thread. Using a small step stool, she completed her decoration of the piece in the lacquered black vase.

"All right, Mandy. We need to take this next door. Along with the other small Aladdin's lamp piece."

David went to the glass front door, stared out at the pedestrian traffic on the street and frowned. "Is there a back entrance?"

"Yes, of course. But we'll go through the front. The rear of the jewelry shop is locked up like Fort Knox." She lifted the upper piece. "If you want to make yourself useful, David, you might carry the vase. It's a little cumbersome and I try not to have Mandy do any lifting."

"Fine." He grasped the lip of the vase with one hand.

"Careful! That thing cost twenty bucks."

"I would have guessed more."

"I ordered it from a potter and did the painting and design myself. Please watch what you're doing."

He gave her a wry smile. "I think I can manage to protect a vase."

"Then maybe I need you, after all. You can body-guard all the crockery in my shop."

"It wouldn't be the first time I've worked with crackpots." David stepped outside and held the door for the two women. He scanned the street. Constant traffic, he thought. Too many people milling about. This was going to be a difficult assignment, especially with Tasha's attitude.

"Aren't you going to lock up?" he asked.

"I turned the catch. The door locks automatically. I've got the keys in my pocket."

"Good." He carried the vase in his left hand, leaving his gun hand free. Though this sun-dappled street with traffic that included minivans, Porsches and even a limo seemed totally safe, he was alert. Danger often came in unexpected surroundings. Just when you thought you were safe, pow! A bullet. An explosion.

A uniformed armed guard held open the door to Pola and Tweed Jewelry, and David felt far more comfortable when they were inside. He set the vase where Tasha instructed, then stepped back, drawing into himself, assuming an unobtrusive position.

There was less need for vigilance here, and so he watched her, trying to get a clue about who or what might be threatening this petite woman who was more spunk than smarts when it came to her own safety.

Never before had David encountered a reaction like hers. His services were usually welcomed. Though clients often bristled at what they considered limitations to their personal freedom, they were glad to have a bodyguard. But Tasha had been angry. After that first instant of vulnerability when she gazed at him with bold, naked curiosity, her defenses shielded her emotions. It was almost as if she resented his presence, and he wondered if she had something to hide.

As she tidied up her floral creation, concentration consumed her. Her slender arms reached up to straighten a leaf. She twisted the stem of a tall, waxy red flower so it showed to greater advantage. Her busy hands in yellow gloves poked and plucked and adjusted the elaborate display. She darted back to study the effect. A slight frown pinched the corners of her mouth as she stared. Her huge, liquid brown eyes fascinated him. There were secrets in those eyes.

When she squatted down to wipe a nearly invisible smudge from the vase, he marveled at how she made such an ungainly posture seem almost balletic. In spite of her funky yellow miniskirt and her goofy short black hair with dangling tendrils that made it look as if she'd groomed with an eggbeater, she looked every inch a lady. Well-bred, he knew from the minimal dossier PEI had provided him with. Tasha's mother claimed to have descended from Russian aristocracy.

Tasha herself was delicate, feminine... David stopped himself before acknowledging his opinion that she was also sexy. In his line of work, it was important to maintain a discreet distance between himself and his clients.

But she was adorable. He would have liked to hold her face in his hands, to plunge into the depths of those incredible dark eyes. He would have liked to touch the blushing softness of her cheek, to feel her slender body moving against him.

David looked away from her. He didn't generally jump from "hello" to desire. Tasha Lancer, he decided, was remarkable.

"Hello, there," said a high-pitched female voice. "And who might you be?"

"I might be David Marquis," he said.

She was a full-bodied woman, dressed in Donna Karan with a tasteful hint of cleavage. Her curly blond-streaked hair was so thoroughly sprayed into place that the tresses didn't move a millimeter when she tossed her head. "I'm Janet Pola. I own this shop."

"Congratulations. This is a beautiful store."

"Well, it's not usually draped in silk, but I was trying to create the effect of a desert sheikh's opulent tent. Does it work?"

"Very nicely."

"Are you Tasha's new beau?"

Before David could reply, Tasha leapt between them. "He's with me," she said. "Everything looks splendid, Janet."

"I'm pleased. And tonight will be a very Cherry Creek event. You've done the flowers. I ordered the wine from that specialty shop on Second Avenue. And catering will be done by Desiree's Deli."

"I'm glad you're supporting the area."

"Makes sense, doesn't it?" Her high-pitched voice rose another octave. "I've always said that the best of the best is here in Cherry Creek."

"Not to mention that we give one another discounts."

"That, too." She turned back toward David. "Be sure to bring your new boyfriend tonight."

"He's not my..." Tasha stopped herself. How was she going to explain that David was a bodyguard? "We'll be here."

"Seven o'clock," she said to David. Her voice was a shrill purr, almost a whine. "Tuxedos are optional."

Tasha hurried David and Mandy back onto the street and returned, once again, to the sanctuary of her own shop. After she twisted the key in the lock, David reached around her to grasp the doorknob.

"What are you doing?" she demanded. At the same time, she was very much aware of how close he was.

"I'll go first," he said. "This is going to be standard procedure, so I suggest you get accustomed to it."

"I never knew that rudeness could be standard procedure."

"If you'll allow me to explain . . ."

"Don't bother." She stalked inside her shop, then whirled around to face him. "This is the last time I'm going to say this, David. I don't need a bodyguard."

"Too late. I've already been hired to protect you."

"I've been taking care of myself since I was fifteen, and I'm doing just fine."

Her temper kicked in, and Tasha fought to control herself. Her sister, Anastasia, had always said that was the big difference between them. Tasha reacted with fire. Stacey was ice.

Tasha could feel the flush in her cheeks, the heat that arose to consume her common sense. "Please leave, David. I don't want a bodyguard."

"Here's what I suggest," he said calmly. "Tomorrow morning, we'll order blinds or shades for the windows here. Tonight, I'll go home with you and secure your apartment. Depending upon the arrangement of the building, we can decide whether or not it's possible for me to keep an eye on you from the hall outside your door."

"What? You'd sleep in the hall?"

"It's best if I can be inside with you, but—"

"In my apartment? No way!"

"I'll check out your car. And, of course, I'll be driving you everywhere."

"Get out!" The fire inside her erupted in a volcanic burst. Who did this guy think he was? "I'm not going to put up with this!"

"Tasha, someone has reason to believe you're in extreme danger. I'm doing my job."

"If you don't leave right now, I'll call a policeman. A real policeman. And I'll slap you with a restraining order."

"PEI will send someone else."

"And I'll get a restraining order against them, too. I'm not going to be pushed around." She yanked off her gloves, flung them into the drawer behind the counter and slammed it. "For the last time, get out!"

"Be reasonable, Tasha. You might not know where the danger is coming from, but it's there. Waiting for you around a dark corner, in the closet in your bedroom, in the back seat of your car. You're vulnerable."

"I'm not!"

"Everybody is. Nobody can go through their entire day looking over their shoulder. That's why they hire me."

"Tasha?" Mandy stepped forward. "Maybe he's right. It's better to be safe."

"Nobody's after me." Tasha tried to reassure the girl who looked at her with worried eyes, and she mentally cursed David for upsetting Mandy. Being seventeen, unmarried and pregnant was hassle enough. "Don't give this a second thought, Mandy. Come on, you know me. Why, I don't have anything worth stealing. There's absolutely no reason I should be in danger."

Except for Stacey. Despite her sister's coolness, she was wild. Sometimes her escapades landed her on the wrong side of the law. But Tasha hadn't even seen her sister in more than five years. The last she heard, Stacey was living in London.

When Tasha patted Mandy's shoulder, the girl flinched. She looked so very young. How could this child be about to give birth? "Don't be concerned," Tasha soothed. "Everything is just fine. Sugar dandy. Couldn't be better."

"What if David is right?"

"He's not." She glared at him. "He's leaving now. Aren't you, David?"

"I'll wait outside."

When the door closed behind him, Tasha said, "I could just slap him for making you nervous. You don't need that kind of stress."

"But I liked him. He was real nice to me."

"I know, Mandy. But—"

"And he likes you."

"Nonsense," Tasha said. But she felt an annoying tingle of pleasure. "Why would you say that?"

"He was watching you. When we were over at the jewelry store. And he had that look in his eyes. You know, like he's starving, and you're a chocolate cake."

"Oh, really?" Her assistant's explanation brought a smile to Tasha's lips. She felt her anger fading as quickly as it had arisen. "The chocolate cake look?"

Mandy stroked her protruding belly. "Believe it, Tasha. I know that look."

"I guess you do. I keep forgetting that you're young and old at the same time. Almost a mother."

"I can't wait for this to be over. I'm starving all the time. I hate being pregnant. I feel like a hippo."

"But you're so beautiful," Tasha said. And she wasn't lying. There were times when Mandy seemed to glow with a special serenity. Sometimes Tasha was almost envious. "You're bursting with life."

"That's me, all right." She treated Tasha to one of her infrequent grins. "Busting out all over."

"Are you sure you won't come to the premier showing tonight at the jewelry store? Might be fun."

"Hanging out with all those snobs? I'd rather sit in poison ivy."

"Would you do me a favor and close up the shop at six? I'd like to leave now and start getting ready."

"Sure."

Tasha ran the figures from the cash register, processed the charge slips and checks and deposited the extra cash in the wall safe in her office. Since there was less than five hundred dollars in cash, she wouldn't bother with a run to the bank tonight. She wanted as much time as possible to get ready for the premier showing of the Sheikh's Rubies. All of these potential customers would be watching her as much as they noted her floral designs. It was important to present herself well.

She bade Mandy goodbye and stepped out onto the street. David was nowhere in sight, and she felt a contrary sense of disappointment. She'd ordered him to leave, after all. She'd threatened him with a restraining order. "Good riddance," she murmured to herself. "I should just forget him."

But she wasn't convinced. It might have been nice to meet him in different circumstances. He was certainly an attractive man, and she'd felt that pull when she first saw him. The only way to describe it was, *Wow! Those eyes! Those shoulders! Wow!*

Obviously, there was something very wrong with her. David was the first man who had truly excited her in a long time, and there he'd stood, offering to stay with her twenty-four hours a day. And what had she done? She'd thrown him out!

Maybe she should have played along. Where was the harm in pretending that she needed a bodyguard?

As always, she'd parked a few blocks away from the store. The most negative aspect of this shopping district was the lack of adequate parking, and she didn't want to take up a precious space near her shop.

Within two blocks, she was on a residential street that was a hundred times more quiet than Third Avenue. The early dusk was pleasant. Another beautiful cloudless day in Colorado. When she stepped into the street to cross toward her car, her mind was a million miles away, thinking of the simple black dress she would wear tonight and mentally trying to decide how to accessorize.

Car keys in hand, she approached the driver's side door. Then she heard the rumble. Her head turned. She saw headlights, though it wasn't dark. A black sedan raced down the street. Moving too fast. Speeding. The car bore down upon her.

She felt herself being lifted, thrown between the hood of her car and the bumper of the car parked in front of her. Tasha didn't scream until she hit the grass. She heard the scrape of metal against metal. Someone was lying on top of her. David!

He flipped her over. "Are you all right?"

"I don't know. I think so." She looked up into his gray eyes. "What happened?"

"Somebody tried to kill you."

Chapter Two

Tasha shoved at David's chest, pushing him away. She sat up, scrambled to her feet. It seemed important to be upright, as if being vertical meant being in control. But once she was standing, she felt dizzy. Was she in shock?

Hurriedly, she patted her thighs and arms, assuring herself that everything was still intact. She seemed to be amazingly unhurt. There wasn't even a rip in her clothing.

Yet, when she looked at David, her vision blurred. The stark awareness of danger pressed around her, smothering her, and she braced herself against the hood of her car so she wouldn't keel over.

"Do you believe me now?" David demanded. His voice was harsh. "You're in danger. Somebody tried to run over you with a car."

He slipped his gun back into the shoulder holster. The gesture was swift and efficient. He fairly bristled with an excess of adrenaline. Tasha half expected to see him race down the street, attempting to overtake the speeding vehicle on foot. But the black sedan had vanished.

"HGB 344," David said. "That was the license plate. I'll bet it was a rental."

"How did you notice all that?"

"It's my job, Tasha. I'm a bodyguard."

When she touched her fingertips to her temples, she realized that her palms hurt from hard contact with the grassy strip beside the street. There was no apparent bruise, no mark of any kind. But her sense of touch was unusually sensitive.

She tucked both hands away, folding her arms beneath her breasts. For a long second, she squeezed her eyes closed, then opened them again. Not injured. She was okay, and she didn't want to seem weak in front of David.

"Listen, David. I'm not trying to be difficult, but I just can't believe that somebody would purposely try to run me down. It's far more likely that this was a random traffic accident. The guy was a careless driver. That's all."

"The guy? Did you get a look at him?"

"Didn't you?" she sniped. "I thought you bodyguards were trained to notice everything."

As soon as she spoke, Tasha regretted her words. She ought to be thanking David. Even if this was only an accident, he had saved her from what might have been a serious injury.

"Come here, Tasha." He summoned her with a brisk wave of his hand. "Come around the car."

Slowly, she obeyed. The trembling in her knees had subsided enough that she could walk.

"Look." He pointed to the driver's side door of her car where there was a huge dent. "That's where you were standing. How can you think this was an accident? The other car was aiming directly at you. He was parked up the street. When he saw you, he pulled out. It *was* a 'he,' wasn't it? I couldn't tell through the tinted windows."

"It was somebody big," she said. "At least, that was my impression. I really couldn't tell if it was a man or a woman. But I know this—it was an accident."

Her denial became more vehement each time she stated the words. She was not in danger. She refused to be. Tasha had worked damn hard to be a responsible, law-abiding citizen. People like her weren't supposed to be threatened. "An accident," she said. "Not on purpose."

"Then why was he waiting? Why did he pull out as soon as you started across the street?"

"Maybe he was drunk. That would explain why he didn't stop. Didn't want to deal with a DUI."

"You are the most stubborn woman I have ever met." David's jaw clenched tight. "Come with me. I'll take you home."

"You don't need to. I think my car is drivable." She struggled with the door for a moment, finally wrenching it open. "It's fine. Only a dent. I don't need for you to hover around watching me."

"What's it going to take to convince you? A bullet in the head?"

"I don't need a bodyguard."

"Dammit, Tasha." He held her by the shoulders, peering into her face, trying to force her to believe him. "Somebody is out to get you. I don't know who. I don't know why. But this attack proves it."

She shook free from his grasp. She wasn't a silly little girl anymore. It had been years since she'd gotten herself into trouble, and she wouldn't allow anyone to treat her like a fool. She'd done nothing wrong. She didn't need protection. "I don't need you, David. I don't need anybody."

She dove behind the steering wheel of her car. It took three tries to finally slam the door, and she had the feeling that it wouldn't open ever again. But she didn't care. She just wanted to be gone, to run away and hide from this strange confusion that had settled upon her when she first laid eyes on David.

Cranking the engine, she pulled away from the curb and left him standing, staring at her exhaust pipe.

Other men had promised to take care of her. Other men had offered their "protection" against the big, cruel world. But they never really meant it. They couldn't be trusted. Tasha had learned that lesson long ago. She'd been taught by her parents. First her father left when he divorced her mother, then he died. And her mother . . .

Tasha had been forced to make it on her own, and the struggle had not been easy. But she was close to having her life arranged exactly the way she wanted—not depending upon anyone but herself. Her flower shop was doing well. Her expenses were covered, and she was making regular payments on her small business loan. She refused to believe that her comfortable life was in jeopardy.

Less than fifteen minutes away from her shop, she parked on the street in front of her four-story, early-American-style, redbrick apartment building. Though dusk had lengthened the shadows, there was still plenty of sunlight. She didn't see anything that looked like a threat in front of the clean, well-kept building. Surely, if someone was after her, they would come here. There were few witnesses on this quiet, residential street with its tall, old, heavy-limbed oak trees and elms. Though many parts of this area called Capitol Hill were run-down, Tasha lived in the center of urban renewal. This neighborhood was relatively safe. Still, she scanned the street, looking for that black sedan. Nothing! There was nothing suspicious at all.

She fought with her car door for a moment before giving up and climbing out the passenger side. Only an accident, she told herself. The driver who hit her car must have been blind drunk. There wasn't any reason for anyone to threaten her.

After picking up her mail in the tiled foyer, she unlocked the main door and climbed the stairs to the second floor. She hesitated for a moment before unlocking her door. What if she was wrong? What if someone was after her? What if they were here, inside her apartment, waiting to grab her?

With a burst of determination, she strode inside and was rewarded with the pleasant air of comfort that she always found in her home. The front room was sparsely furnished with a lovely beige brocade sofa in the Queen Anne style with rosewood trim. An antique coffee table matched perfectly. The artwork decorating the walls included a couple of very good lithographs and an oil that Tasha had done herself when she was in art school. And, there was a rack of drying flowers hanging upside down in the front window.

Tasha left her mail on the refinished library table in her second bedroom and meandered into her bedroom. The puffy white spread and gleaming dark furniture pleased her eye. In here, she kept two bouquets of baby's breath and fragrant jacaranda roses, using whatever colors weren't selling at the shop. Right now, the fully opened blossoms were white, tinged with fragile pink.

She sank down on the bed and remained there, motionless. From outside her window, she heard the harsh cries of migrating Canadian geese. At one time in her life, she'd fled from danger. Only once. Never again. There was no reason for anyone to be after her.

Tasha flexed her hands and lightly rubbed the tips of her sensitive fingers together. *No reason for fear.* With a sigh, she allowed her worries to fly away on the great gray wings of the geese. Rising from the bed, she began to prepare herself for the premier showing of the Sheikh's Rubies.

AT FIFTEEN MINUTES before seven o'clock, Tasha studied her reflection in the full-length oval mirror that stood in her bedroom. She was satisfied with the simple, formfitting black sheath hemmed just above her knees. And she loved the hot pink satin gloves that stretched above her elbow. Her short black hair had pouffed out nicely and the long tendrils at her cheek and neck were held in place with a light mousse. Her lipstick matched the pink of the gloves. She looked pretty good. Except for the jewelry.

She'd planned to wear matching earrings and choker necklace of cubic zirconia, but it was too faux. She was on her way to see the Sheikh's Rubies, a genuine treasure, and it seemed tacky not to wear real gems—precious stones she did not own.

Finally, she opted for a simple gold necklace, earrings and bracelet worn over the gloves. Now, she was ready.

With perfect synchronization, the telephone rang and she answered. "Hello?"

"This is David. If you're ready, I'll pick you up in the back alley."

"What makes you think you're coming to the premier showing?"

"I was invited this afternoon by Ms. Pola herself."

Tasha was so accustomed to attending various events by herself that having a handsome escort might be a charming novelty. But this was David the bodyguard, she reminded herself. She didn't want to encourage him. "Why are you in the alley?"

"You're parked on the street. If anyone followed you home, they'll be watching for you to come out the front door."

"Nobody followed me."

"Are you sure?"

She'd taken a look around after she parked. There hadn't been anybody lurking in the shadows. More emphatically, she said, "I wasn't followed."

"It never hurts to be extra cautious."

Overzealous was what she would call his attitude. Hadn't she told him to back off? Tasha had to wonder at his motivation. Why was he so anxious to protect her?

"I'll be waiting," he said.

"Fine."

She hung up the phone. For all she cared, he could wait in the back alley until her cubic zirconia turned into real diamonds. She didn't intend to be ordered around. Nor did she find David's overly aggressive caring to be reassuring. All this protection was downright suspicious.

Tasha grabbed her black purse, a short black jacket and her car keys, then went down the stairs to the front door. With any luck, she could be gone and at the party before David realized what she was up to. She hurried along the sidewalk as fast as she could in three-inch-high spiked heels.

A gaunt, almost emaciated, man wearing a long, dark trenchcoat blocked her way. He spoke in Russian. "I must apologize for my comrade's clumsiness this afternoon."

Tasha was shocked. First, because she actually recalled enough of her Russian to understand him. Second, because of what he was saying. "Who are you?"

"Call me Mr. Brown. If you come with me for only a few moments, I will explain everything."

"Speak English, for goodness' sake."

He started over in heavily accented English, "If you will please come with me—"

"I heard you the first time," she interrupted.

"You will come. I will explain."

She was almost tempted to go with him and satisfy her curiosity. This man didn't seem to mean her any harm. His manner was reasonable. Then the creases of his face folded into a grotesque death's head smile, and her instincts told her to get away fast.

"I'm in a bit of a hurry," she said. "We could make an appointment for tomorrow, Mr. Brown. Is there a telephone number where I can reach you? Do you have a card?"

"You will come." He withdrew his skeletal hand from his pocket. The corner street lamp shone on the dull pewter of his pistol. "You will come now."

Her heart slammed against her rib cage. Her reaction was equal parts of fear and outrage. How dare he! A man with a gun was accosting her on the street outside her house, in the middle of her quiet neighborhood, and there wasn't much chance of running away from him in these high heels.

Stalling for time, she spoke to him in halting Russian. "Please do not hurt me." She opened her purse. "I will give you all my money."

"I do not want your money." He sneered, an expression that looked much more typical than his smile. "We go now."

Her hand closed around her spray bottle of Opium cologne. In her other hand, she still held the keys to her apartment. Feigning terror, Tasha took a few backward steps, closer to the front door of her apartment building. Still speaking Russian, she said, "I am afraid."

"Silly goose. I will not hurt you if you do as I say."

Another two steps. She was almost to the walk leading back inside. "I cannot move. I am too afraid."

Her arm shot out straight. She sprayed him directly in the eyes with her cologne.

He screamed.

She ran. Damn these shoes. Her steps were wobbly, but she made it into the foyer without wrenching her ankle. Frantically, she opened the interior door with her key, darted inside and yanked it shut as she heard the outer door opening.

Tasha kicked off her shoes, picked them up and sprinted down the hallway to the alley exit. In an instant, she was down the steps and leapt into David's car.

"Go!" she ordered.

Without questioning, he obeyed, jamming into drive and whipping onto Eleventh Avenue without looking in either direction.

Gasping for breath, Tasha sank back in the bucket seat of his car. She couldn't believe what she'd done—attacked an armed man with Opium cologne.

David turned south on York Street. "What happened?"

"You were right." She didn't feel like talking. She'd just had a narrow escape, and her brain wasn't connected with her mouth. "Who knows what would have happened if he'd gotten me in his car."

"Who?" David demanded.

"The Russian." She laced her pink-gloved fingers together. Her palms were still sore from when David threw her to the ground. None of this danger had started until David arrived. Coincidence? Were bodyguards supposed to bring their own danger with them? The only reference she had for him was a New York phone number. "You don't happen to know a Mr. Brown, do you?"

"It's not an uncommon name."

"What about a Mr. Brown who looks like the poster boy for anorexia and speaks Russian?"

"Tasha, are you going to tell me what happened?"

"Maybe." It had been several years since she'd had to survive by her wits, but she remembered the first rule: Trust nobody. Nobody except her sister, Stacey.

David tried again to pry information from her, "Did this Mr. Brown attack you?"

"He had a gun." Saying it out loud seemed to release some of her tension. The knot in her stomach slowly uncurled, and she reached down to put on her shoes. "Damn, I have a run in my panty hose."

He swerved right into the Polo Grounds where the houses were as big as medieval castles, and he parked. "Let me get this straight. You were attacked by a skinny Russian with a gun, and you're worried about your panty hose?"

"Well, I can't go to the premier showing of the Sheikh's Rubies with a run, can I?"

"I assume you got a good look at this guy."

"You bet I did. And he wasn't a pretty sight."

David started the car engine. "We're going to the police station to look at mug shots."

"No, we're not. I'm going to Pola and Tweed."

David weaved through the tangled streets of the gracious Polo Grounds. "Identifying the man who assaulted you is more important than a party."

"Let me explain something to you, David. This isn't just a party. This is my opportunity to meet several of the wealthy elite, the people who live in these mansions, the A list. Hopefully, they'll like the arrangements I did for Janet Pola. If I'm really lucky, they'll like me and want to hire me to do flower arrangements for all their social affairs. This event is hugely important to my business."

"It's best to look at the mug shots when his face is clear in your mind."

The practical side of her brain agreed with him. Tasha was ready to accept the fact that she was in danger and needed to cope with it. But she wasn't going to put her life on hold. "I've got a better idea. Go to my shop."

"Why?" he asked suspiciously.

"In the first place, because I have an extra pair of panty hose there. In the second, I have a sketch pad. I'll draw this guy."

"You can do that?"

"I studied art," she informed him. "That's how I got into flower arranging. And I'm pretty good with portraits."

Though she directed him to the rear parking behind the shops, the small lot was filled with other cars and the caterer's trucks. At the back entrance to Pola and Tweed, there were two armed guards. They found a space just around the corner.

Since Tasha's panty hose were already ruined, she walked barefoot and comfortable along the sidewalk. When David fell into step beside her, she realized that he was wearing a tux. He'd been handsome in a sports jacket. In the tuxedo, he was breathtaking. "Nice suit," she said. "Typical bodyguard clothes?"

"Actually, yes. I need to be able to blend in at all sorts of social occasions, including black tie."

"Sure," she said. As if somebody as outrageously gorgeous as David could ever blend in. That was like saying Arnold Schwarzenegger wouldn't be noticed at a librarian's conference, like saying that an Elvis impersonator blended into an accountant's office.

When she unlocked the rear door to her shop, he again reached around her and grasped the knob. This time, she didn't object when he went first. Almost docile, she followed him inside and turned on the lights beside the door.

She glanced up at him. He really did look great in his tux with the snowy white shirt. "I never did thank you for this afternoon. I could have been hurt."

He gave her a little salute. "Just doing my job."

"Well, thank you."

"You're welcome."

The little shop, heady with the scent of flowers, felt intimate. The most natural thing in the world, Tasha thought, would have been to glide into his embrace, to cling to him and let all her fear and anger drift away. *Let him protect me.* But she still didn't know enough about him. Tasha made it a rule not to grant her trust too easily.

She broke eye contact and turned away from him. "I'm going into my office to change my panty hose."

"I'll be here."

Finally, he thought as he watched the subtle roll of her hips. Finally, she was beginning to accept that she was in danger. Tasha was one stubborn woman. It took a Russian with a gun to convince her, but finally she knew. She needed a bodyguard. She needed him.

Somehow, that fact gratified him more than it should have. David knew better than to become personally involved with his clients, but he'd never been confronted with an assignment like this one. Tasha Lancer appeared to be an average person who didn't have a clue as to why she might be in danger. And yet, she had managed to escape from an armed man. That confrontation had barely ruffled her pretty little feathers. Therefore, he could assume, she wasn't quite as innocent as she pretended to be. She'd been in danger before. From whom? Why?

He really didn't expect her to look him in the eye and tell him what was going on. This lady had secrets.

But he'd find them out. As a trained observer of human nature, with a master's degree in sociology from Yale, David sought answers in inference, not fact. Thus far, he'd only spoken to Mandy, her assistant, who idolized her employer and was appropriately grateful for the job. Tasha had hired her at a decent salary when no one else would. Tasha was more concerned about Mandy's well-being than her own mother who was embarrassed by her daughter's pregnancy.

And what did that say about Tasha? Was she merely a good-hearted person who was willing to help out a teenager in distress? Or did she have a special reason for empathy? Her teen years had been rocky. From the short dossier on her, he knew that she'd run away from home when she was fifteen. She'd been to Europe, returned to Denver. She'd never been arrested. Never married. She had attended art school, off and on, for three years.

She emerged from her office wearing her high heels and carrying a sketch pad and charcoals.

"I'm curious," he said. "How did you manage to escape from the man with the gun?"

"Opium."

"I beg your pardon?"

"Opium cologne. I sprayed it in his face and took off running."

She perched on a stool behind the counter and began to draw. In a few swift strokes, she'd captured the shape of the face. Her hands were quick. Her concentration intense.

Almost obsessive, he thought. When she focused on her creative work, there was nothing else in the world. Would she notice if he reached out and stroked the tendrils that curled at the nape of her long, slender neck? He wondered if she'd hear his words if he whispered in her ear, if she'd look up when he bit the tender lobe.

Her honest concentration appealed greatly to him. But all those secrets warned him away.

In minutes, she completed a detailed sketch of a grotesquely skinny man with thin, black hair pasted across a high forehead. His features included hollow cheeks and sunken eyes. The space between his nostrils and his upper lip was extremely long.

"Height?" David asked.

"Five foot eight or five foot nine."

"Age?"

"That's a tough one. He looked like he'd been ill, like he'd had a hard life. He could have been anywhere between thirty-five and fifty." She cocked her head to one side as she remembered. "But he wasn't dressed like a bum. He had on a long, dark gray trenchcoat. It wasn't stylish, but it was quality. Know what I mean?"

David nodded.

She hopped down from the stool. "Let me wash off my hands, then we can go to the party. Is there anything special I should do? I've never had my own bodyguard before."

"Let's not alert everyone to my occupation. There seems to be a mystery to why someone would be after you, and it might be easier to figure out if they don't know you're under my protection."

"That suits me just fine," she said.

She hadn't been looking forward to explaining why she needed a personal bodyguard. Also, she thought, a bodyguard might scare off potential customers for Bloom's.

At a wall sink beside the refrigerated unit, she rinsed the charcoal off her fingers and dried them carefully with an absorbent paper towel to prevent chafing.

"Tell people that I'm an old boyfriend," David said.

"We'll need more of a cover story than that. Women are curious. They'll want to know who I'm dating." She pulled on her long hot-pink gloves. "Janet Pola was all over you like a spandex leotard this afternoon."

"Let's stick as close to the truth as possible. Say that I'm visiting from New York. My occupation is psychology, private practice in Manhattan. I attended Yale."

"You did?"

His eyebrows raised. "Do you have a problem with that?"

"No, it's just that I think of bodyguards as attending the School of Hard Knocks."

"I try not to be a thug," he said, offering her his elbow. "Shall we go?"

She rested her gloved hand on his arm. It felt classy to be escorted for a change. She liked being near him. Physical contact was...reassuring. "Is there anything else I should do? Keep my back to the wall? Don't drink the wine until you've tasted it first?"

"Just circulate as you usually would. Let me know a few moments before you plan to leave."

"I'd do that anyway, boyfriend."

"I'm sure you would, girlfriend."

His easygoing grin was his best feature, she thought. His whole face lit up. His gray eyes twinkled. He had light, endearing laugh lines at the corners of his eyes.

There was no fanfare when she and David entered Pola and Tweed, but Tasha sensed that people were looking. She and David were different, not part of the regular crowd. And, Tasha thought with justifiable conceit, they made a striking couple. She felt more beautiful and glamorous than she ever had in her life.

The interior of Pola and Tweed had been transformed for this occasion. The silky drapes, suggesting the tent of a desert sheikh, added a touch of decadence. Almost everyone was beautifully dressed, except for the two armed guards that stood at the front door and the two others who flanked a central display case that was draped with a black cloth.

At each of the glass display cases, an employee was posted to assist with showing the jewelry, and Tasha decided to indulge herself. Still holding David's arm, she went to a long case and scanned the contents.

"Hi, Tasha," said the clerk.

Tasha introduced David as an old boyfriend from New York, and the clerk brightened. "Looking for a diamond ring?"

"I wouldn't let him off that cheap," Tasha said. She pointed to a necklace that had caught her eye on several other visits to the store. "Let's see that one."

"You're incredible," the clerk said. "That's the most expensive piece in the store, apart from the Sheikh's Rubies, of course. Blue diamonds, set in silver."

"From the De Beers mines?" Tasha asked, though she knew the answer. Quality stones like this had to be from South Africa.

"Yes."

"May I?" Tasha picked up a loupe and studied the stones. "Remarkable. Almost flawless. The design is, however, modern. I'd guess that the jewelsmith was Carole Tannenbaum."

"Right, again. You know a lot about gems."

"My mother had an incredible collection."

She stripped off her glove to feel the stones against her skin. Jewelry was a sensual experience for her. The coolness of the stones absorbed her body heat and warmed, glowed from within with an incandescent light. Tasha allowed the necklace to slide through her fingers. The shimmer was more perfect than a waterfall.

Her heart was beating fast. Her throat felt dry as the Sahara. "Beautiful," was all she could say.

But she wasn't here to fondle the jewelry. She handed the necklace back to the clerk. "So, who are some of the important people I should meet here? People who need flowers."

"The woman in the green silk suit has a daughter getting married next year. The tall man wearing cowboy boots with his tuxedo organizes the debutante ball in the spring. The priest is Father Gregory, and I'm sure he'd love to have flower donations."

Tasha nodded her thanks and turned to David. "Okay, let's mingle."

The only people she was acquainted with at this event were other Cherry Creek merchants, and they were generous in sharing their contacts. She found herself passing out business cards right and left. Coming to this party was a great idea! If only half of the people who said they were interested gave her a call, she'd have to hire another full-time designer.

At half past eight, Janet Pola called for attention. She had dressed for this occasion in formfitting silver with tons of sequins that emphasized her heaving bosom. Her hair was so massive that it almost took on a life of its own. Janet might have been ridiculous, Tasha thought, if she hadn't been so wholeheartedly enthusiastic. Her premier showing was a total success, and she deserved this opportunity to preen.

Janet's high-pitched voice trilled above the general hubbub. "Ladies and gentlemen, I am privileged to present the Sheikh's Rubies."

Conversations stilled. Everyone moved in a circle around the central display case. Tasha was fortunate to be in the front row.

Janet claimed their attention, and she continued, only slightly less shrill. "This legendary necklace and bracelet set is touring the country under the auspices of the International Jeweler's Association. It will not be for sale until the end of the tour when IJA will conduct a closed auction via conference call. If you are interested in the bidding, please let me know."

"What's the floor bid?" asked the tall man in cowboy boots.

"One million, nine." Janet reached for the black drape, then lowered her hand, allowing the suspense to build. "Let me tell you a bit of the legend of these jewels. The rubies came from Siam, nearly two hundred years ago. They were set in this elaborate golden necklace and bracelets by an anonymous, genius jewelsmith in the Middle East and were delivered to the palace of Sheikh Hajib Sahad who maintained a harem that sometimes numbered over one hundred. The sheikh would present these rubies to his favored wife. The drawback was that if the wife fell from his good graces, she would not only sacrifice the jewelry but also her life."

Janet paused dramatically. Her voice dropped as low as it could go. "They say that the red of the rubies was deepened by the blood of twelve beautiful women."

Tasha felt her anticipation growing. She couldn't wait to see the rubies. Of course, no one would be allowed to touch them. But the vision alone should be incredible.

Janet continued, "Finally, the aging sheikh fell deeply in love with a young woman, Aziza. Some said she was a sorceress who enchanted him. His dying wish was that she keep the rubies for all eternity. And she did. She escaped her country with a fortune in other jewels and lived in Paris for a time.

"The rubies have passed through the hands of royalty and noblewomen. They are reputed to bring good luck to a favored lady who is beloved by a powerful man. Otherwise, misfortune."

Dramatically, the lights in the shop dimmed. Tasha could feel David standing very near to her. Track lighting made spotlights shine on the black draped case.

Janet whipped off the veil. The rubies were displayed against a creamy satin drape. As Tasha gazed upon them, she held her breath. Magically, she was transported to a different place and time. Her ears rang with the wail of desert winds. Her eyes scorched. Fire from the deep red stone leapt into her soul. Her fingers itched. Desperately, she wanted to hold the necklace, to feel the weight of it against her throat.

When the lights came up, she had to look away.

"Are you all right?" David asked.

"The gems. They're so magnificent." She exhaled the breath she'd been holding and fanned herself with her pink-gloved hand. "Seems hot in here. Could we step outside?"

"Yes, of course. I'll go first."

Her reaction to the Sheikh's Rubies intrigued him. She'd flushed when she looked upon them. Her eyes misted. Even now, when she placed her hand on his arm, he felt a tremor in her fingertips. Her yearning was so ferocious that he could feel it, and he wondered if her visceral attraction to precious gems had anything to do with the danger.

He was about to ask her how and why she knew so much about jewelry when Janet came up to them outside. Though David was trying to like this woman, she reminded him of an overinflated Kewpie doll. She was bubbling with excitement, almost squeaking. "Isn't this wonderful! I had my doubts, but it's all turned out so very well."

"It's fantastic," Tasha said with honest enthusiasm. "It's a great crowd, and your presentation was marvelous."

"Not too fanciful?"

"You were perfect," David lied gallantly.

"Thank you." She batted her eyelashes at him, then turned her head. "Oh, here's someone interesting for you two to meet. Yoo-hoo!"

She called to a heavy-set gentleman in a black suit, and he joined them. David thought his eyes lit up when he spotted Tasha. He stared rudely at her while Janet made the introductions.

"This is Inspector George Henning of Scotland Yard," Janet said. "He's accompanying the Sheikh's Rubies on their tour, and he's world renowned for nabbing jewel thieves."

She beamed at him. "Inspector, I'd like you to meet the young lady who has the shop next door to mine."

He clasped Tasha's hand. "I know Miss Lancer very well. Very well, indeed."

Chapter Three

David's protective instincts cranked into high gear when Inspector Henning gripped Tasha's hand. This wasn't a friendly handshake. Despite the inspector's round, cherubic face and curling gray hair, his mouth had a cruel twist. His features sharpened as he gazed at Tasha. His blue eyes, set in a ruddy complexion, were cold as ice.

"I haven't seen you for quite some time, Miss Lancer." He spoke in a British accent, tinged with a Scot's burr that rolled his r's. "Not since the SoHo affair. That was—let me think now—that must have been four years ago."

"You're mistaken," Tasha said.

She matched his ice with a frosty disdain. She was less than half his girth and, even in her high heels, she was much shorter than the inspector. Yet she managed to tilt her head in such a way that she appeared to be looking down at him. David would have been amused by her trick if he hadn't caught the undercurrent of real, possibly dangerous, hostility between them.

"The last time I saw you was in Miami," Tasha corrected. "And that was six years ago. I remember because it was one day after my twenty-first birthday."

"And what a birthday present you gave yourself. An emerald tiara, wasn't it? Quite a remarkable piece of antique jewelry."

"I was there to sell the tiara, not to acquire," she said. "It belonged to my mother."

"And it went so nicely with those emerald earrings."

Janet Pola, like David, stood at the fringe of this brittle confrontation. Janet, however, was so wrapped up in the excitement of her premier showing that she was oblivious to the uneasy tension between Tasha and the inspector. She spied another acquaintance, trilled a farewell and flitted away from them like a weird silver bird with big hair.

"Inspector, this is David Marquis," Tasha said.

David nodded but did not extend his hand. The ritual of handshaking was one that bodyguards avoided. His job was to be alert, not congenial.

The inspector sized him up in a glance. "You must be her new beau. I warn you, this young lady has broken many hearts in her day."

"I'll be careful," David said. He wondered if the inspector numbered himself among those whose hearts had been broken. His antipathy toward Tasha had a distinctly personal edge, almost like that of a jilted lover.

Inspector Henning scowled at him. "Tell me, David. Do you have a permit for that gun you're carrying?"

"Yes, sir. I do." Interesting, David thought. His tuxedo was tailored to conceal the bulge of his shoulder holster, and he doubted that anyone else at the party had noticed that he was armed. But the inspector was, of course, from Scotland Yard. He was a professional.

"One should always stay on the right side of the law." The inspector turned his attention back to Tasha. "Shouldn't one?"

"Absolutely."

"Quite a temptation for you, Miss Lancer. Having your shop right next door to the Sheikh's Rubies."

"Not at all," she said.

"Come now, my dear lady. Wouldn't you like to touch them? Wouldn't you like to wear the necklace around your throat like the bewitching Aziza, favored wife of the sheikh?"

"Too dangerous," she replied. "If I made the sheikh angry, I'd lose my life. I never take such risks."

"Never, eh? But I thought a cat or, should I say, a cat burglar?—had nine lives."

A cat burglar? Though Henning spoke to Tasha, his gaze was riveted on David, watching him for a reaction. And it took all of David's self-control to maintain his attitude of impassivity. He didn't flinch. His gaze was steady. Thanks to years of training, he betrayed nothing of the turmoil that ricocheted inside his head. Tasha was a cat burglar? That sure as hell explained her knowledge of fine jewelry and her passionate reaction to the Sheikh's Rubies. And why hadn't she mentioned this little, tiny, infinitesimal detail about her life? Why had she adamantly insisted that there was no reason for anyone to be after her?

She'd lied to him. Wrapped in a mantle of offended innocence, she'd cleverly disguised her true motivations.

Damn her lies! Beneath his perfectly tailored tuxedo, David began to sweat. He glanced down at her, waiting for her to deny the inspector's oblique accusation.

Instead, she said, "David, I'd like to go back inside. There was one more person I wanted to chat with."

"Certainly," he said. When he took her hand and placed it on his arm to escort her back into Pola and Tweed, his grasp tightened like a handcuff on her slender wrist. She had some explaining to do, and he wouldn't be satisfied until he had some answers. Honest answers.

"I'll be seeing you again," the inspector said. "For the next two weeks, I'll be staying close to the rubies."

"That sounds like a warning," Tasha said.

Inspector Henning didn't bother to put up a facade of politeness. He glared at her. "Quite right."

As they stepped past him, heading back inside, she turned for a parting comment. "It wasn't me in SoHo."

"So you say."

Inside Pola and Tweed, David automatically scanned the crowd. The presence of armed guards and the number of people crammed inside the silk-draped store made this into a fairly safe surrounding. The question was, should he be protecting Tasha from them or vice versa?

"Over there," she said. "I want to talk with that woman who—"

"Not just yet." His voice was low and hard. His anger simmered close to the surface.

Grasping her elbow, he propelled her to a relatively quiet corner of the room. "You have one chance to explain."

"What do you mean?"

"The agency I work for, PEI, doesn't extend bodyguard protection to criminals."

Her dark eyes flashed. Her chin quivered. She tried to wrench her elbow away from him, but he held on tightly. If he hadn't just heard a Scotland Yard inspector refer to her as a cat burglar, he might have fallen for her delicate, wide-eyed look of offended virtue.

"I'm not a cat burglar," she whispered.

"Glad to hear it." As if she would confess to him without a struggle! David's patience wore thin. It was killing him to be subtle. He wanted to pry the truth from her delicate pink-tinted lips. "Tell me how you happened to be acquainted with Inspector Henning?"

"What an obnoxious creep! It's going to be hell having him right next door for two weeks."

"What happened in Miami?"

She winced. "It's complicated, David. Do we have to go into it right now?"

"Yes."

"All right. You asked for it." She snagged two wineglasses from a passing waiter and held one out to David.

He refused. "I don't drink on the job."

"Just as well. I might need both of these." She took a long swallow. "My mother came from Russia. When she emigrated to this country, in the late 1950s, it was the height of the Cold War. Though her family was aristocracy and she hated Communism more than anyone in the United States could possibly imagine, she was virtually unemployable. Nobody trusted a Russian woman. She had no job skills, spoke very little English and didn't have a big bankroll to support her. What she did have was jewelry, a fortune in family jewels."

"I see," David said. Did he believe her? In this exotic setting, with draped silks and desert flowers, he thought of the legendary storyteller Scheherazade in the *Arabian Nights* who enchanted her enemies with fanciful tales. David refused to be so easily duped. "Continue."

"I learned about gemstones at my mother's knee. Literally." She polished off one of the glasses of wine and set it down on a countertop. "When we were little, Mother used to insist that my sister and I sit by her side as she painstakingly cataloged her jewels, explaining the history of the piece, the carats, the workmanship. Some people have family albums. We had the family jewels."

"Fascinating," David said tersely.

"Insane might be a more accurate word."

"All families have their idiosyncracies."

"I'll bet yours didn't." Her voice snapped like a whip. "I'll bet you're white bread through and through. I'd guess that you played football in high school, or maybe in prep school, dated a cheerleader and matriculated to Yale."

"You're wrong." But he didn't intend to be sidetracked by his own dysfunctional family history. "Let's get back to the family jewels, shall we?"

"My mother, Martina, was married and divorced and then married again to my father. She had me and my sister. Then, she and my father divorced. I was six. It really hurt, but I can't blame my father." She frowned into her wine. "Here's what you've got to understand, David. My mother is a tragic kind of person. She has that deep, Russian gloom—a darkness that's heavy as the snows of Moscow in winter. After the two failed marriages, she was bitter toward men and vowed to never marry again."

David was beginning to get a clearer picture of why Tasha was so adamantly independent. Her mother sounded like a classic man-hating witch.

"It was horrible when I started thinking about dating," Tasha said. "Who was that monster in Greek mythology? The one who had snakes for hair and turned men into stone?"

"Medusa?"

"That was my mom. Any guy who came into my house got the Medusa glare right between the eyes."

"So you weren't dating the captain of the football team."

"Not hardly."

He knew that they had gone far afield in her explanation, and he suspected that her digression was purposeful, leading him away from the real story. "Tasha, what does this have to do with Miami?"

"It's like this. Morty Lancer was fairly good about child support, but there was never enough money. Mother had to keep selling off her jewels, one at a time. Each time, it was an exercise in depression. You would have thought she was hacking off parts of her body, selling her lifeblood. Finally, my sister and I said we'd take care of the jewelry sales for her."

"And you went to Miami," David prompted.

"I'd located a buyer there for this incredible tiara, and it was worth the expense of the trip for what this woman would pay. Unfortunately, at the same time, a pair of emerald earrings were stolen in a particularly daring cat burglary. Inspector Henning was called in to help the investigators. He got wind of the tiara, and—for some ridiculous reason—I became his number-one suspect."

"A ridiculous reason," David said coldly. Finally, she had led him to the meat of her story. But it seemed that Tasha was leaving out the most important facts. "In my experience, the police don't often zero in on a suspect without some rational basis."

"What?"

"This supposedly 'ridiculous reason,' what was it?"

"Oh, come on, David. You can't possibly be on Henning's side."

"I want the truth."

"If I was a cat burglar, would I be running a flower shop? I'd be filthy rich and living in Monte Carlo. And I meant it when I said I wasn't in SoHo four years ago. You can check my passport."

Which could be faked, he thought.

She stared up at him with her huge liquid brown eyes, the eyes that he thought from the first were secretive and mysterious. "David, you believe me, don't you?"

God help him, he wanted to believe her. He might be making the biggest mistake of his career, but he hoped that Tasha was telling him the truth. "You haven't told me the whole story."

"You're right." Her voice was low, almost a whisper. "There's more. But I don't understand, David. Why do you need to know everything?"

"To save your life."

Startled, she glanced up at him. Her eyes were haunted. In their liquid depths, he saw a shimmer of fear, like the flicker of moonlight across a midnight pond. When she looked at him like this, he wanted to hold her close, to be her haven in a world that had been cruel.

Then her lips quirked in a grin, banishing the naked vulnerability in her eyes. There was a spark, a flash of her teasing wit. "Maybe I'll tell you, David. But only if I decide I can trust you."

In a blink, she'd turned the tables. They weren't talking about *her* dubious past, they were talking about him. Completely taken aback, David sputtered. "Me? You don't know if you can trust me?"

"That's right."

"How can you say that?" He struggled to control himself. "I'm a bodyguard. I work for PEI, one of the most reputable agencies in the country."

"All I know is that I wasn't in danger until you arrived."

She sipped at the second glass of wine, which David knew was her fourth drink of the night because he'd been counting. And he'd only seen her nibble at a couple of canapés. She did not, however, appear to be the least bit out of control. Apparently, little Tasha could hold her liquor. She was full of surprises. The greatest of which might be that she was a cat burglar.

She glanced back toward the party, which had begun to break up. "I want to talk to that woman with the daughter who's getting married. Then we can leave."

"Go ahead. I'll wait here."

David stood beside the elaborate floral display of anthurium provided by Bloom's and glared as Tasha worked the crowd. Moving through the clusters of people, she was graceful. Men were captivated by her. Their appreciative glances followed her around the room. And the women seemed to warm to her, too. She made them smile. So easily, she disarmed everyone who came in contact with her.

He could see that Tasha would fit in anywhere. She'd be welcomed at a hoedown or a debutante ball. She was loaded with charm and sophistication—both were handy traits for a jewel thief. In order to pull off any caper, inside information was essential. Was that why she was in danger? She'd cleverly sidestepped his questions about the inspector's "ridiculous reasons" for suspecting her. She hadn't actually said that she *wasn't* a cat burglar.

As he watched, she glanced over her shoulder and winked at him. A sudden heat flowed through his veins. Without thinking, he smiled back at her. She made him glad to be with her, proud to be her escort. And if she was a thief? How could he be exchanging warm grins with a criminal? That went against everything he believed in.

When she came back toward him, a touch of laughter lingered on her soft pink lips. With her short black hair, she looked like a gamine, more mischievous than mysterious.

"Okay," she said. "Let's hit the road."

Mindful of his duties as a bodyguard, he took her arm and escorted her onto the street. Even this slight physical contact, the nearness of her, aroused him, and David was annoyed at himself for allowing his emotions to go haywire. He shouldn't be feeling this way about a client, especially not when the client might be a criminal.

They were parked nearby and the streets were well lit. It seemed safe enough to walk. He'd only gone a few paces, however, when he sensed a threat.

In the entrance to her shop, he noticed a thickening in the shadows. Someone was standing there, hiding.

David halted, stepped in front of Tasha.

A match flared in the doorway, illuminating the features of Inspector Henning. David smelled the rich smoke of a good cigar.

"Odd place for a smoke," David said.

"Didn't want to offend any of the party goers," the Inspector said. "Nobody appreciates a fine Cuban cigar anymore."

Tasha peeked out from behind David. "Perhaps it's you that people find offensive."

He chuckled. "Ah, Miss Lancer. You're always a challenge."

"Don't play with me, Inspector Henning. You'll never win."

His laughter vanished in a puff of cigar smoke.

David whisked her to the car, held her door and hurried around to the driver's side. Whoever was after Tasha had not made a move at the party. But were they still watching her apartment building?

On the short drive home, Tasha fumed, "Do you believe that Inspector Henning? What a snake! No, he's too fat to be a snake. But a reptile, for sure. A lizard!"

"The thing with the tiara in Miami wasn't the first time you met him, was it?"

"Oh, gosh, no. He's been harassing me since I was just a kid. Seventeen. The first time was in London."

"And I suppose that had something to do with jewels."

"Of course, it did. That's why he was so quick to jump to the wrong conclusions in Miami. What a jerk!"

But she didn't want to dwell on the nasty Inspector Henning. Tonight had been a very successful evening for her, and she wouldn't let old disasters ruin her rosy glow of success.

She glanced over toward David. His jaw clenched tight as if he were forcing himself not to speak. She, too, was silent. She'd left her story half-told. Had she said too much? Or too little?

Tasha cleared her throat. "When we get to my apartment, is there anything special I should do?"

"I'll accompany you inside. Just do as I say." He kept his attention on the road, but his eyebrows pulled down in a frown. "Returning tonight, after dark, would be a lot easier if I'd secured your apartment before we left."

"I'm sorry," she said. "I should have listened to you when you said I was in danger, but I couldn't believe it. I still can't. I still don't know why anybody would be after me."

"Come off it, Tasha. You're a woman who has been suspected of burglary on an international scale. Hardly an innocent, law-abiding citizen."

"Don't be absurd! I can explain everything."

"And you will," he said. "As soon as we're in your apartment."

David drove slowly past the front entrance to her building. "Looks okay," he said. "Get your keys out and ready. As soon as I stop the car, jump out and run to the door."

"Should I take off my heels?"

"Yes. You need to move fast. I'll be right behind you."

He went around to the alley entrance. They were in luck and found a parking place next to the back door. David swerved neatly into the space. "Go!"

She darted from the car, raced up the four concrete stairs to the door and fitted her key in the lock. She could feel David right behind her. In less than a minute, they were inside her building, cocooned by soundproofed silence. The beige-carpeted hallway was deserted.

Hers was a relatively small building, four stories high. On Tasha's floor, the second, there were only four apartments. Each was a two-bedroom.

With gun in hand, David preceded her up the stairs to the second floor where, once again, they met with quiet.

At the door to her apartment, he instructed, "You stay out here. Face the hallway. If you see any movement at all, yell. I'll check out the inside."

She unlocked the door, and he disappeared into her apartment. It seemed strange to be standing in her own hallway, watching for a threat. Everything looked exactly the same as usual. Well lit by precisely spaced ceiling fixtures. Textured white walls. Natural wood baseboards. Perfectly quiet. If it hadn't been for that Russian man with the gun, she wouldn't have thought it possible that she was in danger.

Despite what David and Henning thought, Tasha had no reason to be threatened.

David was back in the doorway, no longer carrying his gun. "It's clear. Come on in. Quickly."

Inside, she fastened the dead bolt, dragged herself over to the couch and collapsed onto it. She exhaled a deep sigh of relief. At last, she was home. Safe.

David also seemed to relax by several degrees. No longer on the alert as a bodyguard, he tugged at his bow tie, untied the knot and allowed the ends to hang loose on his snowy white shirt. When he unfastened the top button on his shirt and rubbed at his throat, she noticed an enticing glimpse of chest hair, and Tasha smiled to herself. She was seeing him with—no pun intended—his guard down.

David shrugged out of his tuxedo jacket. "Mind if I hang this in the front closet?"

"Not at all."

He put away his jacket and rolled up his shirtsleeves. His forearms were strong. The crisp hair, like the hair at his throat, was darker than the thick, chestnut brown hair on his head. His black shoulder holster was clearly visible above the cummerbund, and she couldn't help staring at it. Tasha wasn't afraid of guns. In fact, she kept a .32 revolver locked in her bottom desk drawer in the office, thinking that it might be some kind of deterrent against robbery. Still, it seemed odd to have an armed man in her living room, casually relaxing as he pulled over a chair from the dining room table and sat opposite her. "Apparently, these people who are threatening you don't want to kill you."

"No? Running me down with a car and sticking a gun in my face seem like pretty fatal gestures."

"If the gunman wanted you dead, he wouldn't have talked to you. There was plenty of time to pull the trigger."

"That's true," she agreed. "He told me to come with him, and he'd explain everything."

"What was he talking about?"

"I don't know." She saw the disbelief in his gaze. "Listen, David, I know it seems weird that I don't know what these people are after. But it's even more strange from my perspective. I really don't have a clue."

"There's no political or terrorist thing, right?"

"Absolutely not."

"No reason to believe they would kidnap you for a ransom?"

She laughed. "Mother would never exchange one of her jewels for something as trivial as my life."

"What about other relatives? You have a sister, don't you?"

Tasha wasn't ready to discuss Stacey, not while Inspector Henning was in town. "I seriously doubt that anyone would expect ransom from my sister. We haven't seen each other in years. She'll usually call at Christmas and my birthday, but I don't even have a current address for her."

"You don't know where she lives?"

"She travels a lot. Part of her job."

"Which is?"

"Buying and selling. Import and export," she said vaguely.

"And what does she buy and sell? Jewelry?"

"I don't really know." She'd never questioned Stacey too closely. Tasha wasn't sure that she wanted to know the truth. "I could try to get ahold of her."

"That might be wise." David stretched back in his chair and folded his hands behind his head. "So, the Russian must be after something you have. Information of some kind?"

Wearily, she said, "Not unless he wanted to consult about the proper floral arrangement for a Russian thug dinner party."

"Do you own anything worth killing for? Do you have any of your mother's jewelry stashed around here?"

"No. Mother has it all."

Tasha pushed herself off the sofa, and when she stood, she realized how tired she was. All this talk about her family was exhausting. Too many of the memories were painful. Pointedly, she said, "Good night, David."

"Dammit, Tasha. You're not going to bed yet. Not until I have some answers."

"Don't give me orders," she warned.

When he stood suddenly, she was aware of his strength. His long fingers clenched into fists. His thighs flexed as he took two steps toward her. His blazing gray eyes told her that he wanted to grab her and shake her until he heard the answers he so much wanted to hear. The sheer physical power in his masculinity should have been intimidating, but Tasha did not cower before him.

She would match his strength with her wits. She'd done it before, and could do it again. Standing, she faced him. "I'm going to bed."

"What could you possibly have that these people want?"

"I don't know. Why don't I sleep on it? I'll tell you in the morning if I've thought of anything."

"In the morning." The fury in his eyes subsided until the gray irises were glowing embers. "I'm not an impatient man, but I'll wait only so long."

"For what?"

"Answers." He turned away from her. "Sleep with your windows closed and your door open. I'll stay out here on the sofa."

Tasha hadn't thought that far ahead. He was supposed to protect her twenty-four hours a day. And that meant night as well as day. At the shop, he'd mentioned sleeping arrangements. And, really, it shouldn't be any trouble for him to camp out here. But she didn't like the idea. There was something terribly disconcerting about having David sleep only a few steps away.

She drew herself up. "I don't think that's necessary."

"Of course it is."

"I'm on the second floor. There's nothing outside that anyone could climb up to get in the windows. The door is double locked with a dead bolt." Even as she spoke, Tasha knew that anyone who was determined and skilled could get into her apartment. Any lock could be picked. Any height could be scaled. But she still didn't want David staying here. "I'll be fine."

"It's my job to make sure that you are." He took the straight-back chair back to the dining area and returned to stand toe-to-toe with her. "There will be no discussion on this point, Tasha. I'm staying."

As she looked up at him, she realized that her reluctance to have him here had nothing to do with threats on her life. The danger was David himself, the magnetism he exuded without even trying. His strength challenged and aroused her at the same time. "Please leave. I'll see you in the morning."

"Yes, you will. And tonight, too. I've never lost a client, and I don't intend to start with you. If I was going strictly by the rules, I'd insist upon staying in your bedroom."

She swallowed hard. The idea of David in her bedroom was not altogether unappealing. The opposite, in fact. "In my bedroom?"

"That's right."

"I thought you were from a bodyguard service. Not a gigolo."

It was a low blow, but he wasn't in the least bit shaken. Instead, he grinned. The fire within him had cooled. "Don't flatter yourself, Tasha."

"What's that supposed to mean?"

"In the course of my job, I've come into close contact with some of the most glamorous, beautiful celebrities in the world. Why would I be interested in you?"

"I don't know." They were so near to each other. She was eye level with his chest, and her contrary attraction to him urged her to unbutton his shirt, to run her fingers across the dark crisp hair on his chest. She looked up into his molten gray eyes. "You're interested in me, David. You've thought about being in my bed."

His gaze wavered, and she knew she was right. He'd thought about it. Just as she had.

But he said, "No."

"Don't lie." She was playing with fire, but Tasha couldn't help herself. She wanted so desperately to touch him, to feel his strength melting into an embrace. "Those gorgeous celebrities didn't turn you on the way I do."

"You're mistaken."

"Am I?"

Her hands rested on his shirtfront. The heat of his body seared the sensitive skin of her fingertips as she glided her hands higher, avoiding his gun.

When her fingers laced behind his neck, she felt his grasp. He pulled her against his body. Her breasts crushed against him. His head lowered, and he nuzzled her throat, setting off delicious shock waves of desire. Then his mouth claimed hers. My God, the sensations! His kiss was like nothing she'd ever experienced before. She trembled convulsively, clinging to him.

She felt small and delicate in his arms. With one fierce kiss, he tamed her teasing nature. In one instant, he vanquished the defenses it had taken her a lifetime to build. His tongue penetrated her mouth, and she offered no resistance. She was utterly submissive in his embrace, unthinking and yet aware of every molecule in her being. This moment was serious. It was the most important thing that had ever happened to her.

Her longing was palpable, undeniable. She wanted this kiss to go on forever. She needed him in her bed, making love to her. Then she would curl up beside him, and she would never be frightened again.

But David ended the kiss. He took two quick steps backward, away from her, and stood staring in shock at what he had done. His breath came in harsh gasps. "I'm sorry."

"No, you're not." It wasn't over! It couldn't be over! "And neither am I."

"I shouldn't have..." He turned his back on her. "Give me a blanket. I'll sleep on the sofa."

"I want you closer than that."

She stepped up behind him. Her hands lightly traced the holster strap that spanned his back. How could she convince him? What could she say? In his arms, she'd found something that had been sadly lacking in her life. His kiss was the answer to a question she'd been afraid to ask.

"I can't," he repeated.

"Please, David."

She didn't want to beg. Tasha wasn't accustomed to being so vulnerable. Her mind didn't work along those lines. She guarded herself with teasing and flippancy. "Come on, David. Isn't it in the bodyguard rule book? Stay close to the person you're guarding. I mean, what if one of the bad guys slung a rope down from the roof of the apartment building and climbed into my bedroom window?''

''Like a cat burglar?'' He pivoted so quickly that her hands were thrown back. ''Maybe you're familiar with that line of work.''

''What are you saying?''

''Inspector Henning of Scotland Yard had some reason to suspect you. What was it?''

A chasm opened between them, a yawning canyon. She could feel him receding, pulling away from her. ''Let's not talk about Inspector Henning. Not now.''

''Then I'll have to say good-night, Tasha.''

She stormed to the linen closet, grabbed a blanket and threw it at him. This night could have been so different, so wonderful. Harshly, she said, ''Sweet dreams, David.''

''Thank you.''

He watched her flounce into her bedroom. Her door slammed.

David cursed his lack of willpower. He should have resisted her. It wasn't all that unusual for a client to come on to him, but tonight marked the first time he had succumbed. He couldn't help himself.

She was the most alluring creature he had ever encountered.

Was she also a master criminal? A cat burglar?

Chapter Four

After a wretched, uncomfortable, mostly sleepless night on Tasha's living room sofa, David was awake at first light. There was a stiffness in his lower back from sacking out on the attractive brocade sofa that was intended to be used for tea parties, not for sleeping. But his deeper pain came with conscious remembering of what had happened the night before.

He never should have kissed her. Never. There was no excuse for his behavior. Not only had he been unprofessional but stupid, as well. Because her kiss blinded his suspicions and made him forget that she might be a criminal.

David vowed it wouldn't happen again. There would be no unnecessary touching, no physical contact. He wouldn't even think about her. Yeah, right. As if he could control that section of his brain that was already obsessed with her, imagining her in bed, urging him to peek into the open door of her bedroom and watch her sleep.

Well, that was his job, wasn't it? He needed to make sure she was okay.

Wearing only his silk boxer shorts, he moved silently and stood in her bedroom doorway. Her drapes were closed against the dawn, but he saw her clearly in the glow from the kitchen lights.

Tasha lay on her back with one arm thrown artlessly above her head. Her pastel green sheets tangled around her slender legs as if she, too, had trouble sleeping. Her white polished-cotton gown twisted across the fullness of her breasts. She wasn't a bosomy woman, but her tiny waist and the flare of her hips was beautifully feminine. Her body, he thought, was perfect. He wanted to touch her, hold her, feel her respond to him.

He came closer to her bed.

Her rich black hair contrasted with the pale pillowcase. Her face, devoid of makeup, looked sweet and innocent. Luxurious black eyelashes formed crescents above her high cheekbones. Her lips parted, breathing sonorously. She was achingly lovely.

Could it be possible that this fragile beauty was, in fact, a cat burglar of such infamy that she was known to Scotland Yard? David knew he'd never coax the truth from her. Even if he asked all the right questions, Tasha was far too clever at deflecting his inquiries. When she wasn't directly lying, she was holding back, shielding herself behind a wall of independence, pretending that she needed no one.

David turned away from the delectable vision that lay before him. He meant to find the answers. Today.

Fortunately, he had a contact in Denver, somebody he'd planned to look up while he was in town. The guy's name was Earl Rockman, and he owned a detective agency, a handy resource for the information that Tasha refused to give.

David dragged on his tuxedo trousers and last night's shirt. With gun in hand, he hurried through the halls of her apartment building to the rear and checked his rental car. The vehicle had not been tampered with. David had left a nearly invisible wax seal on the trunk. It had not been broken. As far as he could tell, there had been no surveillance during the night.

Taking his suitcase, he returned to her apartment. He showered, shaved and dressed in a white shirt, khaki trousers and shoulder holster. It was just after seven o'clock when his morning brew finished trickling through the coffeemaker in her kitchen, and he closed the door to her bedroom.

Nine o'clock in New York, David thought. He sat at her dining room table and dialed the phone number for PEI. "This is David Marquis. I need to talk with Delia Marie."

Almost immediately, she came on the line. "You're awake early, David. Rough night?"

"You have no idea how rough."

"Sounds yummy." So did her warm, husky voice. "Are you having a problem, darling?"

"It's about the client I'm guarding. Natasha Lancer. I need more information about her."

"You already have our dossier."

The information on Tasha had been only half a page, stating her age, physical condition, the fact that her father was deceased and her mother was from Russia, and that she had a sister. Tasha had run away from home when she was fifteen, dropped out of high school. After traveling across the United States and in Europe, she'd returned to Denver, obtained a GED and had gone to art school. Her flower shop, Bloom's, was opened six months ago using a combination of savings and a bank loan to cover expenses.

"I need to do further investigation," he said.

"Why?"

"This client is different. She's not rich or famous. I don't know why anybody would be after her. Not knowing where the threat is coming from makes it hard to protect her. I don't know which way to look."

"You'll just have to look in all directions at once."

"Come on, Delia Marie. I need some help."

"You're not a detective." Her voice held a chiding note.

He imagined a frown, though he had no idea what Delia Marie looked like. Because of PEI's valued reputation for discreet services, the upper management—Joseph Singleton, the owner, and his right-hand woman, Delia Marie—remained unseen and as anonymous as possible.

Still, David's relationship with the office manager was comfortable. He joked with her on the phone, and they exchanged silly notes on assignments. His favorite was after he'd been fired while doing bodyguard duty for a sultry female rock star. Delia Marie had written, *"Client terminated contract. Reason: No rock 'n' roll in the boudoir. Congrats, D. You're the only man on earth to share her bedroom and not her bed."*

"Here's the problem." He exhaled a deep breath. "I think Tasha might be involved in criminal activities."

"She has no police record. She's never been arrested. Let me remind you, lamb chop, that you're not there to pry into her personal life. Remember, our reputation at PEI is discretion first."

"But golly gee, honey pie, PEI doesn't protect crooks."

"Don't even joke about that." He heard a shudder in her voice. "We're really careful about the people we take on."

"Isn't there anything you can tell me?"

"Your assignment is for two weeks, twenty-four-hour-a-day protection. That's all I know."

"What can you tell me about the individual who hired me as a bodyguard to watch Tasha?"

"I don't have a name for you. This job was hired through a telephone contact on a personal recommendation from top-level management. The payment for your two-week assignment was wired. A cash transaction. I don't have a name."

"Doesn't that seem weird to you?"

"Not particularly." She paused. "I don't understand this, David. It almost sounds like you're getting personally involved on this assignment. That's not happening, is it?"

"I can handle myself." Except for last night, he thought. Except for the fact that he'd succumbed to a desire that was more powerful than anything he'd felt in a very long time. "I'm a pro, Delia."

"Glad to hear it, darling. Is there anything else you need?"

"Yes. Neither her home nor her shop are secure, and I'll need authorization to purchase alarm equipment."

"Approved."

"Also, I'd like to hire a backup to relieve me for a couple of hours a day."

"You've never required backup before."

"Like I said, this is different. Usually, I protect people who live in mansions that are completely secure. I only need to be sharp when they're going out. Tasha is an average person without a butler, chauffeur, maid or guard dogs. I need to be alert twenty-four hours a day."

"Approved," said Delia Marie. "Anything else?"

For a moment, he considered. He also wanted to run the portrait Tasha had sketched of her Russian attacker through the FBI files of known criminals and through Interpol, but it was probably better not to use PEI resources. Delia Marie was clearly against investigating, and he didn't want to be pulled from this assignment. Though David would quit if he discovered that Tasha was, in fact, a thief, he wanted that to be his own decision.

"David? Is there anything else you need or want to know?"

"There is one more thing." He took a familiar teasing tone with her. "What are you wearing, right at this minute?"

"A black lace teddy with a rose at the cleavage."

"Lovely talking with you, Delia Marie."

"Same here, cutie. Stay safe."

David looked up to see Tasha leaning against the hallway arch. How much had she overheard? Did she know he was investigating her? "Good morning, Tasha."

"Hi, David." She yawned, apparently untroubled by his conversation. "Who were you talking to?"

"My office. Delia Marie."

Tasha's smile was lazy and warm. "So? What was she wearing?"

"Black lace."

"At this hour of the morning?" She'd covered her white nightie with an oversize brown wool bathrobe, designed for warmth, not sex appeal. "How come you're calling your office?"

He didn't want to start off the morning with an argument about how he intended to make her shop more secure. "S.O.P.," he said. "Standard operating procedure."

"Did you find out who hired a bodyguard for me?"

Apparently, she'd heard that much of the conversation. David shook his head. "No."

"Delia Marie wouldn't tell me, either."

She shrugged within the oversize robe. With the warmth of sleep still clinging to her, she looked tousled and cuddly. Her eyelids were heavy. Her mouth, untouched by lipstick, curled innocently.

But David refused to be charmed by her. Efficiently, he moved on to the necessary business of the day. "I have a number of security measures that need to be put into effect immediately. What time do you usually leave for work?"

"In about an hour. So, if you'll excuse me, I'll hop into the shower and get dressed."

"Tasha!" His voice halted her before she could pad down the hall to the bathroom. "There's one thing I've figured out."

"What's that?"

"Keep in mind that there are no coincidences. Everything happens for a reason."

"Yes?"

"I've been hired to protect you for two weeks."

She nodded. Her expression was blank.

"The Sheikh's Rubies are on display at Pola and Tweed for two weeks." He held up two fingers. "Two weeks. The same two weeks that I've been hired to guard you. There's got to be a connection. The danger to you is connected to those gems."

AT THE STORE, Tasha took delivery of fresh-cut roses, lilies, irises and assorted other specialty flowers for the day's arrangements. This was a Saturday, not a heavy schedule, but there was usually more walk-in traffic. After the flowers were stripped and cut, the cash register filled and the Yes, We're Open sign placed in the window, Tasha went into her office and closed the door. Mandy could wait on the customers for a while.

Tasha needed time to think, to consider David's deduction. She sat behind her desk with a fresh mug of coffee cradled in her hands.

The rubies represented a threat—as much of a danger to her as to any of the sheikh's unsatisfactory wives. Though she didn't know why, she'd expected as much when she'd seen Inspector Henning at the premier showing. The creepy inspector from Scotland Yard emanated trouble.

Also, if the danger came from jewels, Tasha was sure that it also connected in some way with her mother and sister. The passion for precious gems was a family trait. The desire to acquire such stones had, more than once, been the family's undoing.

She sipped her coffee and stared at the five-by-seven portrait photograph on her desk. The formal picture showed her mother from the waist up, seated in a thronelike chair. *Long live Queen Martina!* In a better world, that would have been her aristocratic calling. She was imperious and lovely in a black velvet gown, an elaborate diamond-and-emerald necklace and the tiara that Tasha had sold in Miami. Martina Lancer was a handsome woman with strong features and dark, tragic eyes.

Far less imposing at age ten were her two daughters. Tasha and Stacey stood on either side of their mother. Their bodies were in profile, but they looked toward the camera. Simple white dresses, ridiculously expensive for two young girls, contrasted with their long black hair. Ten-year-old Tasha was serious in her expression and her pose. Her hand gripped the arm of the throne. Her slight smile did not mask the worry in her eyes. Stacey grinned impishly. Even at that age, she had an air that suggested she was ready to take off and fly at any given moment.

"Oh, Stacey," Tasha murmured, "I hope you're not in trouble."

There was a tap on her door. "Come in."

David was accompanied by a large, rumpled-looking man whose bulging belly dropped over his large silver belt buckle. "This is Jimmy Jenson. He's going to be your bodyguard during those times when I need to be gone."

Tasha shook Jenson's meaty hand, but her comment was directed toward David. "Do you really think I need two bodyguards?"

"I can't be with you twenty-four hours a day." David glanced around the room. "By the way, this office is perfect for security. No windows. A telephone where you can dial 911. Only one door to guard. After I pick up a brace lock for the door, this is the place you should hide if someone threatens you in the shop."

"You don't think that's likely to happen, do you?"

He shrugged. "I'm not sure what to expect."

"I'm a little concerned about Mandy. I couldn't bear it if there was any danger to her. Even if she was frightened, in her condition, the results might be disastrous."

"Are we talking about the kid?" Jenson asked. "The pregnant kid?"

"Her name is Mandy," Tasha informed him coolly. She didn't particularly like Jenson. "And yes, we are."

"You should give her the sack, right now. A stakeout is no place for a pregnant kid."

"Thank you ever so much for your opinion." Tasha's voice dripped venom. She definitely didn't like this guy.

"It's more than an opinion, lady. I've been in this business for six years, and I'm telling you—"

"You're telling me nothing." She flew from behind her desk to confront him. "This is my shop, Mr. Jenson. I make the decisions."

"Not while I'm taking care of you. Not if you want to stay in one piece with all of your arms and legs attached."

David intervened. Physically reaching across Jenson's broad belly, he turned his backup bodyguard around and dragged him toward the door. "Tell you what, Jenson. You go out front and keep an eye on the door. I'll be with you in just a minute."

"You got it, pal." He waggled a warning finger at Tasha. "And you pay attention to what I'm saying, young lady."

David closed the door behind him.

"Where did you find him?" Tasha demanded. "Did you rent him from Morons 'R' Us?"

"He's from a reputable detective agency here in town."

"Really?" She hiked up an eyebrow.

"Yes, really. I know the owner, Earl Rockman. He's former CIA, and he's generously offered me the use of facilities and personnel to check things out, like tracking down the license plate on the car that tried to run you down yesterday."

"How reputable?" she demanded.

"Very. Earl retired to Colorado to ski, and his firm regularly provides security for visiting royalty while they're in the mountains. That was how I got to know him. I was bodyguard for a duchess who came out here on a ski vacation, and I needed some help keeping track of her on the slopes."

Though Tasha had to admit that Earl Rockman sounded okay, she still wasn't impressed. "Is Jenson the best he can offer?"

"He's the best I can get on short notice. Try to get along with him today, Tasha. He'll only be here for a few hours."

"An eternity," she muttered.

"It's not that bad. In spite of his manner, Jenson's qualifications are excellent."

"I don't care if he's guarded Di and Charles and Queen Elizabeth on skis, Jenson's not going to tell me how to run my shop."

"I understand."

"He's probably out there right now upsetting Mandy. You know, she's due to deliver her baby in three weeks. She doesn't need any kind of hassle."

David held up both hands, warding off further argument. "Hey, I agree with you. Next time we'll get somebody else. But for today, we're stuck with Jenson."

He sat in the chair opposite her desk, reached into his inner jacket pocket and pulled out a small spiral notebook and a gold Cross pen. His eyebrows furrowed as he stared at the page and made a scribble.

"What are you doing, David? What's that?"

"My list." He held up the lined page that was covered with chicken scratching. "These are my brains on paper."

Wryly, she said, "I take it that logic isn't your strong suit."

"If I write it down, I don't have to think about it. I can keep my brain free for more important things."

"Such as?"

"Making sure nobody runs you down with a car. Or sticks a gun in your face." He consulted the page. "When do you want to go down to the police station and run through mug shots?"

"I don't."

"Tasha, if the Russian man who attacked you is a known criminal, the police can pick him up."

"Well, he told me his name was Mr. Brown."

"That's great," David said. "There can't be more than two or three hundred Browns in the local phone book."

Remembering, she said, "There was something else he said. He apologized for his comrade's behavior. Do you think he was talking about the guy who tried to run me down with his car?"

"Yes," David said tersely. "Why didn't you mention this before?"

"Didn't think of it." It was still hard for her to take this seriously. Even though she'd been attacked, even though she truly believed in the danger, Tasha had other things to worry about. Her shop, for one. Mandy, for another. And the rubies. In the back of her mind, Tasha was painfully aware of the fabulous fortune in precious stones that was right next door. If the odious Inspector Henning had not been standing guard, she would have slipped over to Pola and Tweed and begged until Janet allowed her to touch the stones. If only for a moment, she longed to wear that necklace and fasten those bracelets to her wrists.

David rose from the chair and glanced at his wrist-watch. "It's ten-thirty right now. I have a few errands to run, and I'll be back at about noon."

"Jenson will be here until then?" she said with obvious disgust.

"Until noon."

Tasha followed him to the front of the store. Fortunately, Mandy was busy with the guy who did deliveries for Bloom's and Jenson hadn't had a chance to pester either one of them.

"Let me tell you something, ma'am," he said. When he walked, his stomach preceded him. "This is no way to—"

"Excuse me," Tasha interrupted. "I am running a business here. And if you don't mind, I would very much appreciate if you stayed out of the way."

"Listen to her," David said. "She's the boss."

"Hell, she ain't no bigger than a minute. How can she be telling me what to do?"

"I'm telling you," David said. He pointed to a padded leather chair beside the rear exit. "You sit there and listen. If there's a disturbance, get up here fast."

Muttering to himself, Jenson obeyed.

That was exactly what Tasha wanted, but she didn't need David to give orders. This was her shop. She was the boss. Archly, she informed David, "I could have done that."

"I know. And the next time somebody needs telling off, it's your turn."

He went out the front door as a customer came inside. The man who entered was so big that he filled the doorway. The blond, Nordic-looking man moved in a lumbering manner, like a bodybuilder whose neck was too developed to turn his head. Tasha could tell without asking that he had a name for each of his muscle groups: Pecs. Abs. Gluts. But he was sophisticated for a jock. His beige suit jacket, worn over a green polo shirt, was marvelously tailored.

"I'll be right with you," Tasha called out with a smile.

Before she could get to him, Janet Pola swept through the door. "Tasha! When you have a chance, stop by. The small display with the brass lamp needs freshening."

Another customer arrived. This was quite a rush for a regular Saturday that wasn't Mother's Day or Valentine's Day.

The tall man leaned toward her across the counter. "You're busy. I'll come back."

"I should only be a minute. Please wait." When she looked up at him, she was struck by the dullness of his gaze. His greenish eyes were flat and cold as a reptile's.

"Before noon," he said. "I'll be back."

Mr. Green left her shop and stood outside, inhaling the crisp September air. A beautiful day with blue skies, even if it was only Denver. He could wait to see Miss Lancer. There was no safe way to talk to her when the shop was crowded, anyway.

He crossed Third Avenue to the coffee boutique on the opposite corner. Before entering, he flipped open a cellular phone and speed dialed. "Cerise," he said.

"Yes, Green. What is it?"

"I will postpone contact until noon."

"Don't bring her here."

"I know." Miss Cerise treated him as if he was a fool. Green knew better than to bring Miss Lancer to their hideout. He couldn't help adding a dig. "Maybe you'd rather send Brown to fetch her?"

"How many times do I have to apologize? It was a mistake to send Brown."

"A big mistake." Brown might be a genius when it came to computers, but he'd let Miss Lancer get the best of him last night. His eyes still smarted and he stank of perfume.

Still, Green was glad that it had happened. Sometimes, Cerise took his talents for granted. "Where should I bring Miss Lancer?"

"West side of the Capitol Building. At the top of the hill. Let her out of the car, and I'll meet her."

"Yes."

"Green? Don't be impatient. We have two weeks."

"Yes," he said.

"Don't hurt her, Green."

He disconnected the telephone. All this planning and effort for one lousy necklace and bracelets? Green didn't like it. After expenses, his total profit would probably be only six hundred thousand. Less if they had to give Miss Lancer a share.

He went into the coffee boutique and ordered a double shot of espresso. With at least an hour to kill, he ambled along Third Avenue. He was tempted to cross the street and enter Pola and Tweed so he could have a peek at these damned rubies. But the gun in his shoulder holster might set off alarms. It wouldn't be smart to get himself caught before the caper had begun.

No matter what Cerise and Brown thought, Mr. Green was smart.

At a quarter to twelve, he returned to Bloom's. This time, the store was deserted. Miss Lancer and her homely, pregnant assistant were standing at the front counter, fussing with a flat arrangement of red and white flowers.

Miss Lancer grinned when she looked up and saw him. "You've come back," she said. "I'm so glad. Now, how may I help you?"

He pointed to a hanging plant near the door. "Tell me about this one."

"It's a Boston fern," she said.

"Easy to take care of?"

"It depends on what you consider easy." Tasha pulled off a pair of red gloves that matched her red-and-white striped blouse, accented by a pair of oversize red crystal earrings that weren't rubies but glittered brightly nonetheless. She came around the counter and stood beside him.

Up close, she couldn't help being impressed by the sheer size of this man. The top of her head didn't even reach his shoulder, and his torso was wide as the trunk of a sequoia. Usually, the idea of such a large person being interested in small, delicate plants was endearing. But something in this man's attitude alerted her to potential danger. "Are you looking for a houseplant?" she asked.

With his back turned to the counter so Mandy couldn't see, he opened his suit jacket. His right hand reached inside, grasping the handle of a gun. "I'm looking for you, Miss Lancer."

"I'll do whatever you say." Her heart leapt up in her throat. God, if anything happened to Mandy... "Let me get rid of my assistant."

"Fast. No funny business."

Tasha kept her voice unwaveringly calm as she glanced toward the counter. "Mandy, would you mind taking lunch now?"

"I thought you'd never ask. I'm starving." Mandy dropped the shears that she'd been using to clip ends on the banquet arrangement of red ginger and white stephanotis. She reached under the counter for her purse. Every movement was laborious. Her fist dug into the small of her back, and she stretched. "Can I bring you anything?"

"I'll be fine," Tasha said with considerably more confidence than she felt. For an instant, she considered giving Mandy a clue, saying something about wanting tuna—her most despised food—for lunch. But she decided against it. She wanted Mandy out of there. She wanted Mandy to be safe. "Go ahead, now. Hurry up. I'll see you later."

After Mandy had waddled past them and out the front door of the shop, Tasha turned to the man. "What do you want?"

"Come with me. Don't make trouble."

"Who are you?"

"Green."

She would have laughed if Mr. Green hadn't been so scary, if his eyes hadn't been so cold, if he hadn't been big enough to break her in half. Sheer bravado compelled her to say, "Green? You must be a friend of Mr. Brown."

"That's right." He took out his gun and held the barrel against her rib cage. "We'll go out the back door."

Tasha balked. The problem was Jenson. Once the substitute bodyguard had settled himself on the chair in the rear, he hadn't moved. For the past hour and a half, he'd divided his time between complaining whenever she came near him and dozing when he thought she wasn't looking.

Tasha preferred not to have Jenson involved. Something in Green's manner told her that he wouldn't hesitate to shoot. And he would shoot to kill.

"We're right here by the front door," she said. "Why not just go out here?"

"So you can shout for help?"

"I wouldn't say a word. I promise." She kept her voice quiet so Jenson wouldn't hear. "I know that you'd shoot me if I did."

"I'm not supposed to hurt you," he said.

She tried a smile. "I'm glad for that."

"But I don't mind disobeying orders." His lip curled in a sneer. "Have you ever had a broken bone?"

"Never." There was a sick taste in her mouth. His implied threat was more effective than an outright demand. He wanted her to be frightened. And she was. Tasha felt as if she was going to vomit.

"You can hear the bone snap. The pain is very bad. Most people pass out."

"I'll do whatever you say."

"Back door."

He nudged the gun painfully into her side. When she winced, he pressed harder. "Go."

She'd reached the counter when Jenson appeared from the rear of the shop. He stretched and yawned. "You got pretty quiet out here, missy."

"No problem," she said, talking fast and praying that Jenson would be too lazy to notice that this huge man was standing far too close to her. Or that he was armed. Or that he was willing to break her arm if Jenson got in the way. "I'm going to take this gentleman out in back so he can see more of the inventory."

"Okay. I'd offer to help, but I don't know beans about plants."

Cautiously, she maneuvered past him. "Keep an eye on the front," Tasha said. "Thanks."

They were at the back door. Tasha fumbled with the lock. Her fingers trembled so badly that she could barely manipulate the key. What would Green do when they were alone? How could she get away from him?

And where was David? This never would have happened if David had been in the shop, protecting her, taking care of her, making sure that everything was all right.

She heard Jenson's growl. "Freeze, mister."

"No," Tasha pleaded. As she turned, Green caught hold of her. With his huge arm, he held her in front of him like a shield. She didn't attempt to struggle. There was no point. But she was talking fast. "Please don't get in the way, Mr. Jenson. Everything's all right."

Jenson stood with his own gun braced in front of him with two hands. "All right, mister. You put your gun down on the floor. Do it, now. If you don't, by God, I'll shoot."

"No," Tasha said. She pointed out the obvious. "Mr. Jenson? If you shoot at him, he's going to kill me."

"Well, now. We don't know that, do we?"

"I think we can assume." She couldn't believe this was happening. Calm, she thought. If she wanted to get away with her life, she needed to stay calm. "Mr. Jenson, if you shoot, you'll probably hit me."

"Not a chance. I'm a crack shot."

"Please." Her voice quavered. "Please turn around, walk away and pretend you didn't notice a thing."

"He'll shoot me in the back."

Finally, Green spoke. "Put down your gun. Or I will kill the girl."

"Well, I don't know about that."

Green tightened his hold on Tasha. His massive arm constricted below her breasts. The pressure on her ribs was painful. All the air went out of her lungs. She couldn't breathe. Though she tried to struggle, her arms were pinned.

"Put down your gun," Green repeated.

Jenson whined, "You'll shoot me."

"I won't," said the man. "You have my word."

Tasha fought for every gasp. She was losing consciousness. With her last breath, she whimpered, "Please."

Jenson set his handgun down on the floor and took a step backward. "I won't call the cops," he said. "You have my word."

"Very funny." Green gestured to Jenson with the gun. "Come here. Right over here beside me."

"What for? Are you going to tie me up? You don't have to do that."

"Over here. Turn around. Put your hands behind your back."

As Jenson obeyed, Green released Tasha. The breath rushed back into her body. The sudden release of tension was stunning. Her knees went weak, and she had to brace herself against the wall to keep from collapsing.

Green moved toward Jenson. He grasped the body-guard's wrist and made a quick movement. Tasha heard a sickening snap.

Before Jenson could scream, Green whacked him on the back of his head with the butt of his gun. Jenson sagged to the floor like a sack of potatoes.

When Green turned back to her, his face was slightly flushed. His sneer became a grin. "I love my work," he said.

He tucked his gun back into the shoulder holster. "I don't think I need this, anymore. Do you?"

She shook her head, unable to speak.

"You won't try to run or call for help?"

"No."

"This is very good, Miss Lancer. Now, let's go."

She didn't need to be told twice. Fighting her nausea and her panic, she opened the door and stepped through. Outside, the sun was shining. The usual sounds of traffic and chattering shoppers wafted on the light autumnal breeze.

The world had never looked so dark to Tasha. Blinded by terror, she stumbled, and Mr. Green took her arm. With this monster holding on to her, she'd never felt so much alone.

Chapter Five

The minute he saw Tasha on the street, David knew something was wrong. It wasn't just the fact that she'd left the shop when he'd told her not to. Nor was he particularly alarmed by the giant man who strode beside her. David knew something was wrong because he saw fear in Tasha's face.

His heart wrenched in his chest as he watched her. The sassy, defiant attitude was gone. Her shoulders hunched inward. Her usual bouncy stride looked more like a shuffle, as if her ankles were locked in invisible shackles. My God, what had happened?

David had been sitting at the curb, checking items off his list of things to do, when he saw Tasha and this huge man emerge from the rear of Bloom's. As David watched, they stopped beside a light-colored sedan with tinted windows. Colorado license plates.

David's attaché case was open on the seat beside him. He reached inside, took out a .35 mm camera and shot three quick photos of the thug. God, this guy was big. Approximately six feet, seven inches tall. Probably weighed three hundred and ten pounds.

Tasha entered the car voluntarily and sat quietly with

her head down while the behemoth climbed into the driver's side.

David was puzzled. Was she going with him of her own free will? What had he done to her?

Where the hell was Jenson? David glanced back at her shop, fearful of what he might find inside. But that would have to wait. By sheer luck, he'd seen Tasha leaving, and he had to follow her.

He picked the cellular phone out of his case and called the offices of Earl Rockman as he merged into the halting traffic pattern of Cherry Creek. David had already visited Earl's north Denver offices to drop off a copy of the sketch Tasha had made of the Russian man and to request a replacement for Jenson.

Earl come on the phone. "What's up, David?"

"We've got trouble with a capital *T.* Somebody grabbed Tasha Lancer."

"Where's Jenson?"

"I didn't see him."

"That's not good," Earl said. "Jenson's no genius, but he's a bulldog. He wouldn't let somebody snatch the girl without a fight."

"Can you check out Bloom's Flowers without calling out the National Guard? My client wouldn't want a disturbance with sirens and cops. This is a classy area."

"Don't tell me about class, Davey boy. I was playing protocol with the crowned heads of Europe when you were still collecting baseball cards. Don't worry. I'll take care of it. What are you doing?"

"Tailing the car that grabbed her." He read off the license plate. "And I've got some more photos to run through FBI and Interpol."

"I'm on it."

"Thanks." David hung up the phone and concentrated on his driving. The four-way stop signs at every corner made it easy to tail the pale sedan. David fell into line, two cars back. They were headed toward the main intersections. One street went north. The other went south.

The north direction, which went toward downtown Denver, was far easier to track. Once again, David was in luck because the other car headed north.

Hiding behind trucks and minivans, David kept them in sight. His fine-tuned reflexes aided his reactions as he threaded through traffic. He was thinking two moves ahead, anticipating the lane changes of the other car.

David wouldn't lose them. He couldn't. Tasha's life might hang on his skill and ability. So far, he thought ruefully, his protection had been virtually worthless. So far, she'd been threatened with vehicular homicide, accosted by a man with a gun and now abducted by a guy who looked as if he could play on the defensive line of the Denver Broncos.

David's job was to keep her safe, and he was blowing it. He should have stayed with her this morning, shouldn't have trusted Jenson. In his years as a bodyguard, David had seldom made so many errors in judgment.

He should have known better. Delia Marie was right when she told him that he wasn't a detective. He was a bodyguard. No matter what suspicions he had about Tasha, he should have been protecting her—as he was hired to do—twenty-four hours a day.

On Colfax, the other car turned left, toward downtown.

David's hands were tight on the steering wheel. He was following too close, only one car behind them, but he couldn't risk losing sight of the other car. If he got stuck in traffic, they'd be lost. Beautiful, feisty, independent Tasha would be lost.

If that giant hurt her... Rage swelled within David and he fought it back. He needed to be cool. He needed his wits about him. But if that creep harmed one hair on her head, David swore he'd track the bastard down. He'd pay, dammit. He'd pay for frightening Tasha.

The other car made an unexpected swerve into the circular drive around the gold-domed state capitol building. Recklessly, David followed. He slowed, stopped.

The cream-colored sedan had also halted. Tasha got out, and the car drove away.

She stumbled forward a few steps and looked around as if she'd just landed on a strange planet. Her gaily striped red-and-white blouse and denim miniskirt seemed crumpled. Her shimmering red crystal earrings contrasted with the dull pallor of her complexion.

David whipped into a parking place. She was all right! Relief flooded through him. Now, he could go to her, pull her into his arms, reassure her. He'd make damn sure that no one ever threatened her again.

He was halfway out of his car when he saw Tasha undergo a stunning transformation. It was as if she suddenly regained her spunk. She threw back her shoulders. Her step became more confident as she approached a sophisticated blond woman, dressed all in red.

Unsmiling, the two women shook hands. Side by side, they began to stroll slowly. Was this a predesignated meeting? Who was the woman that Tasha had met? They put their heads together. Then they both laughed.

There wasn't time for a major disguise, but David needed to get close and find out what was being said without Tasha knowing that he was eavesdropping. Dark

Ray•Ban sunglasses. His white shirt, unbuttoned, over his T-shirt. A baseball cap, turned backward on his head. He left his shoulder holster in the car, but took his camera. He'd be a tourist, snapping photographs of the capitol.

The two women sat on a black wrought-iron bench.

Subtly keeping outside their peripheral vision, David eased within listening range.

"I knew you were planning a heist," said the woman in red. "I knew from the moment I started my research and I saw a glimpse of you in a photograph by your store. I recognized you immediately. After all, we did spend quite a lot of time together in SoHo."

"Very clever, Cerise." Tasha's voice was calm. "Did you know that Inspector Henning is here?"

"He's such a snake!"

"My thoughts exactly. Reptilian."

The woman in red, Cerise, rose to her feet. "Let's walk. I find it easier to think when I'm in motion."

When they stood, David snapped photos. He drew no conclusions, but it sounded as if these two females were putting their heads together to pull off a caper—the theft of the Sheikh's Rubies.

Keeping a distance, he trailed after them, catching bits of their conversation.

"...old-fashioned security system. Concrete walls and subflooring..."

"...alarms are manually operated. Child's play to disarm. They aren't even motion-activated laser..."

"The safe itself," said Cerise, "within the storage vault, is a rather difficult combination lock. But I believe you're familiar with the device."

"Possibly."

"And there are two armed guards at night."

Tasha said firmly, "They mustn't be hurt. You have to promise, Cerise, or I won't have any part of this job."

"You have such a delightful sense of ethics. In your book, it's all right to steal millions of dollars worth of jewels, but you put a ridiculously high value on human life. You always have. It's gotten you into trouble before."

"I despise what your Mr. Green did to the man in my shop."

David winced. What had happened to Jenson? Was he dead?

"Who was he?" asked Cerise.

"My bodyguard," Tasha said. "After Green tried to run me down with the car and Brown waved the gun in my face, I felt I needed some kind of backup."

"What about that cute boyfriend who spent last night at your apartment?"

"He is adorable, isn't he? Not very bright, but with a body like that, who cares?"

A slow heat simmered in David's belly. Not very bright? Maybe she was right. He sure as hell didn't feel intelligent at this moment.

Tasha continued, "David came as a surprise visit. He's from New York, thinking about relocating to Denver. I'll keep him around for a few more days."

"Don't let him get in the way."

"I won't," Tasha said to her friend in red. "No man is worth a million and a half."

"We have to talk about that split, Stacey."

Stacey? David paused and let them move away from him. Why had Cerise called her Stacey? If he remembered correctly, Stacey, short for Anastasia, was the name of Tasha's sister.

The two women sauntered casually around the capitol, chatting with the nonchalance of a couple of old friends. No one would guess, by looking at them, that they were discussing a multimillion-dollar jewel heist.

David sure as hell hadn't guessed. Though last night Henning had warned him that she was a cat burglar, he hadn't believed that she was a criminal. Maybe, in his head, he'd known that a Scotland Yard inspector would have no reason to lie. But, in his heart, he'd been willing to listen to her stories. He'd admired her spunk, mistaken her bravery for innocence. He'd been tricked by her huge, liquid brown eyes, taken in by her charm.

His jaw tensed. His rear molars ground together as he recalled last night when he kissed her irresistible lips. What a jerk he'd been! She'd played him like a hooked trout.

Disgusted with himself, he turned away from the capitol lawn. He'd heard enough. Leaving the two thieves, he went back to his car and returned to Bloom's.

The best he could do, right now, was damage control. As soon as possible, he would call Delia Marie, inform her of circumstances and remove himself from the job. PEI wouldn't want to be caught protecting a thief.

At the flower shop, he saw an ambulance parked by the rear door. The lights weren't on. The siren held silence. Either this was a good sign or a very bad one.

When David hurried inside, he heard Jenson's voice, complaining as usual.

"I can walk," said Jenson. "It's my arm that's busted, not my leg."

A young paramedic tried to reason with him. "Sir, you've had a concussion."

"This little bump on the noggin? Ain't nothing to worry about. Now, if you don't mind, I'd rather not ride in your ambulance. I'll catch a cab to the hospital."

David took in the situation at a glance. Jenson slumped in the chair by the door. A splint held his right arm straight. White gauze bandages swathed his head.

At the front counter, he caught a glimpse of Mandy. She actually looked worse than Jenson. A greenish hue tinted the pale skin of her cheeks. Her hair dangled in limp strands. Her hands clenched in fists, kneading the voluminous black fabric of her jumper.

David went to her. "Mandy? Are you okay?"

"It hurts," she whispered. "My stomach hurts."

"Are you going into labor?"

"How should I know? I've never had a baby before." Her eyes squeezed shut in a grimace. "I can't be going into labor. Tasha was supposed to be with me. Where is she?"

"She's fine." Depending upon the definition of the word. A fine jewel thief? "Don't you worry about Tasha."

"This is the worst day of my life," she said. "I came back here after lunch and I found that Jenson guy moaning in the back, and his head was all bloody. I called 911, but it took them forever to get here."

She clutched her pregnant belly. "Ow!"

"Hey!" he shouted to the paramedics. "You've got a real emergency over here. This woman is going into labor."

"No," Mandy groaned, "I can't be. It isn't time."

"You're going to the hospital," David said. His anger at Tasha vanished in a surge of masculine helplessness. Poor Mandy was in pain, and there was nothing he could do to stop it. David swallowed hard. He didn't know nothing about birthing no babies. Frantically, he waved to the ambulance staff. "What's the matter with you people? Get the hell over here!"

"Calm down." It was Tasha's voice. She strode through the front door and went directly to Mandy's side. "I'm here, Mandy. Everything will be just fine."

"It hurts, Tasha."

"You're having a contraction. Remember? They talked about contractions in the birthing class. It's your muscles getting ready to have a baby."

"Make it stop."

"The pain is going to pass. Try to breathe through it, okay?" She stroked Mandy's forehead. "There, it's starting to ease, isn't it?"

Mandy sighed. "I do feel better."

"You'll be great!"

"Wish I thought so." Her eyes were wet with tears, but she forced a grin. "I like your earrings. They look like the Sheikh's Rubies."

"They're only red crystal, but I wish they were rubies. I'd give them all to you. For the baby."

"I'm scared, Tasha."

"It's all right to be scared." She held the girl's face in her small delicate hands. Tasha's smile was the perfect combination of encouragement and empathy. "You're going to have this baby, Mandy. Don't you worry about a thing. I'll get you to the hospital."

"Okay."

"Let's put her in the ambulance," David said. "Come on, let's do it."

"I'm sure she's got some time," Tasha informed him. "First babies usually don't come too fast. We can drive. And Mandy is all registered at Rose Hospital. Would you stay with her for a minute?"

"What do you mean? What am I supposed to do?"

"Hold her hand. Don't panic."

"Easy for you to say," David muttered. He'd rather hang on to the tail of a raging bull than take care of a woman in labor. "Where are you going?"

"I'll be right back." She went to the rear of the store and knelt down beside Jenson. "Thank God, you're all right."

He blustered. "I wouldn't call a busted arm all right."

"I was afraid it might be more serious."

The paramedic informed her, "He won't ride in the ambulance."

"You've got to cooperate, Mr. Jenson," she chided. "These people are here to help you."

"My supervisor from work is on his way. And I want to wait for the cops, to fill out a report."

"We'll do that later. Both of us. It's important that you get yourself taken care of."

"Maybe you're right." He gave her a sheepish grin. "How'd you get away from that guy? Jeez, he was big."

"He let me go. Just let me out of the car by the capitol. I guess he just wanted to scare me."

David would have been impressed by her take-charge manner if he hadn't known she was lying. Tasha wasn't about to help the police locate Green or Brown or Cerise. She was working with them. She was the newest member of their thieving gang.

Beside him, Mandy began to groan.

Before Tasha left Jenson, she planted a light kiss on his forehead. "Thank you for trying to help me. You were incredibly brave."

"Just doing my job."

"Now it's your job to get better. Go with the ambulance people."

She saw Mandy through one more contraction while Jenson walked out to the ambulance. Then Tasha looked up at David. "I want you to go into my office. The phone number for Mandy's parents is written on the front page of my calendar. Call her mother, and tell her that we're taking Mandy to Rose Hospital."

David had no choice but to obey. No matter how much he wanted to confront Tasha, there were more important concerns.

In her office, he found the number and dialed. The mother was as calm as Tasha and said she'd meet them at the hospital within an hour. How could women handle these things with such complacency? They made giving birth seem like the most natural thing in the world.

David sank into the chair behind her desk, grabbing this moment of quiet, not wanting to go back out front and deal with Mandy. His gaze landed on the photograph Tasha had on her desk behind the pen set. A dark woman, wearing a ton of jewelry, and two little girls with long black hair. He recognized Tasha and . . . Tasha. The girls were identical.

She stuck her head in the door. "Did you reach Mandy's mother?"

He held up the photo. "You're a twin."

"That's right."

"Your sister, Stacey. She's your twin sister."

"Brilliant deduction, David. I can tell that you're a highly trained detective. Now would you bring your car around to the front door. I'll lock up. Then we can go."

"Go where?'

"Rose Hospital, silly."

As David ran for his car, he wondered exactly when he'd lost control of this situation. Was it the first time he saw Tasha and she told him that she didn't need or want a bodyguard? Last night, when he convinced her that he should stay in her apartment, it felt as if he knew what he was doing. But then he kissed her. He felt like a hare-brained marionette, and Tasha was pulling all the strings.

As soon as he double-parked, Tasha came out of the store with Mandy leaning heavily on her arm. Clumsily, she loaded Mandy in the back seat and got in beside her. "Go, David. Rose is really close. Straight up to Colorado Boulevard, then north to Eighth."

David figured that now wasn't the best time to confront Tasha regarding her criminal activities. Not while she was caring for a pregnant teenager who was about to give birth. But he wasn't going to let her off the hook.

"Slow down," she ordered. "The baby isn't coming in the next five minutes."

"Sorry." He hadn't realized he was speeding, but the speedometer showed him going fifty in a thirty zone. "Are we really close?"

"Yes. Trust me."

There would be a blizzard in Hades before he ever trusted this woman.

TASHA STAYED WITH MANDY until she was checked in, gowned and hooked to a fetal monitor that showed the strong beating of her unborn infant's heart. By then, Mandy's mother had arrived, and Tasha left the two of them in the birthing room.

She took refuge in the four-sink, institutional-style bathroom outside the waiting room, slipped into a beige stall, locked and leaned against the door. Staring at the beige-and-brown tiled wall, she tried to marshal her thoughts. Never before, not even when she and Stacey had been hell-bent-for-trouble teenagers, had Tasha gone through a day like this one. Was this really happening to her? The cat-and-mouse conversation with Cerise had seemed surreal, as if she were looking through crushed glass that distorted every image.

Cerise, Tasha realized, was the name of a shade of red. So that meant she'd met Red, Green and Brown. What kind of gang was this? They sounded like a pack of crayons. If she joined up, would she have to pick her own color? Tasha Blue. Tasha Purple. Puce, she thought. Puce was appropriate because, standing here in front of a sanitized white toilet bowl, she felt like pucing. Puking. Whatever.

She closed her eyes and swallowed hard. At least her sense of humor was coming back. When Green threatened her with broken bones, she feared she would never laugh again.

But now, there was Mandy to worry about. Tasha had been much relieved when the doctors examined the girl and discovered that she was dilated four centimeters. And the heartbeat on the fetal monitor was strong. Though the shock of finding Jenson hurt might have precipitated labor, Mandy's body was ready to deliver. Nothing would go wrong. Tasha prayed with all her heart that Mandy would come through delivery without too much pain and that the baby would be healthy. Nothing else really mattered. Green and Brown and Cerise were utterly unimportant when compared with Mandy and the new life she was about to bring into the world.

An old, familiar ache wrapped around Tasha's heart as she thought of the baby. Though it might have been smarter to be alone with her thoughts, she wanted to see David, her bodyguard. She needed his strength. Even if it was only for a moment, she wanted him to hold her and tell her that everything would be all right.

She left the bathroom and went down the antiseptic hall to the waiting room. Her spirits lifted when she saw him, pacing nervously back and forth like an expectant father.

He came to her and grabbed both of her hands in his own. With worried eyes, he searched her face. "Is she okay? Is it over?"

"Mandy's fine. The doctor says we've probably got several hours to wait."

"That can't be right. She was in a lot of pain."

"Mostly, I think, she was scared. And surprised that it hurt so much. It's one thing to have people tell you that labor is painful, and another to go through it yourself."

"You sound like the voice of experience."

"I had a baby," Tasha said. "It was three months' premature. Stillborn."

The words echoed hollowly in the vast empty cavern of her soul. Though her pregnancy had been seven years ago, the sorrow was sharp as a still-bleeding wound. She had named her infant son Nicholas. He was buried at Crown Hill Cemetery on the west end of Denver. On his birthday and at Christmas, she decorated his grave with bouquets of wildflowers.

Her eyes burned as she looked up at David. Why had she told him? She never talked about Nicholas, not with anyone. The tragedy of his death was still too close. By sharing, she made herself vulnerable.

She longed for David to comfort her, to offer the gentle solace that she'd never accepted from anyone else. But she was afraid that if he did, she wouldn't be able to hold back her tears. And she would never stop crying.

Purposely, she reclaimed her hands from his grasp. She went to a row of chairs and sat. She wasn't tired in the physical sense, but Tasha felt drained of emotions.

David sat beside her. "I'm sorry about your baby. I didn't know. The PEI dossier on you is very incomplete."

"Giving birth changes a woman," she said. "When I found out I was pregnant, I made a lot of decisions about my life. Though my son didn't live, I've tried to be the kind of person he'd be proud of."

When she was pregnant, Tasha willfully rejected the wild, exciting, sometimes glamorous life that she and her sister had been leading. She had wanted to give her child the security of a home. Her baby would have all the love that Tasha could give, all the love she had never known from her own mother and father.

"How did it change you?" David asked.

"For one thing, I had to quit my job as soon as my waist began to thicken. My sister and I worked as assistants for a magician, and I couldn't very well parade around in skimpy, sequined outfits while I was pregnant."

"A magician's assistant?" David's deep voice lifted in astonishment. "My God, I don't know anything about you."

"There's not that much to know. I had a rocky childhood, a crazed adolescence, and then I grew up and became a responsible adult. Ta-da! Nothing magic about it."

"And your sister? Your twin?"

"What about her?" There was something in his voice that disturbed her. "Why would you ask about Stacey?"

"Twins are interesting." He shrugged with too much nonchalance. "Were you a lot alike?"

"We're identical. People who don't know us can't tell us apart. But we're polar opposites when it comes to goals and temperament."

"Then she doesn't share your passion for precious gems."

Tasha grinned. "I guess we have that much in common. We're both extraordinarily fond of beautiful things. Stacey loves designer clothes, flashy cars and a glittering night at the Metropolitan Opera."

"What about you?"

"I'm more likely to find beauty in a clear blue sky. Or a shop full of blooming flowers. Or the lusty cry of a healthy baby." She stood. "Which reminds me. I should be getting back to Mandy."

"Tasha!"

He caught hold of her arm, and she swiveled to face him. His gray eyes seemed darker, as if there were storm clouds in his gaze. His mouth was tight. Holding back something he needed to say? "What is it, David?"

"I'm glad you're safe."

She smiled broadly. "So am I."

Mandy's labor continued, gathering intensity, with Tasha and Mandy's mother alternating time at her side. Every half hour or so, Tasha returned to the waiting room to give David an updated bulletin.

After the second time she emerged from the labor room, he'd taken to foraging in her absence. He had a magazine, a newspaper, a candy bar. At the dinner hour, when she came out to see him, he greeted her with food. Two bagels and a quart of orange juice that Tasha wolfed greedily.

On her next visit to the waiting room, David had a companion, a uniformed policeman. Her first instinct was to run. During her teens and early twenties, Tasha's relationship with cops, like the repulsive Inspector Henning, had been less than cordial. She was older now, impeccably responsible. But she still had something to hide.

David introduced Officer Perry. "He has a few questions for you. It's about the assault on Jenson."

"All right," she said. "Let's be quick about it."

"Yes, ma'am." The officer glanced at David. "Is she always this bossy?"

"Always," he said.

"Here's what happened," Tasha said. She told the story of Green coming into the shop twice.

"And he called himself Green?" the officer queried.

"Mr. Green," she said.

"Do you think that's his real name?"

"Probably not." She glanced over at David. "There was a man who bothered me on the street last night. A Russian-speaking man. He said that he was Mr. Brown."

"I see." Officer Perry made a note. "And do you have any idea why these, um, colors are coming after you?"

Without the slightest hesitation, Tasha lied, "No idea whatsoever."

To tell the truth would be to sign her own death warrant. During their ride in the car, Green had made that perfectly clear. If she betrayed them, he would kill her. Slowly. And he would enjoy every sadistic minute.

To Officer Perry, she quickly described what had happened with Jenson. "Then Mr. Green ordered me into his car. I didn't resist. I was much too afraid."

"I understand. Then what happened?"

It was best, she knew, to stick as close to the truth as possible. "Green took me to the capitol building and dropped me off."

"And that's all?"

"Yes."

"Did he say why he was abducting you?"

"I'm sorry, Officer. He might have said something or done something that would have explained his behavior, but I was so terrified that I wasn't thinking straight. Green is a huge man. Well over six feet tall, with arms that are bigger around than my waist. I can't remember a thing."

"After he dropped you off, what happened?"

"I caught a cab back to Bloom's where I found Mandy in the first stages of labor. Then we came here." She smiled in what she hoped was a disarming manner. "I really should get back to Mandy now."

"Sure," the officer said. "Thanks for your time."

When she glanced back at David, he seemed cool, as if he suspected she was lying. What did he know? What did he suspect? It occurred to her that David's intelligence might be extremely hazardous to her health.

After another hour with Mandy, Tasha returned to the waiting room. The hours of stress were taking their toll on her. She felt haggard, exhausted, wrung out. At first, she didn't see David. What if he'd gone? What if he knew she was lying to the police and had left her? She couldn't bear being alone after she'd had a taste of his companionship and caring. For the first time in her life, Tasha didn't want to be alone.

David strolled around the corner from the gift shop. "There you are," he said.

Relief flooded through her. He wasn't gone! He hadn't left her. Not yet, anyway.

David reached behind his back and produced a homely display of pink and blue daisies in a ridiculous ceramic vase that looked like a duckling.

The arrangement was so tacky, yet so well-intentioned, that she had to laugh.

"I realize," he said, "that bringing flowers to a florist's assistant is a bit like carrying chocolate to Hershey, Pennsylvania."

"A bit."

"I want to do something. Isn't there anything I can do?"

"Mandy's on her own. Like it or not." Tasha gazed into his eyes, wishing he could read her mind and know how much she wanted for him to hold her. "Nothing you can do."

At half past eight o'clock, Mandy went into hard labor. She was wheeled into the delivery room. Tasha scrubbed quickly and followed the gurney. She held Mandy's hand as the girl pushed with all her waning strength. Sweat poured down her forehead. She strained with every muscle.

"Come on, Mandy," Tasha urged. "You can do it."

"I can't." She was weeping loudly. "I can't."

"Push again. I'm so proud of you."

With Mandy's last ferocious effort, the head crowned. Tasha watched in awe as a miracle occurred. The baby girl was born.

Immediately, the attending physician and a nurse bent over the tiny, silent infant. They were working hard.

Tasha's heart stood still. Was something wrong with the baby? Oh, God, no. Remembered horror choked her in an icy grip.

Mandy whispered, "Where's my baby?"

Tasha gripped her hand. Fighting her own panic, she tried to reassure the new mother. "It's a girl, Mandy. A baby girl."

"What's wrong? Where is she?"

Tasha prayed with all her might. "She's fine. Just fine. You did a great job, Mandy. Really. You were wonderful and you worked so—"

A loud cry resounded in the delivery room.

Joy and relief exploded within Tasha. She sang out, "A beautiful baby girl! Oh, Mandy. She's perfect."

The nurse placed the squalling infant upon her mother's breast. "There she is. With all ten fingers and toes. A healthy baby."

In the recovery room, they were joined by Mandy's mother, who also fawned over the new mother and child. Tasha was glad to see this evidence of bonding. Mandy's mother had been consistently disapproving of her daughter and the decision to keep this fatherless child, but now she was warm and kind and everything a grandmother should be.

Mandy rocked the baby against her bosom. Glowing, she asked, "Is David still waiting? I want him to come in and see my baby."

"He'd love that," Tasha said.

"Do you think the hospital would mind?"

"It's probably breaking a rule, but what could it hurt? Only for a minute. Okay?"

She ran to the waiting room, still dressed in the baggy hospital scrubs. When she saw David, she was beaming. "It's a healthy, beautiful baby girl."

He grabbed her in his arms and lifted her off her feet. They were both laughing as if they'd won the lottery. But this was even better. The prize was a precious human life. Tasha could think of few moments in her life that were so unabashedly happy. And it was exactly right that David was there to share this experience with her.

When he set her down, she clasped his hand and pulled. "Come with me. Mandy wants you to see the baby."

"Me?" He pointed to his chest. "She wants to see me?"

"That's right."

When they crept into the recovery room, Mandy smiled at them both. "You two look good together."

David leaned over her. "Not as good as you and this little beauty. Congratulations, Mandy."

"Nothing to it."

"What are you going to name her?"

Mandy tickled the tiny baby under her chin. "I didn't pick out a name ahead of time because I thought it might be bad luck or something."

She was so young, Tasha thought. So young, and yet a mother. "I remember when you talked about that."

"So I kind of figured I'd do something mystical, you know?" Her gaze lifted from the baby and polled the three people in the room. "I figured I'd pick out a name from the first thing I saw when I gave birth."

Tasha really hoped she wasn't going to name her child Light Fixture or Nurse or Doctor. When she glanced at Mandy's mother, she suspected the same thoughts were tracking through her mind.

"Sounds great to me," David said.

Just like a man, Tasha thought. He was oblivious to the potential for a disastrous name choice.

"So?" David asked. "What's the name?"

When Mandy looked directly into her eyes, Tasha caught her breath. Would Mandy name the baby for her? Without thinking, Tasha laced her fingers with David's, wanting him to share this beautiful moment. A child bearing her name? That would be a sweet responsibility.

Mandy's gaze shifted. She was staring at Tasha's bright, oversize, red crystal earrings.

Mandy said, "My daughter's name is Ruby."

Chapter Six

While Mandy slept in her hospital room, Tasha changed out of her hospital scrubs and went to stand at the viewing window of the baby nursery. Nine other infants squalled, wriggled and slept, but Ruby—in Tasha's totally biased opinion—was the most beautiful. Ruby lay very still with her eyes wide open, gazing upon the world with perfect innocence. Her whole life lay ahead of her.

David came up beside her, and Tasha sighed. "She's wonderful, isn't she?"

"A miracle," he agreed.

"Thank you, David, for being here. Not many guys would have hung around for the whole ordeal of labor."

"It's my job," he gruffly reminded her.

"Yes, of course."

Tasha smiled. Of course, it was his job to guard her day and night, but his occupation wasn't the real reason he'd stayed at the hospital, pacing in the waiting room. David was here because he was sincerely concerned. He wanted to support Mandy, a kid he hardly knew. His motives bespoke old-fashioned chivalry and reminded her that not all men were bastards like Green. There were good men, too. Men like David. "It meant a lot to Mandy to know you were here. And to me, too."

"You were pretty cool about the whole thing."

"Me? I was scared to death."

"I didn't think anything frightened you, Tasha."

She didn't reply. There were many things she must not share with him, and her fears had too many faces. There were nervous jitters and screams of shock, hysterical panic and horror. Sometimes, Tasha felt as if she'd known them all.

Her fears for Mandy came from concern and empathy—a clean fear, based on the reality of the physical unknown. Unlike the sickening terror she'd felt when Green had caught her and held her against her will, when he'd broken Jenson's wrist. Tasha shuddered at the memory. Had it only been this afternoon? Less than ten hours ago? She remembered Green and Cerise as if from a distance. Their scheme felt like part of a different life. Yet their evil loomed over her like a tidal wave, poised to crash over her and wash away everything she'd worked so hard to achieve.

A dull fear hammered through her. Why, oh, why was this happening to her?

Seeking relief from her inner torture, Tasha gazed again upon Ruby. The baby's eyes had closed. One tiny fist rested beside her cheek. She relaxed in the dreamless sleep of a pure being, a little angel. Tasha prayed that this infant would never feel pain, would never experience hatred or disappointment, would never be frightened. And when she encountered the inevitable hard times, Tasha wished for Ruby to be strong. These would be her gifts to Mandy's baby: Strength. Wisdom. Bravery.

Tasha reflected upon her own pathetic lack of these three qualities. Facing Green, she'd been weak and helpless. In her conversation to Cerise, she'd agreed to a foolish endeavor. And brave? Now that Mandy's baby was born, the uppermost thought in her mind was running and hiding from a future that could only be catastrophe.

"Tasha?"

She glanced at David. He was the one shining star in the murky darkness that enveloped her. Though she had no idea who had sent her a bodyguard, she offered grateful thanks to her unknown benefactor.

"There's nothing else you can do here," he said. "I'll drive you home."

She blew a kiss to Ruby and fell into step beside him. "I guess it's time to get back to stone-cold reality."

"Guess so."

He seemed quiet and withdrawn, but that didn't necessarily mean anything. This had been an intense day for all of them.

They stepped through automatic doors into the cool September night, and Tasha shivered. She'd left her jacket at Bloom's, hours ago, when the sun still shone warmly. While she was with Mandy, her own physical discomforts had been put on hold. Now the evening air felt chilly, and her stomach growled. "I'm starving. When we get back to my place, can we order a pizza?"

"You can do whatever you want."

She cocked her head and looked up at him. His jaw thrust at a stubborn angle, and he avoided eye contact. "David? Aren't you spending the night?"

"You don't need a bodyguard anymore."

"Why would you think that?" Never before in her life had she felt more threatened.

"Call it a hunch, but I don't think anybody's going to be after you. Not anymore."

With a shock, she realized that he was correct. The bad guys had contacted her, and now they thought she was on their side. There would be no more threats unless she changed her mind. But how did David know?

She halted at the edge of the parking lot beneath a streetlight. What did David know? Had he been contacted by Green or Cerise? Though she hated to suspect him, she couldn't help wondering if he was part of their scheme. But why? Warily, she said, "David, I need to know what you're talking about. What makes you think the danger is over?"

Though he stopped beside her, he refused to meet her gaze. His constantly moving eyes peered into the thick darkness beyond the parking lot. His head turned at the wail of an approaching ambulance, and he watched as the flashing lights careered past them toward the hospital's emergency entrance. This was a man who was accustomed to sudden violence. It was his job to anticipate an ambush before it actually happened. But what if he was part of the attacking force? The shadows that played across his features emphasized the sharp angles of his brow, cheekbones and chin. He looked hard, chiseled in stone, and equally implacable. "It's best if I go."

His low baritone snapped against her. There was a finality in his tone. He would say nothing more.

And Tasha wasn't the sort of woman who liked to beg. She started walking again. "Okay, then. Go, if that's what you want."

But she longed to have him stay with her. Lacking the confidence in her own strength, she yearned for someone to lean on. Not just someone, she corrected herself. David. She needed David.

During those long hours when Mandy was in labor, she had eagerly looked forward to being with him for those few minutes when she could slip out to the waiting room. His silly gifts, his purely masculine confusion, renewed her. She had come to rely upon him in a way she could never express in words. At some point during Mandy's labor, Tasha had come to the conclusion that David Marquis was a good man.

She didn't want him to leave. Even if he was the ringleader of Cerise, Brown and Green, she wished David could be with her.

In silence, she slipped into the rental car beside him. Even now, when he was obviously angry with her, his nearness provided a sustenance that she desperately craved.

Too soon, he parked in front of her apartment building. Still not looking at her, he said, "Goodbye, Tasha."

"It's ironic," she said. "During all that time when you insisted upon staying, I didn't want a bodyguard. Now, when you tell me you're leaving, I want you to stay."

"I'd be in your way."

"Look at me, David."

He leveled a gaze into her eyes, and she saw a reflection of her own sadness. She rested her cold fingers on the sleeve of his blazer. "You don't want to leave," she said.

"I can't be with you." He placed his hand atop hers. There was a poignant warmth in his touch. "It's best if I go now."

"Why?"

"Listen, Tasha, I haven't always been a bodyguard. I've done a lot of things in my life that weren't exactly law-abiding. I've made mistakes. And I got away with it because I came from a wealthy family. But I changed. Permanently and forever."

Tasha nodded. His history sounded like hers, except for the part about the rich family.

David continued, "Now I'm as straight-arrow as they come. I like my job. I like protecting people who are wrongly threatened. My work shifts the balance, you know?"

"I understand."

"So it's better if I don't know exactly what you're involved in. I didn't lie to Officer Perry, but I didn't tell him everything I knew."

What was he talking about? "I haven't done anything wrong."

"Not yet," he said.

"Not for a very long time. Why would you think otherwise?"

"I'd rather not explain. Tasha, I don't want to be forced to turn you in."

How could he presume to know what was going on in her mind? *Forced to turn her in?* Like a criminal? A thief? She'd worked hard. She deserved respect, not suspicion. "Now you listen to me, David Marquis. I haven't been a saint, either, but—"

"Don't bother with excuses."

"What?"

"I won't lie for you," David said. "I won't cheat. And I sure as hell won't steal."

"Nobody asked you to."

"I can't be on your side, Tasha. What you're doing is wrong."

She snatched her hand away from his light grasp. "Of all the self-righteous, judgmental, arrogant—" She fought to control her temper. She wouldn't give him the satisfaction of losing control. "You know nothing, David."

"Give me a little credit. I'm not a complete idiot."

"So you have some reason to suspect. So what! You're wrong! But that doesn't matter to you, Mr. Straight-Arrow. You've already tried and convicted me. Without even talking to me, you've decided I'm up to something illegal. Such a bad girl, so naughty, so evil."

"Am I wrong?"

"I don't have to prove my innocence to you." Her anger erupted like Vesuvius. How could she have thought he was sensitive? He was cold, quick to condemn. "I will tell you this, David. You're making a big mistake."

His eyes hardened. "Would you want me to go to Inspector Henning with my mistaken suspicions?"

"For all I care, you can go straight to blazes!"

She leapt from the car and slammed the door hard. In just a few steps, she was inside her building. Running up the stairs, she went into her apartment and locked the door behind her. "Damn you, David. Damn your—"

Suddenly alert, she went silent. Something was wrong with her apartment. The drapes were drawn.

This morning, they were open. She'd left with sunlight streaming through the south windows.

The light in her bedroom was on. Tasha was certain that she hadn't left any lights burning this morning.

Someone had been here. Or they were still here.

She would have been frightened, but anger consumed her. Storming through the bedroom door, she saw Green stretched out on her queen-size bed. His hands were folded behind his neck, and his head rested on her pillows.

Tasha glared at him. "Now I'll have to scrub my pillowcases with disinfectant."

"Where's the boyfriend?" Green slung his long legs over the edge of her bed.

"He dumped me," she snapped.

"Good. I didn't like the boyfriend hanging around."

"And I don't like you coming into my apartment without permission. What are you doing here?"

"You were supposed to contact Cerise at six o'clock."

"Well, excuse me. It slipped my mind. I was in a hospital labor room, helping deliver a baby."

"Ah, yes. Your little assistant."

"Mandy is her name."

Tasha couldn't believe she was actually snarling at this very large man. If Green had a mind to, he could break her in half without even blinking an eye. But he seemed disinclined toward violence as he pushed himself off the bed, yawned and stretched. His knuckles brushed the ceiling.

As he started toward her, Tasha turned her back on him and strode toward the kitchen. Though she didn't want to appear frightened, she wasn't about to stand in his path and be trampled in order to prove her point.

She yanked open her refrigerator door. Since she couldn't very well order a pizza for only herself, she'd make something here. But what?

"You've got nothing to eat," Green said. "I looked."

"Did you?" It infuriated her that he had been in her apartment, lying on her bed, going through her refrigerator. He had no right to violate her privacy. Under her breath, she muttered, "If I'd known you were coming, I would have stocked up on raw meat."

"What did you say?"

For a big man, he moved quietly. He stood close behind her, so close that she could smell him. The stinky miasma of expensive cologne and acrid masculine sweat reminded her that Green wasn't like other men. He was a barely tamed animal, a monster disguised in a well-tailored suit. He wouldn't stand for teasing. He was dangerous, and she needed to control her hostility.

"I'm sorry," Tasha said. Warily, she closed the refrigerator door and stepped back, bumping her hip against the kitchen counter.

"I don't like you, Miss Lancer. I don't like your attitude. You think you're some kind of princess. Like you're better than me. You think you can tell me what to do."

"Really, I don't. I didn't mean to—"

"Shut up." His mouth didn't smile. His eyes were flat and dull, vacant of humanity. "You do as you're told."

She nodded. "I understand. I'm sorry. I was scared."

"Shut up! I won't hurt you unless you give me reason to. And you don't need to worry." He sneered. "I'm not interested in you as a woman. You're not my type."

That was a major relief!

"Too skinny," he said. "I like my ladies to have some meat on their bones."

Crudely, he cupped his hands in front of his chest. Any woman who could fill those huge hands would have breasts the size of basketballs. But Tasha prudently refrained from making any smart comment. Instead, she asked, "Did you have any other message for me?"

"Call Cerise tomorrow. Six o'clock at night. Same number."

"I will." Timidly, she added, "I guess you can go now."

"What did you say?"

How had she offended him this time? "Nothing. I'm sorry."

His huge hands braced on the kitchen cabinets on either side of her. He leaned down until his big, ugly face was only inches from hers. Panic raced through her. Was he going to hurt her? How had she offended him? She was afraid to ask. In the back of her mind, she heard the sickening snap of bone when he'd attacked Jenson.

He lifted one hand. His thick finger rested on the tip of her nose. "You don't tell me when to go. That's not your job. I decide when I'm going to go. You don't give me orders."

His sneer became a sadistic grin. His finger pressed harder on her nose, and a nauseated ache spread across her face into her sinuses. She gritted her teeth to keep from crying out.

"I told you before, Miss Lancer, that you would do everything I said. You listen to Cerise. You don't go to the cops. You do your part on this job."

"Yes," she whispered.

"You treat me right, Miss Lancer." He removed his finger and stepped back. "Or else I'll show you what it means to be sorry."

She nodded, cowering before him.

"You need another lesson," he said.

"No, please. I understand. I'll do whatever you say."

"Breaking that fool's arm wasn't enough to convince you." Slowly, deliberately, he scanned her kitchen. His gaze rested on two large vases that she planned to take to the shop for displays. Green lifted the vases, one in each hand. "I could break you. Like this."

"I understand. You don't have to—"

He flung them onto the kitchen linoleum with such force that they shattered.

Glass slivers leapt up and bit into her legs like the stinging of bees. She stood frozen, afraid to move, fearful that she might inadvertently irritate him.

"Do you understand me now?" he demanded.

"Yes."

"Don't try anything cute," he warned. "I'll be around, Miss Lancer. When you least expect me."

He left. As soon as the apartment door closed behind him, she ran to lock it. Not that her door lock and dead bolt were the least bit of deterrent. Green had gotten in here easily.

Low sobs rasped in the back of her throat. Her breath came in choking gasps, convulsing her body. She wasn't seriously injured. A few of the cuts on her legs were bleeding through her panty hose, but she hardly felt them. Her pain came from realizing how utterly defenseless she was. *He could break her.*

"Oh, God, what am I going to do?"

Always, Tasha had believed that she could face any challenge. She could dig deep inside and find the courage. If she worked hard and didn't give up, she could succeed at almost anything.

This time, her confidence wavered like an ephemeral mirage. She wasn't safe. There were enemies all around her, closing in for the kill.

"Oh, David . . ." His name slipped through her lips.

He's gone. Though his absence left an emptiness where her strength should have been, it didn't do any good to wish things were different. *He's not coming back.*

She had to go on. Alone. There was no other alternative. "Pull yourself together, Tasha."

She'd been in worse situations. She just couldn't remember when.

Forcing herself to be rational, she cleaned up the glass in the kitchen. *Pull yourself together.*

In the bathroom, she peeled off her panty hose and cleaned the cuts on her legs. Nothing serious. Mostly nicks.

She hardly recognized her own reflection in the bathroom mirror. A sickening terror haunted her eyes. Her jaw trembled weakly. A waxy pallor erased the blush on her cheeks. Even when she scrubbed away the traces of smeared makeup, she wasn't herself.

Dressed in her favorite old flannel nightgown, she stumbled back into the kitchen. Though still hungry, she couldn't face the job of cooking. Instead, she went to the lower cupboard beside the dishwasher and took out a mostly full quart of Stoly.

Grabbing a tumbler from the kitchen cabinets, she splashed the clear vodka over ice cubes and took a healthy swallow. The liquid burned a path down her gullet, and she hoped the warmth would spread like a goosedown quilt, muffling her fear and rage. She needed to escape, but she couldn't run. There was no choice whatsoever. She had to follow orders from Green and Cerise or else. It was best to deaden her emotions, to find solace in the traditional drink of her Russian ancestors.

Making quick work of the first straight vodka, she poured another and sank down into a ladder-back chair beside her kitchen table.

The alcohol spread through her body, gradually easing her tension. False courage in a bottle. That wasn't her way. Tasha wasn't a drinker, though she'd always had the ability to drink hard liquor and not get drunk. Her mother was the same way. And her sister. *Damn you, Stacey. Where are you? How did you get me into this mess?*

Tasha easily imagined her twin's mischievous grin. So many times, Tasha had taken the blame for something her sister had done. Getting into their mother's makeup. Stealing a candy bar from the drugstore. Sneaking through the night, dressed all in black. Breaking and entering.

Somewhere, Stacey would be laughing about the plot to steal the Sheikh's Rubies. But she would be safe, and, somehow, Tasha would have to find her way through this ordeal. Alone.

Without David. Because he'd run out on her. His high and mighty ideals wouldn't allow him to associate with her, a common criminal.

She was totally insulted. She raised her glass. "Common? Let me tell you this, David, there's nothing about me that's common, old boy."

If only he'd given her a chance to explain...

What did it matter? She couldn't have told him about Green.

Tasha sipped at her vodka. She barely knew David, anyway. Why should she care about him?

But she did care. She liked him, admired him.

More than that. Tasha groaned, remembering their brief but wonderful kiss. That would never happen again. She would never have the chance to lie beside him, would never make love to him.

She downed the last of her second vodka. Feeling woozy, she headed off to bed. She tore off the pillowcases where Green's head had made an indentation. Tomorrow, perhaps, she would burn them. But for right now, she was too tired.

As she pulled the covers up to her chin, she glanced at her bedside clock. Three minutes after midnight. Into the darkness, she whispered, "Good night, David."

HER SLUMBER BROKE suddenly. There was a sound in her apartment. It would have been handy to be instantly alert, but Tasha was still dizzy from the vodka. Through blurred vision, she saw the clock. It wasn't even one o'clock yet. What was going on? Why had she wakened? She floundered through a mental fog, so heavy and thick she could barely move.

But she had heard…something. The click of the front door lock? Someone had come through her front door. Was it Green? Had he returned to inflict some new abuse upon her? The man was a bully, a horrible fiend.

There was another noise from the kitchen. Through her half-opened bedroom door, she saw the light being turned on in the front room.

Okay, she wasn't imagining this. There was definitely an intruder. *Wake up, Tasha! Wake up!* She needed to defend herself. Since she kept her handgun at the store, her only protection was.a baseball bat that she hid under the bed.

Tasha reached for the bat, but her arms and legs were tangled in her sheets. Clumsily, she battled free from the twining bedding. Moving with all the stealth of a water buffalo, she groped under the bed for the Louisville Slugger. When she stood, the bedroom twirled slowly, like a merry-go-round in slow motion. Balancing carefully on the balls of her feet, she crept toward the bedroom door.

The silhouette of a man appeared in the doorway.

She took aim. With all her might, she swung. And missed.

The bat clattered against the door frame. The reverberation of the ash wood stung her sensitive fingers, and she dropped her weapon with a little yelp of surprise.

Now what? Trembling and indecisive, she covered her face with her hands. If she were lucky, the pain would be over soon.

"Tasha? What the hell are you doing?"

The baritone voice was gentle and . . . wonderful.

"David!" He'd come back! He couldn't leave her, after all. Despite her angry parting words, she flew into his arms, adjusting her body to fit around the gun in his shoulder holster. "You're here. Thank God, you're here."

He enfolded her in a sweet embrace, and her tension ebbed like the moonlit tide. His strength absorbed the harsh terror that had gripped and shaken her. She could feel her breathing return to normal. Hard-edged, stark reality blurred to a softer focus.

David peeled her off of him and stared into her eyes. "Are you all right?"

"Now I am."

"Tasha, what's wrong?".

"Nothing," she said quickly. But she was still a little shaky on her feet and had to rest against the wall in the hallway to keep from weaving back and forth.

He picked up the bat from the carpeted floor. "Were you planning to protect yourself with this?"

"Maybe." She peered through the semidarkness. He was really here. David had come back to her. He was going to help her. She wasn't alone anymore.

"The Louisville Slugger isn't such a good idea," he said in a sensible tone. "If I'd really been a bad guy coming to attack you, your best defense would probably be to reach over to the phone by your bed and dial 911."

"Really?" Her heart lightened. Though it was the middle of the night, the world seemed rosy and wonderfully bright.

"Yes, really. It's too easy for an intruder to disarm you, then use the weapon against you."

"Really?"

He pulled her toward the light from the kitchen. Again, he studied her eyes. He was worried about her. Illogically, his concern pleased her. She thought his caring was the most marvelous thing in the whole world.

"Tell me more," she said. "About how to fight off the bad guys."

"Never take on somebody bigger and stronger than you are," he advised, "unless you have better weapons and know how to use them."

"Okay."

"Whenever possible, call for backup."

"Reinforcements." She nodded. Her head felt loose and wobbly on the stem of her neck.

"Stay alert and don't get sloshed." A slow grin spread across his handsome face. "But I guess it's too late to tell you that."

"This is a lot to remember, David. All these security things."

"Sometimes," he agreed.

"Know what? I don't think I can handle it all by myself." Hesitantly, she added, "I need a bodyguard."

"If the job's still open, I'll take it."

"Oh, David!" It was all she could say. Happiness welled up within her until she felt that she would burst from the sheer, unmitigated pleasure of having him here.

"Obviously," he said, "you also need a cup of strong, black coffee to sober up."

He hitched his arm around her waist and guided her to the kitchen where the Stoly and single, empty tumbler waited on the dining room table. It looked so pathetic, Tasha thought. A woman alone. Drinking alone.

She felt compelled to make an excuse. "Usually, I'm not much of a drinker. But I didn't have any food, and—"

"It's okay," he said. "Got a headache?"

"I'm not sure." There was a pressure behind her eyes, but it didn't hurt. She reached up and touched her nose, remembering Green's threats. "I'm kind of dizzy."

"Turn around," he said. "Get back into bed and I'll bring you coffee."

Though she was perfectly capable of walking, she leaned on his arm. It felt good to be cared for.

He turned on the bedside lamp and stared questioningly at the tangled sheets and blankets. "Were you bouncing on the bed? Never mind. I don't want to know."

He pulled down all the covers and plumped up the pillows. "Lie down. I'll cover you."

When she scooted into the center of the bed, her long flannel nightie hiked up. She started to pull down the hem, but David caught hold of her hand.

"What happened to your legs?"

She couldn't tell him. Green had warned her about going to the police, and David was one step away from them. "Nothing," she said, reaching down to cover the dozens of tiny cuts.

"This isn't nothing. There are a couple of good-size slices here."

"I dropped a vase in the kitchen," she said. "It shattered and, I guess the glass cut me."

"I don't believe you." But he covered her legs with her soft, old, flannel gown. Not saying another word, David shook out the wrinkles in the pastel sheets and smoothed the comforter over the lower half of her body.

Tasha waited. She knew he would ask questions that she couldn't answer. She didn't want to deceive him, but she couldn't speak the truth. It was too risky.

Finally, he sat on the edge of the bed, facing her. He stroked her bangs off her forehead. "Someone hurt you, Tasha. Was someone waiting for you when you came into your apartment?"

"I can't say." She held herself very still, knowing that he could read her slightest movement.

"Was it that big guy?" David asked. "Was it Green?"

"Could you get me two aspirin from the medicine cabinet in the bathroom? I think I'm getting a headache."

He lifted her hand from her lap, held it to his lips and breathed a light, lingering, warm kiss across her knuckles. "You're afraid to tell me."

She sealed her lips. Fear and common sense warned her not to speak. She'd entered into a pact of silence with the devil. If she betrayed Green—

"You know, Tasha, the first step in ending the abuse is to tell someone. Someone who can help you."

But if she told David, something terrible would happen. She could die. There wasn't a doubt in her mind that Green would kill her, and it wouldn't be a quick, executioner-style death. She remembered what he did to Jenson. She remembered the bits of broken glass slicing into her legs.

She closed her eyes and remembered...a long time ago. Her mind drifted into a distant past, dark threats, painful consequences, the cold disbelief in her mother's eyes. Denial. Only Stacey knew the truth. Only her twin believed her. Even when Tasha said nothing, Stacey knew her pain.

Tasha remembered when she was pregnant... The father of her child. The features of his aristocratic face were no longer clear in her mind, but she would never forget his words when she'd told him that she was carrying his child. "You mustn't tell a soul."

He'd slapped her, hard. Called her a fool. Then slapped her again. Didn't she know he was married?

She hadn't known. Tasha had been blinded by the glitter of his costly gifts. Diamond stud earrings. A strand of pearls. She hadn't seen beyond his Rolls-Royce. She'd been seduced by elegant dinners served by a butler at his London flat.

You mustn't tell a soul. Or else...

But she had to tell Stacey. Tasha had to explain why she was leaving the magic act. And Stacey had taken revenge. His lordship was beaten. His head was shaved.

It wasn't enough to save Tasha. She had suffered the worst possible consequences. Her baby had been stillborn. Baby Nicholas had died.

In her rational mind, she knew there was no connection between her cruel lover's warnings and the death of her child. Still, his words carried weight.

She abandoned her memories, returned to the present danger.

"I can't tell you, David." She searched the depths of his gray eyes, expecting to see rejection and anger. Instead, she found kindness. He was strong enough to be gentle. "Please don't leave me."

"I won't go."

"Promise me."

"I'll be here all night. Tasha, you don't have to be scared anymore. I won't let anything bad happen to you."

Though she had learned never to trust anyone but her twin sister, she believed him. She pulled his hand to her cheek and rubbed against it. For this moment, she felt safe.

When he left the bedroom to get her aspirin and to make coffee, she allowed herself to drift on the warm, secure feeling of being protected. Safe, at last.

She was no longer alone.

Chapter Seven

Though she managed to gulp down a couple of aspirins, Tasha was asleep by the time David had finished brewing a fresh pot of coffee. Standing in her bedroom doorway, he gazed down at her resting figure. The light from the bedside lamp filled the room with a pinkish glow, soft and lovely across her face. Her eyelids were closed. She was so small and slim that she barely made a ripple under her pretty, feminine white comforter.

"Tasha? Are you awake?"

Her lips puffed. She made a muffled, indelicate noise that sounded suspiciously like, "Drop dead, David," and rolled to one side, dragging the bedding askew.

He took a sip of coffee from a blue ceramic mug. "This isn't what I expected," he murmured.

He had wanted to clear the air. Halfway to Denver International Airport, he'd decided that she was right when she accused him of being judge and jury, convicting her without hearing her side of the story. He hadn't given her a chance to explain.

Instead, he'd quit—something he'd never done before on a bodyguard assignment. No matter how difficult the client, David had always managed to ignore the affronts, the rudeness and the outright insults. He granted a great deal of latitude, figuring that these people were under stress, otherwise they wouldn't need bodyguards. Besides, it wasn't his job to get personally involved with his clients. His only responsibility was to make sure they didn't get dead.

Tasha was different.

He grinned as he watched her restlessly kick the sheets. She slept like a gymnast doing floor exercises. If anybody else had been flopping around in the bed, he would have found it annoying. With Tasha, he thought her acrobatics were cute. No matter what she did, she touched him in a way that no other woman could. From the start, he hadn't been able to maintain his professional impartiality.

That was why—when she had deceived him, when he'd overheard her plotting to steal the rubies—David felt betrayed at the deepest level. He'd thought they were a team, but she was playing solo. And that hurt.

Still, he was wrong to quit.

She deserved a chance. Even if she was a thief, she had proved that she was a cat burglar with a heart of gold at the hospital where she selflessly cared for Mandy. There was much good in Tasha.

He set down the coffee mugs on the bedside table, removed his shoulder holster and hung it on the headboard where he could pull his automatic in an instant if he needed to.

Tonight, David would stay in her bedroom instead of attempting to rest on her uncomfortable brocade sofa. As a bodyguard, he'd taught himself how to exist on catnaps and light rest, but he much preferred a bed.

Tasha flipped again, and he frowned. Cuteness not withstanding, it might be impossible to sleep next to someone who bounced around on the bed. Maybe the sofa was better.

He kicked off his loafers, propped himself up on the pillows and stretched out his legs on the queen-size bed. He reached for his coffee and took a sip.

In her gyrations, Tasha now had one leg completely free from the covers. In the light from the bedside lamp, he studied the tiny cuts on her shin. Her injuries could have been a result of an accident she'd had with a vase, as she claimed. But he doubted that her pain was so innocent. Somebody was still terrorizing her. Somebody had inflicted those nicks on her legs.

Green, he thought. That huge guy who had snapped Jenson's wrist in his bare hands. Green. What kind of creep was he, anyway? What kind of man got his kicks by scaring women?

Tomorrow, if David was lucky, he'd have some answers. Earlier this afternoon, he'd given all the photos and her sketch of Brown to Earl Rockman, his friend who owned the detective agency and still maintained connections with the CIA and Interpol. Fingerprints would have been a better source of identification, but the photos might work. Tomorrow, David might have real information instead of these stupid names. Mr. Green. Mr. Brown. Cerise.

And Tasha. How did she fit into their color scheme?

She flung herself across the bed again. In her slumber, she discovered him beside her. Making tiny purring sounds, like a kitten, she snuggled in the crook of his arm. Her lips breathed a contented sigh. And she went limp and motionless.

The warmth of her slender body felt right in his arms.

He should have turned off the lamp and caught some rest. Instead, he looked down at her. Even without makeup, she was striking. Her sculpted eyebrows and lashes were dark as ebony against her creamy complexion. The long tendrils of black hair curled artlessly across her cheeks and forehead.

Mesmerized, he wanted to kiss her. From deep within, he felt an overwhelming urge to taste her mouth, to feel her come alive in his arms.

Oh, yeah! That was a great idea! Not only were they both exhausted from one hell of a stressful day, but he still didn't know if she was a cat burglar. David hardened himself against the tenderness she elicited so easily. He couldn't make love to a criminal. What if she'd been plotting all along to steal the rubies? What if she'd duped him?

Well, then . . . he'd have to change her mind. Somehow, he'd convince her that she couldn't steal the rubies. Why should she? She seemed happy in the flower shop. Her artistic talents were well exercised in creating arrangements. Surely a steady, responsible, law-abiding life was a far better reward than a million-dollar payoff.

Yeah? David had to laugh at his own naiveté. How the hell was he going to convince this beautiful burglar that a life of hard work was better than stealing the rubies? It was more likely that he could slip into a red cape and Superman tights, fly into the stratosphere and heal the hole in the ozone.

He placed his coffee mug on the table, turned off the light and eased down into the bed.

Her hand rested upon his chest. Her slender legs fitted against his. She nuzzled him gently in her sleep, and his body responded. Her nearness was like liquid electricity flowing through his veins. He fought to resist, and tension tightened every muscle in his body. There was an aching heaviness in his groin. God, he wanted to make love to her. It would be so natural. It would be so right.

Or was he lying to himself? Was he willing to ditch a lifetime of lawful restraint for one night with her?

Calling upon every shred of his willpower, David turned in the bed so his back would be to her. Still, she curled around his shoulders. It was going to be hell to ignore her.

DAVID MANAGED to sleep in fitful snatches until the morning light filtered around the edges of the window curtain in her bedroom. As soon as she wakened, he was aware of the change in her breathing, the slight alertness in her body. And yet, she didn't move away from him. With a sigh, she tightened her embrace.

"David," she whispered. Her breath tickled the back of his neck. "I'm so glad you came back to me."

"You're awake," he said.

Immediately, she released him and moved away, putting a space between them on the bed. "Good morning."

Her voice was still husky from sleep.

"Good morning." He rolled over and faced her. During the night, he'd stripped down to his undershirt and shorts. He avoided touching her. All it would take was one caress and his self-control would snap like a frayed thread.

Her dark eyes seemed to ask a question, and he tried to answer. "You don't need to worry, Tasha. Nothing happened between us last night. I didn't, you know, take advantage."

"I know."

"How come you're so sure?"

"First, because you're a gentleman. Second..." She reached toward him and traced the rough morning stubble on his chin. "I would have remembered."

She was incredible! So sexy. So willing. At this moment, she was everything he had ever wanted. After a night of tortured resistance, he couldn't hold back any longer.

He grasped her supple body and pulled her close. Her slender body fit perfectly against his chest. He kissed her hard, with all the pent-up frustration from a night of unfulfilled passion. He needed to make love to her.

He grasped her breast. His thumb flicked the taut bud of her nipple, exciting him beyond reason. Desire consumed him, devouring his common sense.

When she squirmed against him, rubbing his hard arousal, David knew he wouldn't stop. He couldn't.

And yet... He ended their kiss. Groaning, he forced himself away from her. My God, this was the most difficult thing he'd done in his life.

He climbed out of bed and stood. Slowly. Painfully. "I'll make fresh coffee."

"Yes," she said quietly. "That would be best."

It was killing him to walk away from their warm nest, but he had to do it. Making love to a client went against all his principles as a bodyguard. Making love to a cat burglar was insane.

"David," she called to him.

He paused in the bedroom doorway. "Yes?"

"Thank you for last night."

She watched him leave the bedroom. He looked fantastic in his underwear. Most men seemed kind of silly in shorts and a sleeveless T-shirt, like paper dolls waiting to be dressed in cutout clothes. But David had a magnificent, broad-shouldered body with firm torso and narrow hips. His morning erection filled her with desire. His was a butt to die for.

To die for? Tasha frowned at the phrase that had popped innocently into her mind. Death and dying weren't jokes. She glanced over at the headboard where David had hung his shoulder holster. A gun in the bedroom. She couldn't allow herself to relax and feel safe while danger pressed all around. The presence of Green made her future uncertain.

Throwing off the covers, she padded into the bathroom. Why couldn't she have met David in some other way? Why couldn't they be off on a desert island with no horrible distractions? Together they could find perfect contentment with the sun and the surf and stars overhead at night. Dammit, why did life have to be so complicated?

When she emerged from the bathroom, Tasha was wrapped in her old flannel robe. Though she'd managed to splash water on her face and tidy herself up, her mind roiled in chaos. She didn't know how much to tell David. This conversation would be a cautious balancing act, giving him enough information so that he would stay with her as a bodyguard, but not enough for him to go to the police.

He'd slipped into his trousers, but still looked sexy as could be in his bare feet and sleeveless T-shirt that exposed the crisp, curling hair on his chest. She longed to rub her fingers through that hair, to feel the shivering tension of his flesh, to experience the moment when he would abandon restraint and make love to her. He was all man. Looking at him excited the womanly passion within her.

And yet, he set the coffee mugs on the table with the air of someone who was ready to do business. He said, "I guess you're wondering why I came back."

"I try to never look a gift horse in the mouth." She looked away from him, forcing herself to forget her natural yearnings and desires. "I'm just glad that you're here."

"Why?"

"Because I'm in over my head." She sat primly at the table and crossed her ankles. "David, I'm scared."

"Tell me about it."

Slowly, she tasted the coffee. Her habitual wariness kept her from spilling the whole terrifying story. Last night, when he'd driven her home from the hospital, he'd threatened to go to Inspector Henning, and that would be disastrous.

David sat, resting his elbows on the table, and picked up his mug. "I'll start. Yesterday, when Green took you to the capitol, you met a woman. She was dressed in red and called herself Cerise. The two of you put your heads together and started making plans for how you would steal the Sheikh's Rubies."

She gulped and the coffee burned her throat. How did he know? "I suppose that's what our conversation must have looked like."

"That's what it was. I overheard enough to know that."

"You were spying on me?"

"Yes."

"I'm astounded, David. I didn't notice you at all."

"It's my job to be inconspicuous," he reminded her. "I'm not a master of disguise, but I am capable of blending into the local scenery." He frowned. "And don't change the subject. Listen, Tasha, I've got to know what's going on. All the details. Otherwise, I can't protect you."

"But you aren't going to leave me again, are you?"

"If you lie to me? I'll leave in a heartbeat."

She set down her mug and glared at him. She didn't like ultimatums. Her typical response to authority was to flaunt it, but she desperately needed David to stay with her. Without him, she'd be lost. "What do you want to know?"

"Why did Cerise contact you?"

"Because of my brilliant reputation as an international cat burglar who specializes in safecracking. How does that strike you, David?"

His jaw tightened. "Go on."

"The problem is that I'm really not a cat burglar." She exhaled a deep breath. "But my sister is,"

"Stacey." David nodded. From the moment he'd spied the photograph on her desk, he'd known that her twin sister was involved in this strange conspiracy. Now, finally, they were taking baby steps toward the truth. "Cerise thinks you're Stacey."

"She's sure of it."

"Why?"

"We're identical."

He leaned back in the chair at her kitchen table and tried to imagine two of her. Double the energy of Tasha. Double the sassy attitude. Double the charm.

David shuddered. Double the trouble.

"It's not an uncommon mistake," she said. "We look exactly alike. Our voices sound the same. I've been told that we share the same gestures and mannerisms. The only difference is here." She tapped her temple. "We don't think the same way."

"I really hope, Tasha, that you're not going to tell me you're the logical one."

"I'm the patient twin," she said. "I don't mind building my castle in the sky with one brick at a time."

"And Stacey?"

"She loves adventure. Fast cars and skydiving. Designer outfits and fashion shows."

"And jewelry?" He remembered her visceral response to the viewing of the rubies, her expertise in discussing the diamonds with the clerk in Pola and Tweed. "Do you share a passion for precious gems?"

"I guess so."

"You're not complete opposites."

Abruptly, she left her seat and went into her bedroom. Quickly, she returned with a large cedar box and flipped open the lid. The shimmer was blinding. "These are my jewels. Crystal, glitter and paste. There's not a real gem among them."

He ran his fingers across the fake rings and necklaces. "Bitter?"

"Don't get me wrong, David. I love precious stones. In my life, I've owned some lovely pieces. Once, there was a man who gave me flawless diamonds and pearls. I treasured them. They were magnificent." Her lips curled into a frown. "When I sold them, I thought they were the ugliest rocks I had ever seen."

"Why?"

"Because of what they stood for." She sighed. When she looked at him, her eyes were troubled. "I understand the difference between surface beauty and the fire within. The tiniest chip of a diamond, given and accepted in love, is more splendid than the Sheikh's Rubies."

Tasha closed the lid on her jewelry box. "I don't know if Stacey feels the same way. I haven't seen her in five years, but I know she's lived in Europe and New Zealand and New York, for a while."

"It sounds like she has a glamorous life-style."

"I suppose it does, but it's not for me." Tasha shook her head. "That's all I can say about Stacey. I won't give you details about anything she's done. No matter what, she's my sister. My twin. It wouldn't be right to betray her."

"Loyalty is an admirable trait," he said. And, often, a fatal one. "Tell me about what's happening right now. Here. In Denver."

"When Cerise and her gang decided to steal the rubies, they checked out all the places where the necklace and earrings would be displayed. Apparently, they zeroed in on Pola and Tweed because their security system is dreadfully old-fashioned. When they did photo surveillance on the jewelry store, they noticed me in one of the shots."

"And they thought you were your sister."

"Correct. Cerise thinks I set up Bloom's as a front, using Tasha's name, so I could be located next door to Pola and Tweed and could heist the Sheikh's Rubies. Which is, of course, ridiculous."

"Not really," David said.

"Why would I go to all the trouble of setting up a shop as a front?"

"The rubies are worth millions. Even if you'd invested a hundred thousand in opening your shop, you would make a tidy profit."

"But I'm the first person the police would investigate if the rubies were stolen. You saw how Inspector Henning treated me. He'd like nothing more than to lock me up and throw away the key."

"Does he think you're Stacey?"

"No." Her voice got small, and she stared down into her coffee as if searching for answers in the depths of her ceramic blue mug. "It doesn't matter to Henning which of the Lancer twins I am. Though my sister has the better rep among criminals in the know, Henning thinks we're both thieves."

David wasn't sure that he wanted to know, but still he asked, "Was this because of Miami?"

"Because of Paris. And the sapphires."

He squinted across the table at her. The more he learned about Tasha, the more her résumé sounded like a high-class training ground for a cat burglar.

"So," he said. "There were sapphires in Paris, emeralds in Miami and rubies in Denver. I presume there were also precious gems involved in SoHo."

"I think it was diamonds."

"Excuse the pun, but you're a multifaceted woman."

When she tossed back her head and laughed, David thought he had never heard such a lovely, clear, pealing sound. Like wind chimes in the breeze. The tension that had been building between them shattered.

So easily, she charmed him, enchanted him. This was why he'd returned. Though David could pretend he'd come back to fulfill his professional obligations and set Tasha back on the straight and narrow, the real reason was that he needed to be with her again. He wanted to hear her laughter and to see her million-dollar smile.

The merriment lingered in her eyes. "Oh, David, I needed that. As long as I can laugh at my problems, they don't seem quite so huge and horrible."

"But the problems don't go away." He reached across the table and took her hand. He held tightly to her fingers, not letting her pull away, not accepting her quicksilver evasiveness. "Tell me about the plan to steal the rubies. When are they going to do it? How?"

"I don't know that yet. We'll make contact later."

Did he believe her? "When's the next contact?"

"Before I say anything else, David, I've got to know if I can trust you, too. Can you guarantee that you won't go to the police?"

He hesitated, knowing that he couldn't allow her to actually steal the rubies. He wanted to yank her out of this connection with Cerise, even if that wasn't what Tasha wanted.

"David? I need to know. Can I trust you?"

"I would never do anything to hurt you."

"That's not what I asked."

Tasha gently released his hand. She had her answer. Though she desperately wished it could be otherwise, she couldn't tell David everything. Perhaps she'd already said too much.

As her fingertips drew away from his, she leaned back in her chair, putting more physical distance between them. Emotional distance would be more difficult and infinitely more agonizing. Even now, as she gazed at him, she felt the beginning pain of separation.

She was so confused. More than anything, she wanted him with her. But he'd as much as admitted that he would betray her. His good intentions, she feared, would literally be the death of her. If Green found out . . .

"Talk to me, Tasha."

"There's nothing else to say."

"Tell me about Green and Brown."

She shook her head. The smart thing would be to simply tell him to leave, to slap his handsome bottom and send him on his way.

She glanced at the clock on the kitchen wall. "Look at the time. I have a lot to do today. First, I want to run over to the hospital to see Mandy and darling little Ruby. Then I have to rush back over to Bloom's. Leaving early yesterday puts me behind. And I need to place an ad in the paper for a new assistant."

"Quite a schedule," he said dryly. "Whenever will you find time to steal the gold off the capitol dome?"

"Lunch break," she said.

Tasha pushed away from the kitchen table. Though she would have loved to have David as close as possible, protecting her night and day, she simply couldn't trust him. He might prove to be more of a liability than a help. After all, things hadn't worked out too well with Jenson as a bodyguard. "Tell you what, David. You stay here at my apartment and I'll keep you posted on developments."

He gaped at her. "Excuse me? You want me to stay here and keep the home fires burning while you go out and wrestle with the bad guys?"

"Well, I wouldn't put it that way, but . . . yes."

"Honey, I'm not that kind of man."

"That's what I'm afraid of."

"I'll protect you, Tasha, not the other way around."

"Right now, they think you're my boyfriend. If Green finds out you're a bodyguard, it'll blow the whole thing." She pivoted and headed toward the shower. "You're not coming to the shop today. I can handle it."

Firmly resolved, she rushed through her shower, washed and blew dry her hair and slapped on makeup. By the time she was dressed in a long mauve skirt with matching turtleneck and a sequined vest, David was also ready.

"I'll follow your car to the hospital," he said.

"That really isn't necessary. I'm sure I'll be safe."

"I wasn't thinking of you, Tasha. I was hoping Mandy would let me hold the baby again."

SINCE EIGHT-THIRTY in the morning was well before the regular hospital visiting hours, Tasha blithely lied to the nurse on duty at the floor desk. "I know it's early," she said, "but we're immediate family."

The nurse raised her eyebrows and peered over the top of eyeglasses that had slipped to the tip of her long nose. "Both of you?"

Tasha nodded.

The nurse scowled at David. "Are you the father?"

"No, ma'am." His response was immediate as was the sudden frantic blush that reddened his face. "Not the father. No."

"A brother," Tasha said smoothly. "And I'm a sister."

"Not much of a family resemblance, is there?"

"We're all adopted," Tasha explained.

"Well, I suppose it's all right," the nurse said, adjusting her glasses. "Mandy is in a two-person room, but she doesn't have a roommate right now, so you won't disturb anyone else. Be quick about it."

"We will." Tasha led the way down the corridor. Under her breath to David, she said, "Good thing we're in a hospital."

"Why's that?"

"When the nurse asked if you were the father, I was sure you were going to have a heart attack."

"Very funny." But he didn't look the least bit amused.

"Do you have any children, David?"

"No. I was married once. But it didn't last and we didn't have kids." He shrugged his broad shoulders as if shaking off an unpleasant memory. "Someday, though, I want two. A boy and a girl."

Tasha peeked into Mandy's room. She was sitting up on the bed, cradling a tiny, flannel-wrapped bundle in her arms and cooing softly. When she looked up, Mandy beamed a smile that was as brilliant as a rainbow. In all the time she worked at Bloom's, this teenager had never looked so happy.

"Motherhood agrees with you," Tasha said.

"Yeah, it does." Mandy stroked the fine dark hair on her baby's head. "I love Ruby so much."

David hovered on the opposite side of the bed. In his navy blue suit and open-collared white shirt that revealed a glimpse of dark hair at his throat, he looked totally masculine and out of place in this hospital room. Yet he didn't appear to be uncomfortable. "Mandy, can I hold her?"

"You'll be careful, won't you?"

"I'm a bodyguard. I'm always careful."

She eased the baby away from her breast, and David lifted the tiny infant, taking care that she wasn't pressed against the gun in his shoulder holster. His features softened as he gazed down at the little round face. In a low, private voice, he told Ruby that she was the most beautiful girl in the whole world. When she wiggled in his arms, he chuckled with sheer delight. "She smiled at me."

Tasha exchanged a glance with Mandy, and the two women silently acknowledged that the baby's smile was probably gas. But neither of them corrected David's perception. His natural, sincere fascination with Ruby charmed Tasha. The picture of a big, strong, handsome man playing with a fragile infant was a heartbreaker. Someday, she thought, he wanted kids. His warm affection for Ruby made her think that someday might be very soon. His biological clock was ticking even more loudly than her own.

She scooted around the bed to stand beside him. "My turn."

"Come on, Tasha, I've barely had a chance." Little Ruby's hand was barely large enough to reach around his index finger, and he murmured to her, "Not long enough. Huh, pretty girl. You want to play with Uncle David, don't you?"

"Please, David. I have to go to work. You can stay."

With a sigh, he surrendered the child. When Tasha clasped the warm little body to her bosom, a surge of maternal yearning flowed through her. Ruby was beautiful. She was perfect. Ruby's eyes, bright as sapphires, shone at her. The delicate, rosebud lips pursed in an expression that appeared to be both thoughtful and wise. Did babies think? Did these tiny biological miracles come from a magical place, imbued with knowledge that adults could only guess at? Or was it gas?

Ruby made a squeaky noise, and Mandy immediately responded, "She wants her mommy."

"And that's you." Reluctantly, Tasha passed Ruby back to her mother. "Are you breast-feeding?"

"Yeah, but I don't think she's hungry because she just ate. And I burped her." With Ruby safely cuddled in her arms, Mandy smiled again. "You were right about taking those newborn baby care classes, Tasha. I'm not freaked at all, and I have a pretty good idea what to do."

"You're going to be a terrific mommy."

"I hope so. Ruby deserves the best."

With a sigh, Tasha returned her mind to more practical concerns. "I've got to get back to Bloom's."

"I'm sorry we ran out of there yesterday," Mandy said. "I kind of left a mess."

"Don't you worry about a thing. I'm going to hire somebody to fill in for a couple of months, then I want you to come back to work for me."

"I don't know. Day-care is—"

"Unnecessary," Tasha said. "I would be thrilled if you brought Ruby with you to work. We can figure it out. I promise."

"You're the best friend I ever had. Can I ask you something important?"

"Sure."

"Tasha, would you be Ruby's godmother?"

"Oh, yes. That would make me very happy."

If, by some benevolent quirk of fate, Tasha managed to survive the next few weeks, she would be overjoyed to be a godmother. If she were still alive, she would embrace life as never before. She wouldn't waste any time being bitter or frightened. If she survived...

"I'm going now," she said with a glance at David.

"I'll see you later," he said.

"Tonight. At the apartment," she said firmly. She was supposed to telephone Cerise at six o'clock. "I should be home by seven, but if it's later, I'll call."

"Okay. Bye."

He watched her leave the hospital room as he settled into the single chair beside Mandy's bed.

"You look good together," Mandy said. "You and Tasha."

"Do we?"

"I think you kind of like her."

"Kind of," David agreed. Though it seemed slimy to weasel information from Tasha's assistant, David needed more facts. "I don't know too much about her, though."

"I do," Mandy cheerfully volunteered. "What do you want to know?"

"This twin sister of hers. Stacey? Do you think they were close when they were growing up?"

"Totally," Mandy said. "When they were, like, fifteen years old, they ran away from home together and went to work for a magician. Isn't that so bad?"

"Bad?"

"Bad means good," she explained. "Cool? Neat-o? Anyway, it sounded like the best job. They got to travel all over the world. In France and England and everywhere."

"What did they do in the magic act?"

"Tasha said they did all kinds of twin things where one of them would disappear in one place and the other would appear someplace else."

Of course, he thought. A set of twins would be handy for performing illusions.

Mandy's voice changed as she talked to Ruby. "That's right, little girl, I'm talking about Tasha, your godmother."

"What else?" David asked.

"You really want to know about her, don't you?"

He rationalized that he truly did want to know about Tasha. It was part of his job. He wasn't really taking advantage of Mandy's naiveté. "I do."

"Another thing they did with this magician was escapes."

"Like Houdini."

"Whatever. You know, like Tasha would get locked up in handcuffs and chains and stuffed inside a safe. Then she'd break out. She said they would, like, come into a town and the local cops would use their own cuffs. One time, they got locked in a bank vault.''

Swell, he thought, Tasha had expert training from a magician on how to crack a safe. ''I wonder how they did those tricks?''

''Here's the best part. It wasn't a trick.''

''What do you mean?''

''Have you noticed how Tasha always wears gloves?''

He nodded.

''Well, it's because she has this really superdeveloped sense of touch. And her sister, Stacey, has it, too. When this magician guy found out about it, he showed them everything he knew because they were, like, ten times better than anybody. You should see her do card tricks.''

''Great,'' David muttered.

''Oh, yeah, and you have to ask her to show you how to pick somebody's pocket or pick a lock. She's, like, incredible. One time she took a necklace right off my throat and I didn't feel a thing.''

Inwardly, David groaned. He didn't find much assurance in the fact that Tasha had kept up her pickpocket skills. It seemed that she and her twin were naturally gifted with the very talents that a cat burglar would need.

Chapter Eight

Sunday morning at Bloom's was usually a quiet time, but after leaving early on Saturday with none of the regular duties taken care of, Tasha felt as if she'd entered a marathon from two miles behind the starting gate. There were deposits to make, balances to calculate, plants to water, flowers to be arranged, deliveries to be filled. Thank goodness she'd taken care of the church flowers yesterday morning.

She raced through the door, grabbing half a dozen notes that had been shoved through the mail slot and turning on lights. The interior of the store was chilly, and she discovered that the door to the refrigerated unit had been left open. She slammed and latched the door, turned up the thermostat and glared at the hectic, blinking light on the telephone message machine.

A million things to do! On the plus side, this morning promised to be so busy that she wouldn't have a spare minute to think about David. *Oh, David...* Immediately, a series of images flashed across her mind. David, walking from her bedroom in his underwear. David, pacing in the hospital waiting room. David in his tuxedo, the most handsome man at the premier showing. David, David, David.

Desperately, she wished she could tell him the whole truth. But she couldn't take that risk. She couldn't trust David to ignore his principles. If he went to the police...

Forget about David! She needed to keep busy. She couldn't allow herself to think about how cozy it was this morning when she wakened beside his warm body.

With firm resolve, Tasha stacked the notes beside the phone. Only one required immediate attention: A special delivery of African violets had been left next door at Pola and Tweed.

Though the jewelry store didn't officially open until noon, Tasha went around to the rear entrance where an armed security guard sat in a lawn chair, reading the Sunday comic section of the *Denver Post.*

"Excuse me," Tasha said.

The gray-haired guard peeked over the top of the paper. "You're the lady from next door."

"That's right. And I have a bit of a problem. Yesterday, a deliveryman left a shipment here. They're delicate plants, and I'm concerned about them. Can you let me inside?"

"I'm not allowed to do that, miss."

There was a Texas twang in his voice and he appeared to be so relaxed that he was almost comatose. She noticed, however, that his right hand rested on the butt of his revolver, and she suspected that this lanky old Texan would be quick as a rattlesnake if action were required.

"I don't suppose Janet Pola is here yet."

"No, miss. She surely ain't."

Tasha was certain that he had a key to get inside. In fact, he'd probably spent the night on the interior of the shop. "Could you telephone Janet and ask her if it's okay for me to go inside?"

His weathered face pulled into a scowl as he cogitated, then he took the cellular phone off his belt and made the call while Tasha stood waiting impatiently, counting the seconds, thinking of all the tasks she needed to accomplish before she opened her doors for business at noon.

When the security guard disconnected his call, he turned back to her. "Missus Pola says it's okay, but here comes the man you really need to talk to."

Slowly, Tasha wheeled around, knowing who she would see. "Inspector Henning."

"Good morning, Miss Lancer." His burred British accent was crisp. "Bribing the guard?"

"Oh, please don't start."

"I'm wondering why else you might be here."

"All right, have it your way. You're right. I came over here to seduce this gentleman." She gestured to her rather dowdy turtleneck and midiskirt. "As you can see, I'm wearing my highly erotic Dance of the Seven Veils costume."

"Rather snippy for a Sunday, aren't we?"

Tasha could have launched into a sermon about respect and disrespect and presumption of innocence until proven guilty. Instead, she stated the facts. "A delivery of plants to my store was left here. I just want the flowers. Okay?"

The security guard added, "I spoke with Missus Pola, and she gave the go-ahead."

"In future," Henning said, "permission to enter the store when it is not officially open for business comes only from me. Do I make myself clear?"

"Yes, sir, Inspector."

Henning held out his hand for the keys. "I will accompany this lady into the store."

After Henning used three separate keys to unlock the doors, they stepped inside where he deactivated a computer alarm. Tasha followed him. Almost immediately, she spied the flat containing her African violets in the small employee lounge area at the very rear of the store. "Here they are," she said. "I'll be going now."

Henning blocked the exit. "Don't run off, my dear little Tasha. Or is it Stacey?"

"All I want is the flowers."

"Come with me." His snotty arrogance befitted his hefty swagger as he pointed toward the hallway that led past Janet's office toward, as Tasha knew, the vault. "You might as well check out the security."

"I'd rather go," she said.

"My dear, I would prefer not to have you traipsing in and out with ridiculous excuses and pestering the guards. Do allow me to show you our extensive precautions."

"Listen, Henning, I've been in and out of here a million times. Janet and I are friends."

"Then you must be aware that we have upgraded the lock system on the vault. It is timed to open one half hour before the store opens. It closes one half hour after closing time. All computerized. To override the system takes a special key and direct notification of the local police."

Honestly, she said, "I couldn't care less."

He studied her with insultingly frank scrutiny. "I wonder which one you are. The spunky, industrious, little Natasha? Or are you the sophisticated, world-weary Anastasia?"

"I'm Tasha." She picked up the flat of violets. "And I'm leaving."

"I understand there was a disturbance at your so-called shop yesterday. An assault perpetrated by a Mr. Green."

"Yes. And my assistant went into labor."

"Where there's a Green, there's a Brown, and often, a Sienna. Or Cerise." He stepped in front of her to block her exit from the shop. "Their name is Spectrum. They operate primarily in Europe. Jewel thieves. Though they have, on occasion, branched into other endeavors."

"Let me pass. I don't know what you're talking about."

"Very good!" His round, cherubic face became a cold mask. "You and your sister were always the most wonderful liars. Not a twitch or a tic or a blink to betray your perfidy. Come with me."

When he reached toward her, Tasha darted away. She despised Henning's smugness. In Miami, he'd kept her in police custody for twenty-four hours before Stacey could arrange for her release. Henning had perfected the art of tiptoeing around the rules without technically breaking the law.

"How's your mother?"

Tasha was taken aback. "Why are you asking about my mother?"

"I've had cause to consult with her on occasion, to seek her expertise on jewelry. She seems to have a great vitality, a strong acquisitive nature, almost a greed. Family trait?"

Her lips were tight. "Mother is fine."

"Do you suppose she'll be coming into Denver to view the rubies?" His thick lips pursed in a sneer. "Do you know her plans?"

Tasha rolled her eyes. "No doubt she's organized the other residents of her retirement community near Vail into a troupe of geriatric cat burglars. Now, if you don't mind—"

"But I do mind, Miss Lancer. This time you're not going to get away with it."

"Let me by!" she yelled, loudly enough that the lanky Texan guard poked his head inside.

"Very well," Henning said. "I'll be in touch."

As Tasha marched stiffly toward the rear entrance to Bloom's, carrying her tray of violets, she couldn't decide which was worse. Green saying he'd be watching her? Or Henning promising to stay in touch? Both men despised her. Both wanted to hurt her. Both threatened. In her mind, the only difference between them was that Henning was supposedly on the right side of the law and Green was on the other.

After she'd taken care of the bookkeeping chores and answered her most urgent phone messages, Tasha moved on to the more practical, more satisfying tasks of preparing flowers. She opened the heavy door to the large walk-in refrigerator unit.

"Oh, no!" Her heart plummeted as she beheld the chaos. Flowers were strewn in all directions. Carnations, gladiolus, tulips, lilies. Crushed and broken. Long stems of roses snapped and maimed. Tubs of water were overturned. Handfuls of dirt, flung against the walls, dribbled into mud puddles on the linoleum floor.

Why?

Was this a message from Green, showing her that Bloom's was worthless except as a front?

Maybe it was Henning who had done this. He could have slipped in and out easily. But why?

Pure cruelty, she thought. Nothing else could explain the wanton destruction of these beautiful blossoms. She bent down and picked up a single white tulip that had somehow escaped being trampled. Once again, she wished that David were here to help her, to soothe her aching vulnerability.

But she couldn't call on him. If Green knew he was a bodyguard, he'd probably kill David. If Henning knew, he'd suspect her even more than before.

David couldn't help. In spite of her temporary sense of security when he came back to her last night, Tasha couldn't call on him. She couldn't tell him the truth. She was alone.

But not helpless! Her outrage flared, shot to the boiling point so quickly that she didn't even feel the refrigerated chill. Damn them all! This was her life! Bloom's was her future. She wasn't going to give up, wasn't going to dump everything she'd worked for. They weren't going to beat her down. Not without a fight.

Tasha dragged on a pair of yellow rubber cleaning gloves, rolled up her sleeves, hiked up her skirt and dug in, salvaging as many of the blooms as possible, swabbing like a cleaning lady possessed until every surface glistened and every trace of the destruction had been erased. Unfortunately, most of her flower stock was also gone.

It was past one o'clock when she stuck the Yes, We're Open sign in the front window and unlocked the door. It was a matter of pride to stay open for business. Even if she only had one carnation to sell, Tasha would open her doors.

Her determined professionalism belied the fact that she looked like Cinderella after a bad day in the ashes. But how could she go home and change clothes? There was no one else here to watch the store. Tomorrow, she would contact one of the women who worked for her during peak times, like Valentine's Day and Mother's Day. But there was no point in doing so today. On a Sunday when she was only open for a few hours, anyway.

Tasha rested her elbows on the counter and buried her face in her hands. Too much. This was all too much.

Yet, when the tinkling bell over the door announced the arrival of a customer, her smile was ready. "May I help you?"

At a glance, she realized that this fellow definitely needed help. His posture was atrocious, almost deformed, with a nerdlike hunch to his shoulders. His flowered Hawaiian print shirt and too-baggy, too-short trousers worn with sloppy socks and sneakers were not the standard upscale uniform of Cherry Creek shoppers. His baseball cap with a logo for the Oregon Ducks pulled low on his forehead. Tinted-blue glasses obscured his face. His goofy grin was an orthodontist's nightmare.

Though Tasha tried to be charitable, this guy was a mess. Though he wasn't a teenager, he appeared to be stuck in the throes of male adolescent clumsiness. He had a Spiderman tattoo on his forearm, for goodness' sake!

In a nasal voice, he said, "I hear you're looking for an assistant, and I like plants a whole bunch."

"Do you?" The fact that she even considered hiring this guy indicated the level of her desperation.

"You betcha," he said.

He thrust out his jaw, and a spark of recognition went through her. She noticed that his forearms were muscular. The vee collar of his ridiculous shirt revealed crisp, curling, dark chest hair. "David?"

He straightened. The breadth of his shoulders expanded by several inches. "You're perceptive. I thought this was a great disguise."

His voice was its natural baritone but with a lisp, and he spat out the dental appliance that turned his straight white teeth into the world's worst overbite.

Delighted to see him, Tasha laughed. "I knew it was you. Right away."

"No, you didn't."

"I'd have to be an idiot not to recognize you," she said as the door to her shop swung open. "After all, I slept with you last night."

"Tasha!" The person who had entered was Janet Pola. Obviously, she'd heard Tasha admit to spending the night with this grotesque nerd, and Janet was purely appalled. Gaping, she stared at David's back, then at Tasha.

David slipped in his fake teeth, hunched his shoulders and turned around to face her. "Hi ya," he squawked. "I'm Tasha's new assistant."

"Really?" Her upper lip curled in disgust.

"Yuper-duper," David said, sticking out his hand. "My name is Wally Beamis."

"Charmed." Janet allowed him to grasp her fingertips before brushing past him to the counter where she took in Tasha's disheveled clothing and general air of exhaustion. "Darling, are you all right?"

"I've been better," she admitted. "I had a break-in last night, and someone destroyed most of the stock in my refrigerated unit."

"With all my guards next door? I can't believe it."

"Me, neither," David said, clumsily leaning against the countertop. Despite his weird disguise, she saw a glimpse of the real David.

"It's my own fault," Tasha said, addressing her words toward David. "I was in such a hurry to take Mandy to the hospital that I didn't set the alarms. Getting in here was simply a matter of picking a door lock."

"If you'd like," Janet offered, "I can have Inspector Henning pay a visit and revamp your security. I loathe his cigars, but he's quite the expert in his field."

"No, thanks," Tasha said vehemently. "My losses are only a couple of hundred dollars worth of greenery. I'm glad that the African violets weren't damaged because I need them for an order. Thanks, Janet, for allowing the deliveryman to leave them with you."

"No problem." Dismissively, she waved her ring-bedecked hand. "How's Mandy?"

"She had a baby girl, six pounds, eight ounces. Her name is Ruby and she's absolutely perfect."

Glad to think of something other than the break-in, Tasha described Mandy's labor and delivery while Janet listened with rapt feminine attention and empathy. David, alias Wally Beamis, made appropriate nerdlike grunts of disgust.

Glancing toward him, Tasha concluded, "And David was wonderful. He spent the whole time pacing in the waiting room."

"David?" Janet frowned before she remembered. "Oh, yes, your handsome boyfriend."

"Not anymore." Tasha cast a bemused glance at the man in the ghastly Hawaiian print shirt.

"What do you mean?"

"He had to return to New York."

"Such a shame! He was so terribly good-looking, and I think he cares a great deal for you, Tasha. I caught him watching you with very possessive eyes."

Tasha was momentarily pleased by her friend's observation until she realized that a bodyguard's scrutiny would naturally appear to be possessive.

"In any case," Janet continued, "I'm happy for Mandy. And her baby's name gives me a terrific idea for a baby gift. A silver spoon with a tiny, little ruby in the handle."

Though Tasha could hardly think of any gift less practical for a teenaged mother, she said, "Mandy will love it."

Janet headed to the door, turned and regarded David with a critical look. "Don't take this personally, young Wally."

"Huh?"

"Dear boy, you've absolutely got to change your style before you start working in Cherry Creek."

He gave her a huge, dopey smile. "Okeydokey."

With a shudder, Janet left.

"She could be right." Tasha looked him up and down. With mock concern, she said, "I can't have Wally Beamis lurking around Bloom's. You'll frighten my customers."

He popped out the dental appliance. "Come on, Tasha. I might be homely, but I'm not scary."

"Some of my regular customers pay a hundred dollars for a pedicure. Tackiness horrifies them."

"Tacky?" He pantomimed "Who me?" His elbows went flying. His shoulders hunched even higher. *"Moi?"*

She struggled to keep the laughter out of her voice. "Where did you get that dorky outfit?"

"Hey, it wasn't easy to find pants that were both baggy and too short."

"And the teeth?"

"The teeth and the glasses were especially made for me by a Manhattan makeup artist."

"Someone who was, no doubt, going for the stylish Hunchback of Notre Dame look," she suggested.

"Sometimes, in my line of work, I need a disguise." Triumphantly, he added, "And it works, doesn't it? Janet had no idea who I was."

"Congratulations," she said dryly.

"So, what do you think? Can I be your assistant?"

"Well, I suppose I could hide you in the back." Suiting the action to the word, she led him away from the front counter to the back of the store. "I'll explain to people that you're a genius botanist who I've hired to create a special signature flower for Bloom's."

"Then I'm hired?"

"Yes, David." She slid her hand along his forearm. If only he weren't so doggoned honest and law-abiding... "I'm glad you're here."

In one swift gesture, he doffed his baseball cap and the silly-looking, blue-tinted glasses. He straightened up and became her David again. "You know, Tasha, it isn't the clothes that make the man."

"I know." She glided into his embrace.

Whether or not she could trust him remained to be seen, but she very much needed someone to watch her back. She needed him on so many levels. His steadfast presence might be her only anchor in a sea of fear. "I want you with me. Here in the shop. And at home."

"That's handy." He pressed lightly on her spine, and she molded her body against his. "Because I want to stay."

"Does this mean you've decided I'm not a cat burglar?"

He feathered a kiss across her forehead. "It means that I've always liked felines."

"A cat like me might be too independent, David. On a whim, I might scratch your eyes out."

"Your purring makes up for it."

Before he could kiss her, the bell at the door tinkled and the parade of afternoon customers began.

It was just before five o'clock closing when Jenson sauntered into the shop. The white plaster of his wrist cast shone like a warning beacon in Tasha's eyes, reminding her of Green and of danger.

Guiltily, she asked, "How are you feeling?"

He held up the cast. "Doesn't hurt a bit. The docs say I'm going to be fine."

"I'm glad," she said. "And I'm really sorry that you were injured."

"Not your problem, lady. Although if you'd done like I told you and kept me posted at the front door, I would've spotted that guy as a bad cookie. Would've shot him right quick."

Then you might be dead, she thought. Tasha doubted that Jenson could have beaten Green in a showdown.

"Anyhow," he said, "that's not why I came by. I've got a package for David from my boss. Do you know how to reach him?"

"Yes, I do." Over her shoulder, she called, "Wally? I have a package for you to deliver."

David in his disguise loped from the rear of the store. As he approached Jenson, he nearly tripped over his own feet.

"Whoa, there. Who in the heck are you?"

"My new assistant," Tasha said. "You can trust him as much as you'd trust David himself."

"You think so?" Jenson was clearly disbelieving.

"I promise," she said.

Reluctantly, Jenson handed over the eight-by-twelve envelope to David, who pivoted in a grossly ungraceful pirouette and retreated to the rear of the store, into Tasha's office.

Jenson leaned toward her. "That's some strange kid."

"Isn't he?"

A puzzled Jenson left the shop, shaking his head. He hadn't recognized David. Nor had Janet. His disguise masked his appearance, and his klutzy behavior hid his strong masculinity. If Tasha hadn't witnessed the transformation before her very eyes, she wouldn't have believed it was possible.

After finishing with her last customer, Tasha locked the front door and went into the office where David sat in her chair with his feet upon her desktop. He'd discarded the cap, glasses and teeth, and the serious expression in his gaze was purely David. Intelligent. Cool. Ever watchful.

Tasha knew from his look that this was not the time for teasing and joking. "What was in the package from Jenson?"

"Information."

For the past several minutes, he had debated with himself on whether or not he should tell her the findings that Earl Rockman's Detective Agency had discovered after the inquiry to Interpol. If Tasha were in cahoots with this gang that called itself Spectrum, he wouldn't be telling her anything she didn't know.

"David?" Tasha's eyes widened as she closed the office door behind her. "What's wrong?"

She wasn't naive. She had to be aware of Spectrum's reputation for callous cruelty. How could she be involved with these people, even for a moment?

He watched her expression carefully, knowing that she was an accomplished liar, as he tossed his snapshot of Green onto the desktop. "According to Interpol, this man sometimes goes by the name of Green. He has half a dozen other aliases. His real name is Callahan."

Tasha sat in the chair opposite her desk. "What else?"

"He was arrested twice in the United States when he was in his teens. Both times for assault. Both times, the victims dropped charges before he came to trial." He looked up at her. "His first victim was his grandmother. He beat her with a kitchen chair."

Tasha's jaw clenched. Though she sat perfectly still, her eyes were moving, glancing to the right and the left as if she sought escape from his information.

David's instinct was to comfort this delicate woman who seemed as fragile as a broken rose. Deep in his chest, he felt an urge to pull her into his arms and tell her that everything would be all right. But his protectiveness was overbalanced by anger when he thought about her working side by side with Green to pull off this caper.

Harshly, he continued, "In his early twenties, Green moved to the Middle East where he was, apparently, employed as a mercenary for several years. In Europe, he was suspected in four contract murder cases."

"Contract murder?"

"Someone else hired Green to kill the victim. One of these murders was particularly brutal. The woman was bludgeoned almost beyond recognition. Both her legs were broken. The police suspect that death took several hours."

He gazed steadily at Tasha. A sharp pallor cut all the color from her face. Through tight lips, she said, "Go on."

"For the past several years, Green has been working with a gang that calls itself Spectrum. They specialize in theft, and their methods are high-tech. Green is the muscle. There's never been enough evidence to charge him, partly because Spectrum is careful never to leave witnesses."

He tossed her sketch of Brown on the desk. "Interpol had no information whatsoever on this guy."

The next photo showed Tasha and Cerise in conversation. David said, "The lady's real name is Farrah

Mauser. She was born in Australia, moved to California when she was three. She has a record as a juvenile of shoplifting. Five years ago, she was charged in Los Angeles as an accessory to theft, but she got off. Like Green, she's suspected of involvement in several jewel heists and, once, in stealing artwork from a small museum in Barcelona. No hard evidence. No witnesses. In the museum theft, four guards were executed, shot in the head.''

He leaned forward in his chair. ''Do you understand what I'm saying, Tasha? If you cooperate with these people, there's a hell of a good chance that somebody's going to die.''

She kept her silence. Her slender fingers laced primly on her lap. Her knees pressed together. Her ankles were crossed. She appeared to be holding tight to the reins of control.

David looked back at the picture that lay on the desk like an open accusation. ''The other woman in this photo—''

''Me?''

''Yes, Tasha. You.''

Her dark eyes flashed with surprise. ''Interpol has a record on me?''

''They identified you as Natasha or Anastasia Lancer. Neither of you have ever actually been charged, but both of you are suspected in jewel heists that go back ten years. You remember, Tasha? The diamonds, the emeralds, the rubies.''

''But Interpol?'' She seemed honestly appalled. ''What does that mean?''

''When the cops round up the usual suspects, you're going to be included if the crime involves precious gems.''

''That's not fair!'' Color crept back into her face. ''I've never stolen anything. Never!''

"According to this information, you and your sister worked scams, using your identical appearance to provide each other with alibis."

She blinked twice, a small signal of distressed recognition. David knew that he'd hit a chord of truth. "That's what happened, isn't it? Stacey stole the jewels, and you provided the alibi."

Her head lowered. She stared down at her hands.

A typical ploy of liars. David knew that she was shielding her eyes from him, covering up any flicker that might inadvertently betray her.

"Dammit, Tasha!" Frustrated at every turn, he finally erupted, surged to his feet. He circled the desk and stood over her. "What does it take to get at the truth with you?"

She whispered, "I'm not a thief."

He wanted to help her, to save her from herself. "Are you telling me that Interpol is wrong? Henning is wrong? This photograph of you and Cerise, is that wrong?"

He grasped her shoulders and pulled her to her feet. Holding her upper arms, he shook her. "Tasha, look at me."

She lifted her chin. Her thick lashes were spiky and wet with tears, but David steeled himself. There was a poison inside her, the poison of lies, and he needed to exorcise it.

"Tell me," he demanded. "Tell me about the thefts that you and your sister pulled off."

Her voice did not quaver. "I never meant for it to happen. The first time, I thought it was a joke on some of the obnoxious rich people we'd met while performing our magic act. I was sixteen, and the only thing that seemed important was not to get caught."

"You robbed them."

"I was the alibi. I changed clothes twice and went to two different places while Stacey pulled the robbery. I thought we were going to return the jewels after we'd made our point, but Stacey had fenced them. She bought a Volkswagen with the money."

A single teardrop, pure as a crystal, traced a path down her cheek, but David tightened his grip on her upper arms. He would wring the truth from her, no matter how much it hurt.

"It happened again, didn't it?"

She tossed her head. "Let me go. You're hurting me."

"Tell me."

"Don't push me, David. I'm doing the best I can."

"Not good enough." He couldn't stand by and watch as she perpetrated a heist that would likely result in murder. "Tell me, dammit."

"Twice more." She gasped out a sob, then quickly recovered. "Stacey used me two more times. I couldn't turn her in, David. I couldn't. She's my twin. And Stacey's a good person. She really is. I'm sure she would never intentionally hurt anyone."

"Not like Spectrum."

"No. Never." Her eyes pleaded with him. "You've got to believe me."

"Then why? Why, Tasha? Why have you agreed to work with these people?"

She exhaled a ragged sigh. "Don't you understand? Can't you guess?"

"You want the rubies," he said.

"No." With a violent effort, she wrenched free from his grasp. Her breath heaved in her breast. "You might have read Green's record, but you have no idea of what it's like to look into his eyes. He's the soul of darkness.

There's no light of compassion or humanity. None at all.''

''Then whey are you going along with him?''

''If I don't cooperate, if I say one word to anyone—the police or Henning or even you—Green will kill me.''

Chapter Nine

Her cheeks colored with two bright spots. Her dark eyes flared with inner fire. As David stared at her, he saw beyond her slender beauty to the passionate rage within, an anger that was fueled by terror. Her nerves were stretched to the breaking point.

In so many ways, she was as fine and hard as a diamond, created by intense pressure. Her razor-edged determination could cut through almost any obstacle. And yet, the inner woman was as delicate as a rosebud—easily crushed, thoughtlessly broken, unable to flourish without nurturing. The stone and the flower. She was both.

Despite her wiry defiance, she trembled like petals in the wind.

"Is that what you wanted to hear, David?"

"I wanted the truth."

"There you have it. If I don't do everything he says, Green will hurt me in ways I can't even imagine."

David cursed himself for not figuring out the simple explanation for her silence. Tasha had to cooperate. If she didn't, Green would kill her. "You could have told me," he said. "I would have understood."

"Would you? It's still theft. It's still wrong." She looked him straight in the eye. "You want to go to the police."

"That's right. I don't see any other way," he said. "The police can protect you."

"Get real, David." She pointed at the photo of Green on her desktop. "Read the record. This monster has gotten away with assault. He's been a mercenary. He's tortured and killed. And he's not in jail."

"I know, but—"

"Did you hear me? He's not in jail. He's out on the street, free as the night. If I went to the cops and told them that Green was plotting a theft, what could they do?"

"Arrest him."

"For how long? Twenty-four hours? Green has money. He'd have a lawyer. He'd be out on bail. Even if the police could hold him for a week, he'd get out. And he would come after me."

In the back of his mind, David knew she was right. "I'd protect you."

"Imagine my relief!" Her sarcasm stung. "You'll be gone in less than two weeks. Remember? You're only hired to protect me for two weeks."

"Okay, suppose we don't go to the police. Even if you do as Green asks, what's to prevent him from killing you after they have the rubies?"

"I'll have a better chance. Cerise might be able to control him." She wrung her hands. "Oh, David, who am I fooling? I can't believe a word that Green says. He's a sadist. A murderer. I'd rather trust a coiled rattlesnake, but what choice do I have?"

"I've got another idea." He picked up the photo of Green and the report from Interpol. Deliberately, he ripped the papers in half, then ripped again and again until they were torn to confetti. He allowed the scraps to drift through his fingers into the wastebasket beside the desk. "Eliminate Green."

A frightened gasp escaped her lips. "Murder? David, you can't mean that you'd kill him."

"No." Though the idea was tempting, David wasn't an executioner. "But we can make damned sure that there's enough evidence to convict him. Have you ever heard of a sting?"

"A setup," she said. "Where I would play along with Spectrum, do everything they say, and the police would rush in at the last minute and arrest the gang."

He nodded. "I'll be here in the shop with you during the day. At night, I won't leave you alone."

She considered for a moment before shaking her head. "I won't do this with the police. Spectrum has a lot of money for bribes."

"Why would they think of bribes? They contacted you."

"One of the cops could go to them, offer to sell information. Or someone could make a simple mistake, something that would alert Green. It won't work."

"But we could—"

"No. If you talk to the cops, I'm gone. I'll go to the airport and catch the first plane to the farthest location. I'll have plastic surgery. Change my name. Become a different person. Start over."

"I could arrange for private cops. Professionals. People we could trust."

"Like Jenson?"

Jenson was a potbellied bad example and David knew it. But could he do better? They couldn't afford to make any mistakes. An error could cost Tasha her life.

"Forget it," she said. "There's a reason that Green hasn't been in jail. He's very good at what he does. He slithers in and out of my life whenever he wants. Like an apparition. A horrible nightmare. Do you know why he broke Jenson's wrist? To teach me a lesson. So I could hear the snap of bone and imagine what it would feel like. Last night, after you dropped me off, he was waiting in my apartment."

"The cuts on your legs?"

"He shattered two vases at my feet. The splinters of glass cut me."

Bastard! If ever a man needed killing, it was Green.

"David, you've got to promise me that you won't go to the police."

A ragged edge of desperation serrated her voice, and he realized how much courage it had taken for her to trust him. By telling him, she literally placed her life in his hands. "I won't betray you, Tasha."

"Thank you." Her gaze slid away from his face. "Although I wouldn't blame you if you left right now."

"Hell, no. I'm not going anywhere. I won't let you face this alone."

Her lips parted, but before she could object, he placed his finger crosswise on her mouth. "I'm staying, Tasha. With or without the police. We're in this together."

She caught his wrist in her hand. Her grip was surprisingly strong. "Because it's your job?"

"I'm here because I care about you."

"Oh, David."

The tears she had been fighting welled up behind her eyelids. She was nearly overcome. Finally, someone was on her side for all the right reasons. She had to turn away from him before she started blubbering like a pathetic fool.

David held her shoulders. His touch was exquisitely kind. "What's next, Tasha?"

Swabbing the mist from her eyes, she checked her wristwatch. "I'm supposed to call Cerise. At exactly six o'clock."

"Why?"

"I won't know until I make the call. I expect this will be a meet."

"I don't like it. You're too vulnerable."

"You're telling me? Anyway, I have to make the call. I've got to do whatever they tell me to do."

"I'll follow you," he said.

"What if they already suspect me? Green might be watching the store right now."

David nodded. "Here's what we do. I'll leave right now. You make the call. Write down your destination on a scrap of paper, crumple it. When you unlock your car door, drop the scrap. I'll pick it up. If you take your time in reaching the location, I should be there before you."

"Okay." As she looked up at him, she felt the most amazing sensation—a glimmer of hope. "That's very clever."

"Hey, I'm a pro."

"But I didn't think bodyguards did much more than stand around wearing dark glasses and looking tough."

"A couple of times, I've been called on to protect people who didn't want to look like they had a bodyguard."

"Like who? Famous people?"

"I can't tell you that."

"Oh, come on."

"Have I mentioned lately that PEI has a major reputation for discretion?"

She teased him. "Who were they, David? Superstars? Giant celebrities? Supernova celebrities?"

"One was a politician who took an aggressive stance on aid to Latin American countries. He was threatened by both sides, but didn't want to appear intimidated. Another was the author of a Mafia exposé who was zipping across the country on a book tour and didn't want to diminish his macho image by admitting he needed a bodyguard."

"That's why you're good at disguises," she deduced.

"It's always been easy for me to blend in. Standing out in a crowd? Now, that's hard."

"I don't believe that for one minute."

"Why not?"

"Because you're handsome," she said. Tasha wasn't handing out an obligatory compliment, merely stating a fact. "And you're incredibly sexy. Wherever you go, women will notice you."

He stuck the goofy teeth in his mouth and pulled on his Oregon Ducks baseball cap. In his squeaky Wally Beamis voice, he said, "Sexy, huh?"

"Even in that goofy getup. Only a man who's confident in his virility can play the fool." She stepped toward him. Lightly, she stroked the misshapen line of his mouth. "You're a wise fool, David."

"I'm not sure how smart I am. I'd still like to talk to the police."

"But you promised you wouldn't."

"And I will not lie to you." He caught her hand and squeezed lightly. "I'm going. Be careful, Tasha. Agree to anything they ask. I'll meet you back at your apartment."

His shoulders hunched. His chin stuck out. His arms and legs took on an awkward gait as he went to the door of her office. She could hardly believe that Wally Beamis and David Marquis were one and the same. "David?"

He glanced over his shoulder. "Huh?"

Tasha smiled seductively and crooked her index finger, summoning him back to her. "I've always wanted to kiss a guy with an overbite."

"You'll have to keep waiting for that thrill. Fake teeth get in the way." He removed the dental appliance. "It's like kissing with braces."

In two strides, he closed the distance between them. Gazing down, his gray eyes smoldered. Roughly, he pulled her close. With sudden passion, he claimed her with a hard kiss, branding her with the heat of his body, overwhelming her slight resistance with his masculine strength.

She met the challenge, urging his lips apart, plunging her tongue into his mouth. There was no point in resistance. She'd already offered a gift more precious than the Sheikh's Rubies. She'd trusted David with the truth. And she clung to him desperately, fiercely.

When he ended their kiss, he broke away from her.

"Tonight," she whispered, "at my apartment."

"Tonight." Then, quickly, he was gone.

At precisely six o'clock, Tasha made her phone call to Cerise. The voice that answered was heavily accented with Russian. "Mr. Brown," she said. "I apologize for the other night. If I had known who you were, I would have come along quietly."

"My eyes still burn," he complained.

"I'm sorry." Maybe, Tasha thought, she could get Brown on her side. In halting Russian, she repeated her apology.

He responded in the native language of her mother's homeland. "Now, we meet with you. The private room at Cutter's Lodge. You know the place?"

"West Denver." She'd been there once. "Near the mountains."

"Ask for the private room. Go there directly."

The telephone went dead in her hand.

Tasha made a note on a scrap of paper and wadded it up in her hand. A restaurant? Somehow, it bothered her that the location was at least a half hour away from her shop and her apartment. They were trying to get her out of the way. But why? Her apartment was vacant all day. Her shop was vacant all night. If Spectrum wanted access, they had ample time.

Before leaving the shop, she set the electronic alarm. Though it wasn't foolproof, the screaming device that connected with the local police might discourage another break-in.

A few blocks away, she paused beside her car. Since she hadn't bothered to fix the door, she had to enter from the passenger side, and that gave her a chance to take a quick look around. There were a few pedestrians, but she didn't see David. He was extremely talented at subterfuge, becoming part of the scenery. The man was full of surprises. His Wally Beamis disguise was terrific.

Behind the wheel of her car, she wondered how David would respond to a sudden burst of totally unexpected spontaneity. What would he do if, tonight at her apartment, she didn't curl up in the bed wearing her practical flannel gown? What would happen if she dressed in that sexy blue peignoir that she'd worn only once before?

Tasha entertained herself with that fantasy as she drove toward a meeting that promised to be dangerous, a confrontation where she would need to keep her wits about her. The mental respite soothed her as she prolonged her journey by driving on Colfax Avenue instead of taking the highway.

Outside Cutter's Lodge, she took a few more minutes after parking to reapply her lipstick. With any luck, David would have had enough time to get here ahead of her and to situate himself at a table where he could overhear some of their conversation.

That hope was dashed when she entered the restaurant and was shown through swinging, saloon-style doors into a small private dining room. The atmosphere was Old West with heavy beamed ceilings, rough-hewn paneling to suggest a log cabin, and a moss rock fireplace. Deer and elk heads decorated the walls.

Cerise, dressed in a fire engine red suit with black trim, sat at a heavy round oaken table. She gestured to the seat beside her. "Won't you join me?"

Tasha took her place at the left hand of Cerise. Before she could ask about the whereabouts of the others, Green strode through the swinging doors, brandishing a bottle of red wine.

He appeared to be pleased with himself. "This is the best they've got. It's California merlot, but acceptable."

"Green is quite the gourmet," Cerise confided. "And a wine connoisseur."

Though Tasha would reject any drink he offered, fearing poison, she smiled politely. "And where is Mr. Brown?"

"Playing with his computers, as usual. He's patched through a dozen systems to find the precise blueprint of Pola and Tweed's brand-new security system." She nodded to Green. "We will start without Brown."

"I already told the waiter that we're ready for our appetizer. Escargot."

Snails, Tasha translated. Not her favorite snack, but she didn't complain. It was best to appear cooperative. Though she would have felt one hundred times more comfortable if David had been seated at a neighboring table, she took solace in the fact that he was, most likely, nearby.

"I've also ordered Rocky Mountain oysters," Cerise said. Her thin lips arched in an expression too cold to be called a smile. "An amusing local delicacy."

Somehow, Tasha wasn't surprised. Cerise was just the sort of woman who would enjoy the concept of Rocky Mountain oysters, which were made of the testicles of large-range animals.

To Green, Cerise said, "I'll have the wine. And you, Stacey?"

"I'd prefer vodka, straight up. Stolichnaya."

"Take care of the drinks, Green."

He lumbered from the private dining room.

"Vodka. How very Russian," Cerise murmured. "Brown will adore working with you. That is, of course, if you manage to fulfill our expectations, Stacey."

Tasha chafed at the use of her sister's name. She wasn't Stacey. She shouldn't be here. "What do you mean, Cerise?"

"You were supposed to telephone me last night. But you were all caught up in your silly little drama with that pregnant teenager, weren't you?"

Silly little drama? Giving birth was silly? A hostile response poised on the tip of her tongue, but Tasha held back. She couldn't expect Cerise to understand. This scarlet woman with her sculpted eyebrows and beautifully frosted hair and the slash of bloodred lipstick was thoroughly disinterested in human miracles. She was blinded by greed.

"I trust," Cerise said, "that we won't have any more interruptions for your personal business."

"Absolutely not." Tasha matched the coolness of Cerise's gaze. "The only thing I care about is the rubies."

"Good. It would have been annoying to look for someone else with your particular expertise at this late date."

Green returned with an entire bottle of Stoly and two shot glasses. Brown was with him. The two men together were horribly sinister. Green was huge and robust as an ogre. The skeletal Mr. Brown had an unhealthy paleness to his complexion, as if he never went out in daylight. Silent as a shadow, he took the seat beside Tasha and helped himself to vodka.

Cerise touched Tasha's arm. "You seem tired. Why?"

"Someone broke into Bloom's last night and destroyed half of my flower stock. It was a terrible mess to clean up." She glanced at Cerise. "You wouldn't know anything about that, would you?"

"Actually, I don't." Her voice was sharp when she addressed Green. "This wasn't your doing, was it?"

"No."

"Mr. Brown?" Cerise questioned. "Was it you?"

"*Nyet*. Why should I bother with flowers?"

"Inspector Henning," Tasha concluded. That slimeball! He must have broken into her shop, looking for evidence to use against her. When he found nothing, he took revenge by destroying her property. She would remember to tell David about this violation of her rights and her privacy the next time he suggested going to the law. Vehemently, Tasha said, "It must have been Henning. God, how I despise that filthy toad."

Cerise glanced toward Green, who was seated on her right. "You see? I told you she hated the inspector."

"I still don't believe her," he said casually. "There's something about Miss Lancer that worries me a lot."

His suspicion struck a chord of fear that resonated within her. She needed to convince these people that she was on their side, but she was largely ignorant of their procedures. It occurred to her that she should have memorized every detail of David's Interpol report.

"Well, Stacey?" Cerise regarded her coolly. "Are you one of us?"

"Yes. We all want the same thing."

Green sneered. "Why should we trust her?"

Tasha's heart plummeted. Was there a ritual required to prove her loyalty? What was she supposed to do? The possibility for a misstep was huge. She felt as if she was tiptoeing precariously on a precipice with a hundred-foot drop on either side.

The swinging doors to the private room pushed open, and two waiters came through, carrying plates of appetizers. Tasha was afraid to load the small plate at her place setting. Her hands were trembling. She doubted she could even hold a fork.

Then one of the waiters asked, "Shall I pour the wine?"

She knew that voice. David! Careful not to betray her relief, she placed her hand over her wineglass and smiled up at him. "None for me."

He'd slicked back his hair and covered his upper lip with a drooping moustache that befitted the waiter's costume of buckskin trousers and vest. His gray eyes barely acknowledged her as he poured for Cerise.

"Leave us," she ordered.

"Yes, ma'am."

But Taşha knew he'd be right outside the swinging doors. Listening. Waiting. Confidence swelled within her. She raised her shotglass of vodka. "To the rubies."

"Indeed." Cerise held up her wineglass, and the light from a rough-hewn lantern caught the jewellike red sparkle of merlot. "To our latest venture, our success and our profit."

Tasha threw back her vodka and poured herself another shot.

The skeletal Mr. Brown complimented her in Russian. Under his breath, Green muttered, "Vodka. A peasant's drink."

"Too strong for you," Brown said.

"A burn without flavor. What's so strong about that?"

Before a skirmish could break out between the two men, Cerise chided, "Please, boys, let's have none of your petty nonsense. Our first order of business is to name our newest member. Stacey, what color will you be?"

"Is that really necessary?"

"Yes, if you're to be one of us."

"All right." She chose a color that matched her mood. "Black."

Tasha felt three sets of eyes glaring steadily at her. All movement ceased. A frozen quiet settled upon them.

"No," Green whispered. "It can't be you."

Cerise expelled a low chuckle. "You're joking, of course. Black is not an available color of the spectrum."

Tasha knew she'd made a mistake. She decided to bluff. "But I like black. It suits me."

Stiffly, Cerise said, "Black is the absence and the absorption of all the other colors. Only our leader is named Black."

"Didn't you know that?" Green demanded. "You should have known."

Tasha lifted her chin. "I know more than you expect. Don't underestimate me."

"You're not the boss," Green said.

Brown snickered. "Maybe she is. Black could be a woman."

"But it's not me," Tasha said.

"I knew it," Green said.

"I only wanted to make a point," Tasha said. Glad for her facile skills at deception, she continued, "We'll be using my store, Bloom's. And when we're there, I must be in control. Otherwise, it will be impossible to divert suspicion."

Tasha looked each of them in the eye. "I've spent six months creating this cover story. While you are in my store, you must all do exactly as I say."

Though Cerise hiked up an eyebrow, she nodded her agreement. "Now, what color will you be?"

A rainbow flowed through Tasha's mind. Was there significance in each of the colors? Would she make another mistake? Was yellow the color of cowardice, white for purity, blue for sadness? "Silver," she said.

Cerise seemed pleased. "Silver, it shall be."

They proceeded through dinner, and Tasha managed to force down several tasteless bites of food. Though she maintained an aura of friendly camaraderie, her stomach was tied in knots. Her mouth tasted arid and gritty. It took complete concentration not to betray her intense fear as they discussed Denver and the coming ski season in Aspen as compared with true Alpine skiing in Europe.

Nearing the end of their meal, Tasha grew wary. They had not discussed their plans since her mistake in choos-

ing Black. Had she made a fatal error? The only thing
that kept her from disintegrating into a quivering mass of
nerves was the presence of David, gliding into and out of
the room with the other waiters. He wouldn't allow anything bad to happen to her. He would protect her.

Against Green? Tasha almost choked on a bite of her
rare venison steak. "Will you all excuse me? I need to
powder my nose."

On her way to the rest room, David intercepted her. He
spoke only one sentence. "Leave first. Drive like hell
back to your apartment."

"Yes."

In the ladies' room where the frontier motif had been
abandoned in favor of clean white tile, Tasha stepped
into a stall and vomited up her dinner. She groaned. The
tension was unbearable. Every word she spoke, every
phrase, seemed to betray her.

She heard the door to the bathroom open and close.
When she stepped out of the stall, she confronted Cerise, who was casually applying a fresh coat of scarlet
lipstick. Their eyes met in the mirror.

Cerise said, "You shouldn't have joked about the colors."

"I meant no disrespect." She rinsed her hands, dug
into her purse for the Opium cologne and applied a squirt
behind each earlobe, hoping to mask the scent of her
fear. "But I'm tired of Green trying to intimidate me."

"His sophistication doesn't run deep." Cerise smiled
at herself in the mirror. "Generally, he follows my instructions, but he is not a truly civilized man."

"I don't like these games," Tasha said. "Why should
we pretend that we don't know one another? You all
know me."

Cerise turned her head and looked directly into Tasha's eyes. "And do you remember my name, Stacey?"

Tasha thought of David's information from Interpol and nodded. "Farrah. You're Farrah Mauser."

"Good. You really are Stacey Lancer."

"Yes."

"Never speak my real name again."

When they returned to the table, Cerise sketched out the plan.

"The theft will occur three days from now. Brown has determined the best spot to tunnel from the flower shop into the vault of Pola and Tweed. The wall is three feet of concrete and one inch of steel. We will peel through this surface layer by layer, carefully. I think it's best to do this during daylight hours when the shops are open and motion-sensing devices are not in operation." She turned to Tasha. "Don't you?"

"Yes, as long as we're careful about the noise levels." She paused. "By the way, I've hired a new assistant. But don't worry about him. He's a complete idiot. The perfect foil for diverting suspicion."

"Another witness," Green said. "I don't like it."

"She has to have someone," Cerise explained. "And it can't be one of us. We can't take the chance of being too visible. Not with Henning so close."

"I'll start tomorrow," said Brown.

"Fine." Tasha rose from her chair, mindful of David's instructions to leave first. "I'll be at the shop at eight o'clock to take delivery of new flower stock. And I will remain open until nine in the evening."

Green pushed back his chair and stood. "Don't you want to hear your part of the job?"

"It's obvious, isn't it?" Tasha was familiar enough with the vault at Pola and Tweed to make a guess. "You need me to open the safe within the vault where the rubies will be stashed.''

"This is correct," Brown said. "Though they have upgraded the outer perimeter of security, the safe is still the old-fashioned variety. Very clever, really."

"Why?" Green sneered.

"This break-in requires a diversity of skill. My knowledge of computers, electronics and state-of-the-art security will gain entry to the vault. There, we encounter a metal box, five feet square. The weight is nine hundred and forty pounds. The size is cumbersome."

"It's only a safe," Green said.

"Ah, yes." Brown sucked at his vodka. "A five-digit combination lock, magnetized tumblers and a timer to confuse most computerized devices."

"So what?"

"It is possible to break this code, but it might take an hour. It is possible to blow the safe open, but in the confined space of the vault, it would be dangerous." As he glanced at Tasha, he held up his hand and rubbed his fingertips together. "The best method is the time-honored art of safecracking. A sensitive touch. I wonder, Miss Silver, can you do this?"

"Of course," Tasha said. "Why do you think I've gone to all the trouble to set up shop next door to Pola and Tweed? Coincidence?"

Brown said, "I will see you tomorrow at your shop."

Tasha grabbed her purse and headed toward the exit. "Good night. I enjoyed dinner."

As soon as she was outside the restaurant, she dashed to her car and dove in from the passenger side. She fired up her engine, anxious to put as many miles as possible between herself and Green.

"Tasha."

"Yikes!" She jumped in her seat.

"It's David. I'm in the back seat."

"What are you doing?" She gasped. "You scared the poop out of me!"

"Don't go to your apartment."

"But you told me—"

"Drive, Tasha. Take the highway. Go toward the old airport."

She was pulling out of the parking lot just as Green's hulking form appeared in the restaurant doorway. Leaning toward the back seat, she said, "Green's just leaving."

"Excellent! You have a head start. Don't blow it. Go as fast as possible without getting pulled over."

She eased into traffic. "I don't like this, David. I'm not a very good driver."

"Can you tell if anyone is following you?"

"It's night," she said pointedly. "All I can see in my rearview mirror is headlights."

"You can do it, Tasha."

"Why can't I just go back to my apartment?"

"While you were in the bathroom with Cerise, I overheard Green saying that he didn't think you could be trusted. He said he was going to keep an eye on you."

Her fingers tightened on the steering wheel. The danger was still there. Even though she was, supposedly, one of them, Green suspected her. "He's not going to leave me alone, is he?"

"No," David said. "This is his lifework. And, as you pointed out, he's damned good at it."

"Did you hear anything else?"

"Enough to figure that Green and Brown aren't too fond of each other. Cerise has her hands full, trying to control these two." He paused. "Remember what they said about Black?"

How could she forget? "I thought they were going to kill me right there, on the spot. I've never been so scared."

"You handled it well," he said. "You're a gifted liar, Tasha."

"Gosh, thanks." But she knew that he hadn't meant to compliment her. "The only person who has always been able to tell when I'm lying is Stacey. It's one of those twin things. I could always tell what she was thinking, and vice versa."

"Black worries me," he said. "There was no mention in the Interpol information about a mastermind who was running the show for Spectrum. And it seems like his— or her—identity is a secret, even from the rest of the gang."

"How much did you hear about the rest of the plan?"

"Some of it. But give me the details."

While she drove, Tasha recounted the deceptively simple scheme of making a hole in her wall that would connect with the vault at Pola and Tweed. The tricky part, she knew, was Brown's job of disarming the computers and motion sensors.

Leaving the highway, she took the exit that led to the former Stapleton Airport, now a mostly deserted facility. "What next, David?"

"Pick a hotel with covered parking."

As soon as she'd parked, he was out of the car, stretching. Together, they went into the lobby. David checked in. In moments, they were in a fifth-floor room with two double beds. Placing the Do Not Disturb sign on the knob, he locked the door and the dead bolt.

"Are you sure this is necessary?" she asked.

"A simple precaution. I'd rather not have Green barge in on us while we're sleeping."

"I guess you're right." She thought of her earlier plans for this night with David. The gorgeous blue peignoir. The spontaneous seduction. Regretfully, she said, "But I don't have any of my clothes."

He held out his hand to her. "I don't think you'll need them."

Carla Dave

to what wanted to resolve.

"I guess you're right." Returning with the cash he'd
set the table with a sip kindness, he would have to keep to
Il was about her company, he couldn't help but think
Tasha was any bit too thoughtful.

"I'll help you out this morning." I don't want you to be in
here.

Chapter Ten

His gray eyes shimmered with a captivating heat as he
took her hand. Still wearing his waiter's costume of
buckskin trousers and a fringed vest over a white shirt,
David looked handsomely rustic, and Tasha felt an odd,
maidenly hesitation.

"This isn't exactly how I wanted it to be," she said. "I
was fantasizing about my blue peignoir. And maybe a
candle or two. And I'm filthy. I have on the same clothes
I wore this morning to muck out the dead flowers in the
refrigerated unit."

"I don't need anything but you, Tasha."

"But I want to feel pretty."

"You're beautiful." Tenderly, he stroked her hair off
her forehead and dropped a kiss on her temple. "If it
makes you feel better, go ahead and take your bath."

She bobbed her head up and down. What was wrong
with her? She'd been intensely aware of his sexuality
from the first time she laid eyes upon him. For the past
two nights, they'd slept in the same small apartment. Last
night, he shared her bed. And now that the moment was
finally here...it seemed too deliberate, too planned. The
impersonal hotel room lacked the magic she wanted.

Taking a backward step, she said, "I feel silly. It's not like this is the first time."

As soon as she spoke, she realized that this was exactly like the panic she felt on the first time. In fact, it was worse. When she'd lost her virginity, she'd been too young and inexperienced to understand the significance. Now, with David, she was nervous, twittery and trembling with excitement. There was a portent in the air.

Tasha had never felt this way about any other man. She had never trusted so completely, never allowed herself to hope that their lovemaking would be the start of something more enduring. Of course, she'd had sex before. But, perhaps, she had never made love.

Avoiding his gaze, she slipped into the bathroom, ran hot water into the tub and undressed. As she stepped into the steaming liquid, she wished for bath salts, fragrances and soothing oils for her skin. And her makeup. She wanted to be perfect for David.

He rapped on the door. "Take your time, Tasha. I'm going to get food."

"We were just at a restaurant," she shouted back.

"I didn't have time to eat."

Well, of course not, he was too involved in spying on a gang of international jewel thieves. She smiled to herself. Espionage didn't do much for the appetite, but she didn't want him to leave. Had she ruined the mood? Did he regret coming here with her? "Call room service."

"Takes too long. I'll be right back."

Doubts assailed her as she turned off the faucets with her toes and slid down to her chin in the hot, lapping water. What if David didn't really want her? Maybe he felt trapped by the situation and couldn't think of a polite way to tell her. *Wait a minute here. We're talking about David.*

He definitely wasn't shy. If there was anything consistent about the man, it was how he stated his opinions, regardless of what she wanted to hear.

Tasha was pretty sure that he wanted her. But would she be skillful enough to arouse him? Would she disappoint him?

For an instant, she toyed with the idea of calling the whole thing off. David would be an absolute gentleman if she told him that they mustn't make love. After all, they couldn't possibly have anything resembling a relationship. He was leaving in less than two weeks, going back to New York.

And that was why she needed to make love to him. Now. She needed to seize this moment and hold on tight.

Morosely, Tasha soaked until she heard the outer door to their room open.

David called out, "I'm back. I got extra food, if you want any."

"Okay." Whatever he'd gotten, she was sure that it beat snails and buffalo balls. "Save some for me."

She drained the tub, then washed and rinsed her hair in the shower. Fortunately, her short haircut required no more attention than a brisk toweling.

Now, the problem was what to wear. There was no way that Tasha would crawl back into the grungy skirt and turtleneck she'd been wearing all day, but she didn't feel right about strolling out of the bathroom stark naked.

Wrapped in a towel, she opened the bathroom door and peeked out.

David had transformed the plain hotel bedroom. A dozen votive candles in glass holders flickered romantically around the room. And there were flowers. She counted four separate arrangements—two of roses.

"I thought you might feel more at home with the roses," he said. "In your bedroom at home, I noticed that you had two bouquets."

Spread out on the bed nearest the bathroom was a silky pink gown and matching robe. "Oh, David, where did you get all this?"

"Hotel gift shop. I was lucky. They were just getting ready to close."

Contrasting all this seductive elegance was a tray of plain bagels, a container of cream cheese and two extra large coffees.

"It's wonderful, David. *You're* wonderful."

"You deserve more," he said. "I wish that I was a sheikh and you were the beautiful Aziza, draped in precious rubies."

"I wouldn't like that at all. Too dangerous." She drew a line across her throat. "I might lose my head."

"That's precisely what I had in mind."

He yanked out the tail of his shirt, and began unbuttoning. "Help yourself to the bagels. I'm going to take a quick shower."

While he was in the bathroom, she dressed in the silky gown. Though she'd never thought of pink as her color, she loved the way the gown warmed her pale complexion and contrasted with her black hair.

A bag with the logo of the hotel gift shop stood open on the dresser and she found necessary toiletries for herself and shaving equipment for David. She'd begun to nibble at the bagels when he came out of the bathroom.

Apparently, he'd purchased no extra clothing for himself because all he wore was the white towel slung low on his hips. His body was magnificent. His muscular torso and broad chest, sprinkled with crisp black hair, beckoned to her, and she glided away from the bed toward him.

"I should shave," he said.

"Let me be the judge." Her sensitive fingertips stroked the rugged line of his jaw. The roughness of his evening beard excited her.

"Come here," she whispered.

"Does this mean I shouldn't shave?"

"Lie down on the bed."

He didn't need to be told twice. Obediently, David stretched out on the clean, crisp sheets. His hands spanned her waist as he pulled her toward him.

She resisted. "Fold your hands behind your head."

"Why?"

"Because it's my turn." She lifted his muscular arms, crooked his elbows and placed his hands beneath his head. "You've done so much for me. Let me do something for you."

He was so handsome. The swarthiness of his skin made her fingers seem pale as she ruffled his still-damp hair and traced the strong angles of his face.

"Your hands," he said. "God, that feels incredible."

"I've always been good at fine detail work. When Stacey and I were with the magician, he said he'd never seen anything like it."

"So delicate," David murmured.

Tasha concentrated, making her touch softer than a feather sliding across silk. She massaged his chest, teasing his flat nipples into hard buds. The tips of her ultrasensitive fingers claimed his body. She caressed the inner skin of his arms. "What happened to your Spiderman tattoo?"

"A decal. It washed off. If you like it, I could reapply."

"Please don't."

Closing her eyes, she explored his shoulders. His warm skin covered swelling muscles with hard, heavy bone beneath. He felt wonderful. She stroked his neck, teased his earlobes.

Each time he reached for her, she chided, "Not yet. It's still my turn."

She gazed down upon him. Her eyes beheld him, absorbing his virile beauty, memorizing every inch of him.

Then, slowly, she unfastened the towel, revealing him. With light touches, she fondled the ridged hardness.

David's breath caught in his throat. Fiercely, he pulled her down on top of his hard body and held her tightly. Then, he rolled, and he was on top. His mouth descended to hers for a hungry kiss. His hands on her flesh were demanding, swiftly discovering the sensitive points on her body and manipulating them until she writhed beneath his touch.

A moist arousal spread through her body like hot oil. Conscious thought vanished from her mind. There was only sensation, warm and throbbing.

When he peeled away the robe, then the gown, his gray eyes glistened with passion she knew was reflected in her own unfocused gaze. Naked, she arched toward him.

Skillfully, David brought her to the brink of desire and beyond. She yearned for completion. Her thighs opened to him, and he entered her most secret flesh.

A tiny cry escaped her lips as he probed slowly within her, driving her wild.

His voice was husky, rough. "I can't hold back anymore."

"Now, David. Please."

He thrust hard and fast, finding a primal rhythm that pounded like breaking waves on the intimate shores of her soul, and Tasha trembled at the brink, her body racked with pleasure. Together, they reached the fulfillment of perfect lovemaking, and she drifted in unearthly clouds of contentment.

As she snuggled beside him in the candlelight, Tasha felt that truly this night was her first time. She'd given something more precious than her virginity. She'd given her trust.

THOUGH IT SEEMED improbable that life could return to a schedule after a night of such sensual perfection, Tasha was back in her shop at eight o'clock sharp. She'd left David in the hotel room at six-thirty and returned to her apartment, which seemed undisturbed, to change clothes and apply makeup.

Still bedazzled by last night's passion, which had repeated twice more after the wondrous first time, Tasha perched on the stool behind her counter and sighed. She felt tender all over, happily bruised by pleasure.

David had promised to be in by nine o'clock, and she eagerly anticipated the instant she would see him again. Following her routine, she took delivery of dozens of roses, baby's breath, star gazer lilies, asters and clusters of bouvardier. These flowers she stored in tubs of water in the temperature-controlled refrigerated unit.

She checked her calendar. Her major project for the week was a floral arrangement for a banquet at the Natural History Museum on Tuesday. Tomorrow night. On the weekend, she was providing flowers at a small wedding for a rather unimaginative bride who couldn't understand why bowers of iris and lilacs, both springtime blooms, were difficult to obtain and expensive in September.

Tasha began to envision the wedding bouquet, then stopped herself. In three days, on Wednesday night, Spectrum would steal the Sheikh's Rubies. Fatalistically, she realized that it might not be wise to plan beyond that date.

What would happen? She and David hadn't begun to work out the logistics. Without telling the police, how could they perform a sting? How could she amass enough evidence to ensure that Green would be arrested and locked up forever?

At nine o'clock, she opened her doors for business. Five minutes later, David—in his Wally Beamis disguise—stumbled inside. He wore the same baggy-seat trousers and an ugly plaid shirt with long sleeves. His hair was askew. His posture, atrocious. His mouth, with the dental appliance, twisted in a goofy expression.

She'd never seen a more gorgeous man in her life.

Unable to control herself, she smiled widely. She said, "You're late, Wally."

"Sorry." His voice was a nasal whine.

"Come into my office, and we'll go over your schedule."

He closed the door behind him and pulled out the fake teeth. "Darling Tasha, you can't look at me like that when I'm disguised as Wally."

"I can't help it." She slipped into his arms and sighed.

He hugged her, then held her back. "The first rule of disguise is attitude. When I'm Wally, I can't let myself think of how I really feel about you. And it's got to be the same for you."

"But I—"

"No," he said firmly. "If we can't even fool each other, how will we trick Green?"

The mention of that name was a splash of cold water in her face. She stepped away from him and took a seat behind her desk. "You're right."

"Your apartment? When you went back there, was it okay?"

"It didn't seem like anyone had been there. It didn't even look like my answering machine had been played. By the way, I had a message from Mandy. She's gone home from the hospital and is staying with her mother."

"Good for Mandy."

"I'd like to get out and see her, but I don't know when I'll find time."

Dryly, he said, "It's tough working in baby visits while you're trying to foil international jewel thieves."

"David, how are we going to pull off this sting without telling the police?"

"We'll figure something. Your job is to discover as much as you can about their plan. So far, we know that Brown intends to make a large hole in the wall leading to the vault. Try to find out how they plan to deal with the guards."

"Got it."

He slipped in his fake teeth, and they returned to the front of the store. "Okay, Wally, I have a project for you. Over there, near the back exit, is my worktable. I need more surface, so I want you to figure out how to suspend the rolls of ribbons that I have on standing spools."

"Hang something from the ceiling?"

She nodded. "That should keep you out of trouble."

It was after eleven o'clock when Brown slipped through the front entrance to Bloom's. Immediately, he moved away from the windows and sidled behind the counter. It was the first time she'd seen Brown while the sun was shining, and natural light did not improve his cadaverous looks.

Without preface, he said, "Your office."

Though Tasha hated to relinquish her sanctuary, she led him into the windowless back room. She called to David, "Watch the front, will you?"

"Okeydokey, ma'am."

Brown placed a briefcase in the center of her desk. "Today, I will determine the precise location for entry into the vault. Though I have obtained the layout from computerized plans, I wish to make a visual survey."

That seemed very workmanlike and logical. "All right. And what does this have to do with me?"

He held up a circular pendant, five inches in diameter with gold edges and a crystal center. "This is a video camera. You turn it on by reaching underneath." He showed her the tiny switch. "You see?"

"Yes."

"Wear this. Go to Pola and Tweed. Gain access to the vault, and turn on the video. You must obtain a three hundred and sixty-five degree video of the vault's interior. Turn in a complete circle."

"Is that really necessary?" Usually, getting in and out of the vault while visiting with Janet Pola was no problem. But Henning was there. He wouldn't allow her free access to a public toilet, much less the vault. "I've been in the vault before. I can tell you what it looks like."

Brown scoffed. "I need precision, Miss Silver. If our preparations for break-in are to be undetected, we must be exact. You understand?"

She sighed. "I do."

"Someone will be back to pick up the videotape at four o'clock. Tomorrow, we chip away the concrete wall."

"Chip away?" She didn't like the sound of that. "Won't that be awfully noisy?"

"I will use a thermal lance, of course."

"Of course." *What on earth was a thermal lance?*

"Very efficient tool," he said. "Cuts through six inches of tempered steel in fifteen seconds. Removing the concrete will take less than an hour."

"I'll bet it leaves quite a mess."

He did not return her grin. "This sense of humor, Miss Silver, is mostly not funny. Last night, when you said that you were Black? Not funny at all."

"Well, what if I wasn't kidding? What if I really am Black?"

His dark eyes seemed to disappear in sunken sockets. Mournfully, he said, "Then the joke is on me."

He closed up his briefcase and left the office.

Tasha slipped the video camera pendant around her neck. Fortunately, she was wearing a simple black jersey minidress with gold accessories today and the pendant didn't look too odd. But how was she going to convince Janet to show her around the vault? The request would seem odd because Tasha had been inside before. And there were now guards to contend with.

David, she thought. She could pretend to be taking him on a guided tour of the neighborhood shops.

Hurrying to the front counter, she sketched out her plan to him. "So, you act like you're interested in the vault, and Janet will take both of us inside."

"Is it that big?"

"It's huge. At least fifteen feet by eight. This building was constructed in the fifties, and there have been all kinds of shops that moved in and out. Pola and Tweed was once a furrier with a large storage area. That's what Janet turned into a vault."

He nodded. "Okay, show me around."

"First, I'll make sure that Janet is in the shop and, with any luck, that Henning isn't there." She grabbed a watering can. "Besides, I need to freshen up their flower arrangements. Keep an eye on the shop."

"Okaleedokalee, ma'am."

His gaze followed her out the door, and he watched through the windows as she stepped briskly along the sunlit sidewalk. Her black hair was a shining cap. Her eyes were luminous. Again, she reminded him of an exotic flower, graceful and delicate. And resilient. She owned an ability to think fast under pressure and a talent for bouncing back, which was also handy for subterfuge. She kept a lot hidden. It might take years to peel back the petals into a full blossom and find out who she really was.

David wished he had the time to spend with her. At least, there would be tonight. While she was out of the store, he entertained himself with delectable memories and anticipation of tonight's lovemaking.

Quickly, Tasha bustled through the front of the shop. She returned her watering can to the back area near the sink and stepped up to the counter. A slight malaise clung to her.

"What's wrong?" he asked.

"Nothing." Behind her smile lurked a flicker of discontent.

"You're lying, Tasha."

"You're right." She rolled her eyes. "Oh, my God, David. Those rubies! They're magnificent. I can't go near them without breaking out in a cold sweat."

"You want them, don't you?"

"With all my heart. I want to wear them. Just for a minute. I want to feel the stones against my bare skin."

Her mouth twisted in a grimace. "That's terrible to say. They aren't mine. They will never be mine. But is it wrong to want them?"

"No, Tasha. Almost everyone wishes for something they can't have. An impossible dream."

"I almost believe I could steal for those stones. I'd join Spectrum for real." She held out her hands. "Look, I'm trembling."

Her passions, when it came to precious gems, ran close to the surface, and her blatant desire made David want to drape her in ropes of diamonds, merely to see the delight in her eyes.

She drew in a lungful of air. "Okay, I'll be all right as long as I don't get too close to the rubies."

"You obviously love precious gems. Why didn't you open a jewelry store instead of a flower shop?"

"Are you kidding? That would be like an alcoholic running a liquor store. An overeater becoming a pastry chef. I'd never want to sell any of my jewels."

"So, this is an unhealthy passion."

"I saw what happened to my mother," she said. "I'm much better off with flowers. I love them, but they are, by their very nature, a transitory pleasure. Even after they're dried, flowers will eventually disintegrate into fragrant dust."

"And you don't mind that the flowers are dying?"

"Death is part of their beauty," she said. "In *ikebana*, the Japanese art of flower arranging, there is a concept of duality that is necessary for true appreciation."

Her gestures, while explaining, took on a mannered gracefulness. "When you see a field of flowers, you're filled with joy. Who wouldn't be? The color and light and sheer bounty is too wonderful. At the same time, there's a deep sadness, because you know the flowers will lose their bloom and will die. Duality. Life and death.''

"That's very Zen thinking."

"The concept is actually called *miyabi,* elegance contrasted with transition.'' Her left eyebrow raised. "It's kind of like us, isn't it?"

Though her reference was obscure, he understood completely what she was saying. Last night had been the most wonderfully perfect lovemaking he'd ever experienced. And yet, there was a sadness. He would be leaving. Their relationship would not continue forever. "Very Zen."

"Let's go next door and get this videotaping over with." She hung the Be Back In Ten Minutes sign at the front door to Bloom's and pointed the way for David. "I hate deceiving Janet like this, but there's no other way."

In his Wally Beamis persona, David galloped along beside her. Inside Pola and Tweed, a uniformed guard stood watch beside the Sheikh's Rubies. There were two other clerks, one of whom was talking to a customer.

After Tasha made a brief show of introducing him and pointing out the rubies, which she did not go near, she led him through a rear door into the employee's lounge. "Janet?" she called out. "Are you back here?"

Janet looked up from the newspaper she was reading. "Tasha, darling, I've just run my figures for the weekend, and it's safe to say that the rubies were an unqualified success in drawing customers. My business was almost equal to the annual Valentine's Day rush for jewelry."

Her smile faltered as she noticed David. "Oh, how nice," she said in her high-pitched brittle tone. "You've brought your new assistant."

"I thought if I showed Wally around the neighborhood, he might get an idea of the appropriate style for Cherry Creek."

"Excellent idea!"

In his Wally voice, David said, "I like your store. Is all this stuff real?"

"Not everything. In addition to the gemstones, ivory, jade and pearls, we have costume jewelry."

"Costumes?" David squawked. "Like Halloween?"

With a long-suffering sigh, Tasha said, "Would you mind showing him the vault? He keeps talking about jewelry thieves."

"No problem," Janet said, leading the way.

The heavy steel, lead and copper door to the vault was closed but not locked. Janet explained, "I generally don't bother with locking during the day. It would be too much trouble to open and close every time a customer wanted to see a particular stone."

Inside, the walls were a dull metal color. There were four large metal cabinets with doors that swung open to reveal special drawers and shelves for storing the jewelry. In the far corner was an antique-looking black safe, decorated in gold trim with the name Jezebel written in scroll above a combination lock and handle.

"What's that?" David asked.

"I only use the safe for special deposits, like the Sheikh's Rubies. The precision lock is difficult for even me to open, and I know the combination."

"Where did you get it?" Tasha asked casually.

"My father bought it in the 1930s. He was also a jeweler, you know. And he had it upgraded with copper lining and microwave sensors. Rather a lovely antique. And useful, too."

"What do you keep in here?" David continued. "I mean, don't you have all the good stuff out there?" He flung his arm toward the showroom, bumping it against one of the steel cabinets.

"At night, much of the jewelry goes in here. And I have loose stones here." She brightened as she gazed at Tasha. "Oh, my dear, I've just acquired the most wonderful diamond. Marquise cut. It's only three carats, but it's as clear as spring water. Almost flawless. Tweed did himself proud with this purchase."

Before David could ask, Tasha explained, "Tweed is the buyer for the store. He hardly ever comes into the shop. He's always out, traveling the world, buying the most incredible stones. Some of his buys are absolutely brilliant."

"Tweed's a genius," Janet agreed as she pulled open a drawer inside one of the cabinets. "Especially since he leaves the store to me."

Janet found a small brown envelope and tapped it open. In the palm of her hand, she displayed a sparkling stone in a tapering oval shape like a mostly deflated football.

Beside him, David heard Tasha gasp. "Oh, Janet, it's fabulous. Can I look at it?"

"Go crazy." Janet placed the stone in Tasha's hand. "There's a loupe on top of the case behind you."

David watched as Tasha inspected the stone, held it to the light, viewed the facets through the eye loupe. Her complexion had taken on a rosy blush. The pendant video camera hung around her throat, forgotten in her pleasure at handling the diamond.

Reluctantly, she gave it back to Janet. "That's a high-grade stone. Fantastic luster. I could only see a tiny shadow at the far left edge."

"You're good." Janet slipped the diamond back into its envelope. "If you ever decide to close down your flower shop, you must come work for me."

"Me, too?" David asked.

"Not on a bet," Janet chirped. She shooed them from the vault. "Move along. It's high time we all returned to work, isn't it?"

"Thanks so much," Tasha said. Wistfully, she added, "The marquise-cut diamond? Do you have special plans for it?"

"Not yet. It would make a lovely ring, wouldn't it?"

Tasha nodded. In the back of her throat, she purred, and David thought the sound was very much like the noises of her lovemaking.

As they were exiting Pola and Tweed, David caught sight of Inspector Henning. He stood motionlessly near the rear of the store, and David had no doubt that the inspector was completely aware of every step they'd taken inside the store. And yet, he'd passed up the opportunity to bother Tasha. Strange, David thought. The inspector had always seemed intent on harassing her.

Back in Bloom's, David asked, "Did you remember to turn on the video camera?"

"Yes. But I clicked it off before Janet showed me that diamond. There's no reason to alert Spectrum to the existence of that stone."

"Why not? While they're in the vault, they'll clean it out."

"Dammit," she muttered. "This is going to put Janet out of business."

"Not unless they're successful," he reminded her. "Do you think we should talk to Henning?"

"No. Not him."

They spent the rest of the afternoon with customers, and David stretched the simple task of hanging spools of ribbon into an all-day project. At four o'clock, he was still messing with a ladder at the rear of the shop when he heard the bell above the door ring.

In a terse voice, Tasha said, "Mr. Green, how nice to see you."

"You didn't go home last night," he said. "Where were you?"

"I pampered myself by staying in a hotel. I hope that's all right. Cerise didn't say anything about staying in my apartment. I have to get my rest. It's not going to be easy to break into that safe. I need to be in perfect physical condition."

"I'm not threatening you." But, to David's ear, he sounded hostile. "Give me the camera."

David couldn't see what was going on, but he assumed the exchange had been made when the bell jingled again.

"Hi there, boss. Look who I brought to see the shop."

With a groan, David recognized Mandy's voice. The little mother had picked a hell of a time to drop by. The thought of tiny infant Ruby being in the same room with Green filled him with disgust and dread.

Firmly, Tasha said, "Goodbye, Mr. Green."

"Aren't you going to introduce me to this little mother?" The harsh growl of Green's voice made a mockery of gentleness. "And look at the baby. Boy or girl?"

"A girl," Mandy said, cooing softly. "Her name is Ruby."

"Take care of her," Green said. "It would be a shame to have anything happen to such a beautiful baby."

An overwhelming fury galvanized David. In an instant, he'd shed the Wally Beamis attitude and descended from the ladder. In his hand, he gripped a hammer so tightly that his knuckles were white. His baggy-legged trousers concealed a shin holster holding an automatic. In his back pocket, he carried a tiny four-shot derringer. But David wouldn't need a gun to deal with Green. The scumbag had threatened an infant. David felt fully capable of killing Green with his bare hands.

He spat out the dental appliance. When he came up to the front counter, Green was gone.

White-faced, Tasha stared at him with terror in her gaze.

And Mandy looked puzzled as she cradled Ruby against her breasts. "Hi, David. Weird outfit."

Tasha's voice shivered at the brink of panic. "Do you think he would . . ."

"Yes," David said. "If you don't do what he says."

The front door opened behind Mandy as she said, "What's the matter with you guys? What's going on?"

Inspector Henning stepped around her. "My question, exactly."

Chapter Eleven

As David watched, Tasha's face pinched into a snarl and she began to read Inspector Henning the riot act, starting with a lot of strange accusations about spilled water and trampled roses.

Henning warded off Tasha's words with a disdainful expression and a British sort of noise that sounded like "tut-tut-tut."

At the same time, Mandy repeated, "What are you doing? Tasha, you've got to tell me what's going on. What's up with all this?"

And Ruby began a vigorous wail.

"Quiet," David said.

The single word made no difference. If anything, the wall of sound rose higher.

David lifted the hammer above his head and brought it down with a hard clang on the high metal stool behind the counter. Simultaneously, he shouted, "I want quiet!"

The shop went silent. Everyone, including Inspector Henning, froze in place.

"Thank you," David said. He nodded to Mandy. "It's nice to see you. And Ruby, too."

"Don't even think about asking me to leave," Mandy said. "Tasha is upset. After all she's done for me, I'm not going to take off when she's in trouble."

"Swell," David said. He turned to face the beautiful, dark-haired enchantress who had touched his heart and was, at the current moment, making him want to throw a large object through the plate-glass window. "Tasha, I want you to answer in one word. Is there anything you want to say to the Inspector?"

"Yes. I want to tell him that—"

"One word," David interrupted her. "Now, in one sentence, tell me the problem. Tell me, not him."

With her hands braced on her hips, she glared up at David. "If he ever breaks into my shop again, I will press charges."

"That's all, Tasha." David glanced at the inspector. "Did you break into her shop?"

"I have four words, sonny boy."

"I'm not your son, Inspector."

"And you're not Wally Beamis, either." The inspector tilted back on his heels and held up four stubby fingers. "Four words: Spectrum. Rubies. Wednesday night."

Now, it was Tasha's turn to take action. She flew to Mandy's side and ushered her toward the door. "Honey, I'm fine. And David is absolutely right. This is no place for you, and it's especially no place for Ruby. Are you going straight home?"

"Actually, I was going to the hospital first. I wanted to bring some flowers to the nurses. They were all so sweet."

"Fine." Tasha grabbed a fishbowl terrarium with a miniature pagoda and shoved it into Mandy's free arm. "This should do it."

"I can't take this. It costs eighty bucks."

"Take it."

"Wait," David said. He couldn't allow Mandy to charge out into the world unprotected. Not after Green's veiled threat. "It might be best if Mandy stays here for a minute. I'd really like to escort her to her car, maybe even drive her home."

When Tasha swung around to face him, she looked as if she might cry. Or scream. "Do you think Green might—"

"We don't need to take any chances," he said. "Besides, Mandy can watch the shop for a minute while we talk to the inspector."

"Okay," Mandy said as she shuffled to the counter. "Cool."

"May we proceed?" The inspector said. "I suggest we use Miss Lancer's office."

David followed Henning and Tasha. He closed the door with a bang. "All right, Inspector. What do you know?"

"Everything." He meandered to the chair behind the desk and sat as if he owned the place. He crossed his legs, carefully arranged the crease in his trousers and straightened the necktie around his plump throat. "Miss Lancer was quite correct when she accused me of breaking into her shop."

"Why?"

"Looking for evidence. I found nothing incriminating. I did, however, leave a little something behind."

He picked up the photograph of Tasha's mother and the twin daughters dressed in white. On the back side was a small, round, metal object.

"A bugging device," Inspector Henning said. "Extremely effective."

David silently cursed himself. He should have thought of bugs. "You've heard every word that was spoken in this office."

"Indeed, I have." He tossed the bug on the desktop. "So, your little problem about whether or not to tell the stupid coppers is now over. You already have, in effect, told me everything."

With a groan, Tasha deflated into the chair opposite her desk. Her shoulders slumped forward, her head drooped.

"Buck up, Miss Lancer. This is the best thing that could ever happen to you. I will be running this sting operation henceforth." He focused on David. "I suggest that you proceed exactly as you have been. Cooperate with Spectrum in every particular."

"Except for one," David said. "Tasha won't be stealing the rubies."

"Oh, no, that mustn't happen. However, I will need for the Spectrum plan to be carried completely through so that I can catch them red-handed with the Sheikh's Rubies."

Henning was bloated with smugness. He grinned so broadly that David thought his round face might split in two.

"Quite a coup for me," Henning said. "Apprehending three members of the Spectrum gang will be the icing on my retirement cake. Perhaps I shall take the American expedient of selling my memoirs."

Henning was, as Tasha had said repeatedly, a loathsome egomaniac. And yet, David was relieved. At least the police would be alerted and involved in their sting. "Let's get down to details, Inspector. How are we going to arrest the gang?"

"Simple. We allow them to break into the vault. They fill their pockets. Tasha opens the safe and—"

"I can't do it," Tasha mumbled.

"I beg your pardon?"

"You heard me, Henning." Her gaze was pure venom. "I was inside the vault today, and I took a good look at the safe where Janet is keeping the rubies. There is no way I'll be able to get that thing opened. Even when I was working with the magic act, a five-number combination would have been tough. But now? I haven't done safe-cracking in ten years. I doubt that I could pop a pair of handcuffs."

"Then I suggest you begin practicing," Henning said. "I want to arrest these people with the evidence in their hands."

"I have a better idea," David offered. "We can tell Janet Pola about the sting and get the combination from her."

"No," Tasha said. "Janet would be hysterical. The fewer people who know, the better."

"I find myself in agreement with Miss Lancer," Henning said. "I will inform the guards and one other police officer at the last possible moment. I will not have anyone else botching up my operation."

"What about the combination?" David asked. "You could get it for Tasha."

"And I shall. Obviously, she must be able to open the safe. I want them to be holding the loot when they are arrested."

"That's the part I want to hear about," David said. "How are you going to arrest them?"

"As they emerge from the vault."

"No good." David shook his head. This was the part to the sting that had been bothering him. "Tasha has to go into the vault with them, and she'll be with them when they come out. If Green thinks they've been betrayed, he could turn around and kill her in an instant. Or use her as a hostage."

"And wouldn't that be a shame," Henning said. "I'm afraid that Miss Lancer will need to figure out her own escape. Exit first and flee."

Though that solution was unsatisfactory, David had no alternative idea. "And what about the guards? Green and Spectrum are famous for leaving no witnesses."

"The guards will be alerted, well-armed and wearing bulletproof vests. At the last moment, I shall instruct them not to interfere with the robbery in progress."

David was painfully aware of everything that could go wrong. Green might be planning to shoot the guards as a precaution. Brown might have arranged for explosives. Cerise might be standing outside the vault as a lookout. There were dozens of variables, and each one put Tasha in danger.

"In the meantime..." Henning stood and plucked the bug from the desktop. "I shall be removing my device. Various members of Spectrum will be using your shop for the next few days, and one of them might actually be clever enough to search for bugs. We don't wish to tip them off, do we?"

As he approached the office door, David said, "One last thing, Inspector. We will want a written pardon from you regarding Tasha's part in this caper."

"That she's working with the police for a change? Certainly."

"I mean it," David said. "I won't let her go into the vault without it."

Henning looked David in the eye. "Don't tell me my job, sonny boy. I was apprehending jewel thieves when you were playing cops and robbers with your school-mates. I know what I am doing. Right now, I am running this show.''

On that arrogant note, he left them.

David went to Tasha. He rested his hand on her shoulders. "I'm sorry. I should have looked for bugs."

"It's not your fault." Her voice sounded defeated. "And, actually, you were right. We really did need to inform someone in the police. If only it weren't Henning."

"Maybe it's not so bad. Henning does have experience with jewel heists."

"Oh, David." She rose from her chair and came into his arms. Protectively, he held her. She was so small. Her bones were so delicate. "I'm scared. I'm scared for me and for you and for Mandy. You don't really think Green would go after her, do you?"

"Who knows what he might do?" David wished he could offer reassurance. "It might be best if she stays somewhere safe for the next few days."

"If she gets back to her mother's house without Green following, I can't think of any way he could trace her. Mandy's last name and her mother's aren't the same. And it's way out in the suburbs. She ought to be safe there. I'll warn her not to come to the shop."

"I'll ride home with her now," David said. "To make sure she's not followed."

"If he touches Ruby, I swear I'll kill him with my bare hands."

As anger sparked within her, Tasha felt a bit of strength returning to her body. Though she would have wished for anyone other than Henning to be their confidant within the police department, the choice had been taken from her hands. She had to make the best of it. There was no time for wringing her hands and bemoaning her fate. For the next two days, she needed to exercise the wiles she'd learned as a headstrong adolescent and the wisdom that came with maturity.

Leaning back her head, she gazed into David's eyes. "I can do this. We'll make it, David."

The telephone on Tasha's desk rang and she answered, "Bloom's Flowers. Tasha Lancer speaking."

"Cerise here. Inspector Henning paid you a visit."

"He suspects me," Tasha said, suppressing the twitch of fear that came from speaking to a member of Spectrum. "He was warning me not to try anything. The toad! He keeps talking about SoHo. And Miami."

"What happened in Miami?"

"A team operation with my sister," Tasha said. "Emeralds. A tiara and earrings."

"Oh, yes. I believe I heard something about that. Your mother was involved."

Another warning bell trilled in Tasha's head. "You know my mother?"

"Everyone's heard of Martina and her legendary jewel collection. She's never had a piece stolen, and she always gets top dollar when she sells." Cerise lowered her voice. "For a time, I thought she was Black."

"My mother?" Aghast, Tasha stared at the queenly visage in the family photo. Martina? The leader of an international gang of jewel thieves? "She's retired."

"And living in Vail," Cerise concluded. "Be careful of Henning. I think he's up to something."

Tasha hung up the telephone. It seemed as if Spectrum had spread a web that was tangled in every part of her life. Everything she loved, everything she cared about, was touched. Her family. Her friends. Her livelihood.

After the sting, she wasn't sure she could continue in this location. Her history, as a suspected jewel thief, would be common knowledge. Henning would make sure of that. He would paint her in the darkest colors.

She would be ruined.

"Tasha?"

She looked to David. They had only known each other for a few days, yet it seemed he was the single individual who knew her better than anyone. "Yes, David."

"I'll take Mandy home. At the same time, I want you to go to your apartment. Pack for two days. At nine o'clock tonight, when you close the store, I'll pick you up in a dark sedan with tinted windows. We'll go somewhere safe."

"You're not going to quit being Wally Beamis, are you?" She wanted him here in the shop with her tomorrow.

"Do you have a thing for Wally?"

A chuckle caught in the back of her throat. Desperately, she wished she could laugh out loud, to release the constricting tension. "Maybe I like Wally a lot."

"Then I'll be Wally. And David, too." He pulled her against his body. "I'll be anyone or anything you want me to be, Tasha. We'll get through this."

She drew warmth from him. And hope. As long as there was hope, she might survive.

THAT NIGHT, in their hotel room, Tasha unpacked carefully. She'd brought her sexy blue peignoir, but that wasn't the first thing she removed from her suitcase.

"What's that?" David asked as she pulled out a square wooden container that was slightly larger than a shoe box.

"My bag of tricks," she said.

She flipped the lid of the box back on its hinges. To some people, the objects contained within might have seemed sinister, but Tasha picked fondly through the selection of padlocks, combination locks, handcuffs, ropes and chains.

"I used this stuff for escapes when I was a magician's assistant." She held up a pair of cuffs. "I won these from a cop on a bet."

"Nice," David said.

"And this." She ran a short piece of heavy-duty chain through her fingers. "This is part of the chain that I wrapped around myself before I was locked in a box and suspended from the ceiling."

"Was there anything in your early life that resembled normality?"

On the dresser, she spread out a collection of combination and key-in padlocks from various manufacturers. She picked one up and felt the solid weight in her hand. "This is a Citadel. An excellent lock. It almost killed my sister when she was doing an underwater escape and dropped the key."

"But she had a key," David said. He was unpacking his own suitcase, hanging suits in the closet and filing underwear in the drawers of the dresser. "You two girls didn't really pick all these locks, you palmed the keys or used tricks to escape."

"Now I'm offended." She gave him a mock glare. "Mostly, our escapes were real. We'd ask people from the audience to provide the locks."

"Plants," he said. "People who were working with you."

"Sometimes, but not always. The trick to magic is convincing people it's true, getting them to suspend their skepticism."

"And how would you do that?"

"We'd have someone from the audience who had a reputation for being truthful and honest bring up a lock, and we would actually work it open on stage. Stacey and I used to practice with the stuff I have in this box. Late at night, we'd hang out in our hotel room, talking and practicing for hours and hours. We were good, David, very good. The magician we worked with said we had natural talent." She flexed her hands. "Ultrasensitive fingers."

When David unfastened the holster from his shin and checked his automatic pistol, she looked away. Tasha didn't want to be reminded of the real danger that existed. It was far more comforting to think of the sting as a magic trick, an illusion that would end with a puff of smoke.

She took a pack of playing cards from the box. Thumbing through them to get the feel, she showed off by shuffling in a cascade, flipping the cards, one after the other. She fanned the deck in front of David. "Pick one, memorize it, stick it back in the deck."

After he'd done as instructed, she shuffled again and set the deck before David on the dresser. "Cut three times."

She scooped up the cards. She fanned again with both hands. One card poked out, and Tasha flipped it faceup.

"Queen of diamonds. That's the one you picked."

"Very good." David applauded. "I've always wondered. How does that trick work?"

"A real magician never tells."

She grabbed several locks and a tiny pick no larger than an unbent paper clip. Pacing in the hotel room, she manipulated the padlock open with a satisfying, metallic click. "Do you think the sting will work, David?"

"It better."

He removed a small, flat derringer from his trouser pocket, and Tasha turned away, sitting on the bed with another lock in her hands. "Our plan seems much too casual to me. Just go through the motions, and Henning will arrest Spectrum on the other side. You know that Green is going to be armed."

"And dangerous," David said.

"What if he decides to kill the guards before we break inside the vault?"

"I guess they fall down and pretend they're dead. If they're lucky enough to be shot in the bulletproof vest."

She yanked open the padlock. Working these devices had a calming effect on Tasha. "What if one person in the gang stays outside as a guard? They'll notice Henning moving in, and they'll alert the others."

"Then you're stuck inside, and you'll have to do some fast talking to convince them you're not involved," David said. "But you're right, Tasha. I don't like the setup. It's dangerous."

"On the other hand," she said, picking up a combination lock and working the dial without looking at it, "I can't think of anything else to do. Henning can't arrest them now. They haven't done anything."

"And the chances of conviction are much better if they have the evidence."

She concentrated for a moment, feeling the internal mechanism of the lock. The tumblers fell into place, and she eased it open.

Slack-jawed, David stared at the combination lock. "How did you do that? You didn't even look at the numbers."

"I could feel it," she said. "There's an infinitesimal pause when the right number is reached. It's as if the lock remembers the combination from having used it so many times. Of course, I'm familiar with these locks and they're not terribly complex. The safe in Pola and Tweed is an entirely different matter. Without the combination, it might take me an hour to get it open."

"Why wouldn't Brown cut through with a torch?"

She shrugged. "There must be something about the construction of the safe. Sometimes, safe manufacturers use copper along with the steel walls because copper is a quick conductor and can react with an alarm before the lock is open. There might be a manual trigger that can't be disarmed via computer. A microwave sensor. Something like that."

"Did you ever do one of those escapes when you were locked in a safe?"

"Child's play," she said dismissively. "On the interior of a safe, the locking mechanism is right there in front of you. It's easy to break out."

"Harder to break in."

"But I used to do it handcuffed." Tasha snapped the cuffs onto her slender wrists. In seconds, she had picked the lock. She stood before him. With a flourish she pulled the cuffs apart. "Ta-da! Nothing to it."

"Let me try," David said.

"You want me to lock you in cuffs?"

"No, Tasha." He caught her wrists in his hands and held them above her head. In one step, he backed her up against the wall. "I want to try to pin you down so you can't get away. Can you get out of this?"

She gazed into his warm gray eyes. "What makes you think I want to escape?"

He kissed her lips, probing with his tongue, slowly tasting the sweetness of her mouth. Though David couldn't believe their lovemaking would surpass last night, he had eagerly been anticipating his moment when they would join together once again.

Still holding her hands, he nuzzled her throat, nibbled at her earlobe. Her moan of excitement aroused him.

When he released her hands so he could touch her breasts, he found the nipples were already hard, needing him as much as he needed her.

He carried her to the bed and made love to her, finding the most exquisite pleasure in her arms and her willing acceptance of his passion. She was more bold tonight, even more sensual.

David found himself being drawn to her in a way he'd never felt before. He was tied to her with an invisible but unbreakable bond. And he did not want to leave her. Not ever.

THE MORNING CAME too soon, and they had not figured out any sort of magical plan for turning the odds to their advantage. David hated to think of the danger. He lay in the bed beside her, holding her hand and staring up at the bland fixture in the hotel room ceiling. "Tomorrow," he said. "We need to come up with something by tomorrow."

"We could run away," she said. "We could go to the airport and take off for a distant island where we would never be found."

"And how would we live on this island?"

"We'd pick coconuts and mangoes and make our clothing of palm fronds. Like Robinson Crusoe."

"Supposing that such a place existed," he said, turning his head toward her, "I somehow can't believe a sophisticated woman like you would be happy with the life of a noble savage."

"You're probably right," she said, looking back at him with her mysterious dark eyes. "It would only be a matter of time before I started making jewelry from conch shells."

"Organizing the natives."

"Opening a coconut store."

"But it's a nice fantasy," he said. David leaned over to kiss the tip of her nose. "Being with you forever would be like a dream come to life."

Her lips quirked in a grin. "Forever is only about ten more days, David. Then you're done with this assignment."

He didn't have to go back to New York. As far as he knew, there were no assignments pending. "I could stay longer. I have vacation time."

"That won't work," she said wistfully. "No, it's better if you leave when you intended. That's what I'm expecting, and I don't want to say goodbye more than once."

"Do you want me to stay?"

"With all my heart." She lightly kissed him. "But first, we need to concentrate on getting through the next few days."

Tasha left the bed and went into the bathroom. While David lay thinking, directing his mind down one false corridor after another, trying to find a solution, she got ready for work.

All dressed and groomed, she stood beside the bed. "I'll see you in the shop."

"No, you'll see Wally Beamis. Dammit, I feel so impotent."

She caressed his cheek and lovingly kissed his lips. "After last night, David, I promise that's not a realistic concern."

At Bloom's, Tasha had just completed her morning chores when she saw Mr. Brown approaching the front door, and she hurried to open it for him.

He brushed past her. "I will be in your office."

"Was the videotape okay?"

"Very good. We will cut through the refrigerated cabinet where you store your flowers."

She trailed after him. "When will you start?"

Over his shoulder, he said, "When it is time."

"I had an idea," she said.

"What?"

Brown turned at the door to her office and glared down at her. His abruptness startled her, and she retreated a few paces. "I thought," Tasha said, "that I would have my assistant, Wally, do some construction work in the back. He's terribly clumsy, and I'm sure he'll make enough noise to divert attention from anything you're doing."

"Fine." Brown entered her office and closed the door.

Tasha moved to the front counter, wishing there was something she could do, some kind of mindless task that would occupy her hands and keep her from thinking too deeply about what would happen tomorrow.

Last night, she'd completed the arrangement for the Natural History Museum and had pulled all the flowers they would need. It was too early to begin preparations for the weekend wedding.

At ten o'clock, David arrived in his Wally Beamis disguise. She gave him instructions for building another worktable. Having him close by was an awful temptation. But having him gone would be far worse.

Brown left the shop at noon, and she huddled with David. "I have no idea what he's doing in there. Should I take a look?"

"Don't risk it, Tasha. Brown is probably setting up computer stuff that neither you nor I would understand, arranging for the final disarming of the alarm system next door."

"I could mess something up," she said. "I'd pretend it was an accident, that I spilled a glass of water."

"He'd fix it." David caught hold of her arm. "Don't get in their way. Don't let them think you're not on their side. We have to trust that Henning will take care of his end."

"David, this is driving me crazy. I can't take another whole day of waiting. How are we going to get out of this? Have you come up with anything?"

"Let's try Henning. Maybe he's got a plan." David went to the phone at the front desk and punched in a number. "Inspector? We need to talk. Tonight."

He passed the phone to Tasha. She heard the smug, accented tones of Henning's voice say, "I have the combination for you."

He recited five numbers, and she repeated them back to him.

"Don't write them down," Henning warned.

"I don't need to." These were the numbers that might save her life. She would remember.

"Tell your boyfriend that we can meet tonight at eight o'clock. My hotel."

Tasha hung up the phone. "Do we have to meet with him, David? Can't we figure out something on our own?"

"Henning's a part of this. We have no choice."

He returned to his task, and she sat at the front counter, mentally repeating the five numbers that would open the Jezebel safe in Pola and Tweed. What if Henning lied to her? What if he'd given her the wrong combination?

He wouldn't do that. He wanted to catch Spectrum in the act, with the rubies in their hands. Apprehending this gang would be the crowning achievement of his career.

At half past three in the afternoon, Brown returned with Green. The two men were so intent upon their work that they barely glanced at Tasha before entering the refrigerated unit.

She stood in the doorway and watched as Brown took precise measurements. With the point of a Swiss Army knife, he scratched a rectangular outline into the stainless steel surface of the unit. The top edge was only four feet high. "Here is where I make the cut."

"Make it taller," Green said. "I'll have to bend almost in half to get through there."

"A little discomfort, Mr. Green, is to be expected."

"If there's trouble, I need to get out fast. I can't be crawling around if I need to take aim."

"No higher," Brown said. "The floors are uneven. We will step down sixteen centimeters."

"Make it taller," Green repeated.

Muttering to himself in Russian, Brown refigured his calculations and marked about eight inches higher.

As Brown lifted the thermal lance, Green turned toward her. "Go back out front. Make sure nobody gets suspicious."

"Won't the cutting set off alarms next door?"

"Not right now," Brown said. "The motion- and heat-sensing equipment is off while there are customers in the store."

"Are you cutting all the way through?"

"No, I will go through the stainless steel of your refrigerator, then through twelve centimeters of concrete.

I will leave the steel and copper shell of the safe wall." He shrugged. "Tomorrow night, I can cut through that in eleven minutes. If our penetration goes undetected, this entryway will be concealed behind one of the metal cabinets." He glared at Green. "If it's not too tall to be a visible hole."

"Get out," Green ordered her. "Close the door to this unit."

Tasha obeyed. Brown seemed to have a frighteningly thorough grasp of his high-technology equipment and his centimeter measurements. How had he obtained such complete blueprints of both shops? Her videotape from yesterday wouldn't have showed that. How did he know?

She tiptoed toward her office and silently opened the door. A portable computer sat in the middle of her desk. An array of other electronic equipment was displayed neatly inside a metal toolbox. The only object that looked vaguely familiar was a clock face, permanently set at 7:35.

Glancing toward the rear of her shop, she wished she could talk with David. Her instincts told her that something about the caper wasn't going as planned.

It was five o'clock in the afternoon, one hour before closing time, when Green and Brown emerged from the refrigerated unit.

"Is it done?" Tasha asked.

Saying nothing, they went into her office and closed the door.

"A little rude," Tasha muttered, "But what could I expect from a psychopath and a skeleton?"

Just before closing, the volunteer people from the museum came in, and David helped them load the flowers in two minivans.

While he was in the rear of the store, Tasha looked up and saw Cerise. She was dressed in a close-fitting black outfit with a red belt.

"And how are you today, Miss Lancer?"

"I'd be a lot better if somebody would tell me what was going on. Brown and Green are stalking around here in total silence, digging their little holes in the wall."

"The boys are like that," she confided. "Their endless bickering is so annoying."

Tasha nodded. "Yes, it is."

"When this job is done, I think I'll vacation in Paris where I can shop."

"Sounds lovely."

"And you? Where will you be going?"

Tasha thought of her fantasies with David. "An island," she said. "Micronesia, where the sea is blue and pure. And the sun is warm."

"Do you dive?"

"No, but I plan to learn how." With David beside her. Quite easily, she imagined the warmth of the sun, the pleasure of spreading lotion across David's broad shoulders. "I'll live on coconuts and mangoes."

As David stumbled into the front of the shop, Tasha introduced him to this sleek woman in her black outfit. His manner was suitably Wally Beamis—tongue-tied and clumsy.

Tasha glanced at her wristwatch. "Well, I guess it's time to lock up." She glanced toward Cerise. "Yes?"

"Proceed with your usual routine. Don't mind me."

Tasha fastened the front door locks, then they walked toward the rear of the store.

David said, "Guess I'll be going now, ma'am. Unless you need anything else."

"You can leave," she said.

"I think not." Cerise had taken a pistol from her purse and trained it upon David. "Don't move."

"What are you doing?" Tasha said. "This doesn't have anything to do with him."

"Lock the back door, Miss Lancer. Now." Cerise grasped her arm and marched her toward the rear exit.

Tasha felt the muzzle of the loaded gun being held at her chin. Her fingers trembled as she worked the locks.

"There's been a change in plans," Cerise said. "We're breaking in tonight."

Chapter Twelve

Adrenaline sped through David's veins. His heart beat fast. After all this waiting, finally, finally, he could take action.

But there was nothing he could do. Cerise held a gun at Tasha's jaw. There was no way to disarm her.

"You might as well stand up straight," Cerise said to him. "And take out those ridiculous teeth. I know who you are, David Marquis. A professional bodyguard. Right? Working for PEI, out of New York. Right?"

After a long day of stooping and hunching and shuffling helplessly, it was almost a relief to shed his Wally Beamis disguise. David removed the dental appliance and wiggled his jaw from side to side. "How did you know?"

"I have my sources. Put your hands behind your head."

He did as she ordered. The first rule to survival was: Don't argue with a woman holding a gun. But David did not lace his fingers; he held his hands loosely, ready for action. If he could distract Cerise, he might be able to fight back. There were carpentry tools on the bench. An automatic pistol in his shin holster. A derringer in his pocket.

But Cerise had hold of Tasha. The gun dug into the soft white flesh at her throat. The frightened look in his lover's eyes hurt more than death.

In a low voice, David said, "Listen, Cerise, we can work something out. A payoff."

"Like hell." She shouted, "Green! Get out here."

Mr. Green came out of the office like a Brahma bull charging from the chute at a rodeo. In an instant, he comprehended the situation. "Her little assistant was a ringer, eh? A cop?"

"My boyfriend," Tasha said. "I was scared of you, Green, and I wanted him here to help me."

Coolly, the big man eyed David. "You're not very good at protecting her, are you?"

"What would you know about protection?"

"I know a lot about Miss Lancer. I was in her bed. Wasn't I, sweetheart?"

"You snuck into my apartment!"

"She wasn't much good." Green sneered. "Too skinny."

Bastard. Never before had David wanted to kill another human being. But Green didn't deserve the gift of life.

"That's enough," Cerise said. "We have to do the heist tonight, Green. These two were setting up a double-cross for tomorrow."

"And keep the jewels for themselves?"

"Nothing so smart as that," Cerise said. "They planned to turn us in to Henning."

"Henning?" Green scoffed.

"Miss Lancer isn't a cat burglar," Cerise said derisively. "Just a shopkeeper, after all. This woman isn't Stacey. She really is the other twin, Natasha. The hardworking, responsible twin."

"Should I kill them?" Green's voice was calm and casual, as if he were asking about swatting a fly.

"Not yet. Disarm the man." She reminded David, "And don't try any heroics, David. I have a gun to your sweetheart's head."

"You can't kill me," Tasha said. "I'm the only one who can open that safe."

Green had his gun out. A .357 Magnum. "Why don't I just kill this guy and have it over with?"

"No," Tasha whispered.

Her voice was low and intense. In her eyes, David saw the most heart-wrenching terror. It was as if he could peer straight through to her soul, to the darkest despair.

Cerise chuckled. "Don't kill him, Green. He'll be useful in convincing her to cooperate."

Green stepped closer, almost within David's striking range. The .357 was aimed at his gut, but David visualized his attack. A dive at Green's legs. Get him down.

David balanced his weight on the balls of his feet, prepared to spring. If he could knock Green off his feet, he might have time to reach the derringer in his pocket. He could pull off one shot. Maybe two.

Cerise wouldn't kill Tasha. She needed Tasha to open the safe. Green was the problem. David poised to leap. Eliminate Green and the rest would fall into place.

David heard the explosion of the gun before he felt the pain in his upper thigh.

Tasha screamed.

Green was on top of him. He flipped David onto his stomach as if he weighed no more than a child. David felt his arms being jerked behind his back. His wrists were cuffed. Efficiently, Green pulled the automatic from the holster above his right ankle. Then he stepped back.

"Get up," Green snarled. "It's only a flesh wound."

But David's thigh hurt like hell, like a thousand stinging hornets. He felt the hot blood seeping through his pant leg. He gritted his teeth, willing the pain to recede.

"I told you to get up." Green kicked his ribs, setting off another burst of pain. "Be glad that bullet wasn't a few inches to the left or you could have kissed your manhood goodbye."

Forcing himself not to cry out, David floundered to a sitting position on the floor. He tried to give Tasha a sign that he was all right. A wink. A smile. But David's entire being concentrated on self-control, keeping his senses intact, not giving up. Dammit, he wouldn't give up or give in.

Brown came out of the office. "What are you doing?"

"Change in plans," Cerise said. "We do the heist tonight. Are you ready?"

He let loose with a stream of Russian. It didn't take a translator to know that Brown was angry.

"Stop that," Cerise said. "This is not a big deal."

"You know nothing of my plans and preparations. The timer was set for 7:35. Tomorrow night."

"Well, change it."

Brown glanced toward the windows. "It's not even dark yet. There are still people on the street."

"Do it!" Cerise ordered. "You have twenty minutes."

"Everything was set for tomorrow."

"I've had enough of your whining." Green loomed over the scrawny Russian. "If we wait until tomorrow, we're caught. It has to be tonight."

Mumbling to himself, Brown returned to the office.

Twenty minutes, David thought. He had to make something happen in twenty minutes. He looked down at his leg. A circle of blood stained his trousers. He could feel the pulsing, draining the life from him, but there were no broken bones. He could still move his legs. He had mobility. And he still had the derringer in his pocket.

Brown called out, "Green, I need you."

"Go ahead," Cerise said. "These two won't cause me any problem."

David swallowed hard. He fought a vague dizziness in the back of his head and willed himself to ignore the pain from his wound. He had only twenty minutes to save Tasha and himself. Striving for a conversational tone, he asked, "How did you find out, Cerise?"

"Maybe I'm psychic."

She directed Tasha to a high stool and ordered her to sit. The gun was still trained on Tasha's head, but restraint was unnecessary. All the fight had gone out of Tasha. Her movements were weak. Her eyes were dull. She had been literally frightened into shock.

David had to find a way to reach her, to engage her survival instinct. They could get out of this. They had to. He hadn't gone his whole life looking for the right woman only to have her snatched from him.

But how? How could he tear her from this fear-filled stupor? Her anger, David thought. Tasha was quick to flare. If he could make her mad, she'd be back in the game.

"Tasha," he said, "are you okay?"

Cerise drew back her free hand and slapped. Tasha's head snapped. Her eyes closed.

"Don't talk to her," Cerise ordered. "Every word you speak to her will cause pain."

"Can I talk to you?"

She considered for a moment. "Yes. We have twenty minutes. It might be amusing."

David blinked, forcing back the pain. Then he made a wild guess. "You got your information from Black, didn't you?"

"How clever of you to figure that out." She gestured casually with her gun. "I sometimes resent paying five percent of every job, but Black's information is impeccable. From obtaining blueprints to advising on personnel, Black is invaluable."

"But wrong about a couple of things," David said.

"What?"

"The woman sitting beside you isn't Natasha. She's Anastasia Lancer. Stacey." He noticed a glimmer in Tasha's eyes. "Just as she told you. She assumed Tasha's identity to set up this shop as a front."

"No," Cerise said simply. "This is Tasha."

"Think about it, Cerise." The pain in his leg had settled to a dull throb. He hoped he wasn't losing too much blood. "That's how they pulled off their early scams. They set up alibis by pretending to be each other."

"It really doesn't matter which twin she is. Tasha or Stacey, whatever. This little witch was planning a double-cross."

"A double double-cross," David said. He flung his words at Tasha, goading her, seeking a response from her. "She planned to trick me, too. And Henning. She can't be trusted."

Tasha looked up sharply.

Good, David thought. She was beginning to react. He pressed deeper. "She's been lying to me from the minute we met. And she's a damn good liar."

"You're absolutely correct," Cerise said. "I remember when we were talking in the bathroom. She knew my real name. No one knows. No one, except for Stacey."

The color had returned to Tasha's cheeks. Now, David thought, he needed to signal her, to let her know there was a derringer in his pocket. But how? His hands were cuffed behind his back. He couldn't speak to Tasha directly.

"Stacey's smart," he said. "She remembers everything. Names. Places. And jewelry. She's good at remembering every detail about precious stones—" he looked directly at Tasha "—and metals."

"So am I." Cerise laughed brightly. "I can't tell you a person's name, but I can give a detailed account of who manufactured their wristwatch and jewelry."

Distracted and more than a little hazy, David stared for a long second at this woman who always wore a bit of red. She was carrying on a conversation in the tones of someone at a cocktail party. She didn't appear to be affected by the fact that his leg was bleeding or that she held a lethal weapon in her manicured hand.

Contrasting this coldness was Tasha, whose face held so many emotions. Anger, passion, fierce concern and puzzlement. He tried again to give her a hint. "You know, Cerise, I'll bet you could ask Stacey the contents of my wallet or my pockets and she could tell you every single thing."

"Who cares? I doubt that you have more than a hundred dollars in your pockets. Awfully dull."

"Ask her," David said. "Ask the liar what I have in my pockets."

"Shut up, David." Tasha turned to Cerise. "You really don't need to hold the gun on me. I'm not going anywhere."

"I'm not a fool."

"Nor am I."

She felt the danger all around her, squeezing the life from her. Yet, she was alert. And angry. Why was David talking about his pockets? Why had he called her a liar?

"I knew everything she was going to do," David said. "I knew she was Stacey because she drove so recklessly."

What was he talking about? Why was he saying those things?

"And," he said, "she was too fond of my guns."

His guns? She hated his guns. The shoulder holster. The shin holster. The derringer.

Suddenly, she knew what David was doing. He was giving her a clue. He still had the derringer. Green had taken the automatic pistol from this shin holster. But he hadn't gotten the derringer.

She needed to get close to him. She needed to distract Cerise. "I'll make you an offer, Cerise. After I open the safe and liberate those fabulous rubies, you and I can make a getaway together. I already have a fence. You'll make five times the profit."

"And how will I spend this fortune after Green kills me?"

"Shoot him first. Really, Cerise. Green's the one you want to kill. Not me. I have plans after this." She lowered her voice. "The Kimberly Diamond. You and I can work the heist together. A two-way split. I appeal to your greed, sister."

Cerise licked her lips, and Tasha knew she'd struck a chord. She continued in a whisper, "After we break through, kill him."

Green strode past them and went to the front window. "The security next door is shut down."

"Anyone coming? Any sign?"

"It's quiet," Green said. "A few people on the street. That's all. No guards."

"Excellent," Cerise said. "Are you ready for the final cut into the vault?"

"Brown's doing it right now. He'll be done in a minute." Roughly, he grabbed Tasha's arm. "Now it's your turn. Let's see if you're as good as they say."

"Don't bruise me," she snapped. "I need to be able to concentrate on the safe, not worry about a hurt arm."

When she met his gaze, she saw a wealth of hatred, but Tasha was certain that Green's dislike could never equal the pure loathing she felt for him. He'd shot David, the only man she could ever love.

Green released her. "I won't touch you, Miss Lancer. I'll use him."

He went to David and aimed a sharp kick at the bleeding wound on his thigh. "Get up."

David didn't cry out, but his jaw clenched. His eyes hardened in a squint.

Tasha wanted to run to him, to comfort him and hold him. But she had to be smart, to figure out a way to escape.

Together, they moved into the refrigerated unit. With dismay, Tasha noted the destruction. Heavy chunks of concrete were scattered on the floor. The stainless steel had been cut in perfectly square chunks. The heavier surface of the vault wall was piled in larger pieces.

The entryway into Pola and Tweed was nearly two feet thick. On the other side, the way was blocked.

Despite the chill in the cooler, Brown had stripped down to his shirtsleeves. His arms were so skinny that every vein and tendon stood out in sharp relief against his pasty white skin. "Green," he said in a whisper, "you must push the metal cabinet on the other side. Be careful not to tip it over.''

"No problem.''

"It's heavy,'' Brown cautioned. "Over two hundred pounds.''

"I said it would be no problem.''

The big man wedged himself into the space between the walls. The muscles in his back strained. He made grunting noises like an animal. He backed out. "Dammit, Brown. I told you there wasn't enough room.''

"You told me you could—''

"I'll do it.''

He wedged sideways and pushed. Tasha saw a sliver of light on the other side.

Green shoved with all his might. The sliver widened.

Another effort and the case was moved.

Green climbed back out. "The rest of you go first. I'll bring up the rear.''

Tasha was sandwiched between Cerise and Brown. She stepped down into the vault. Then Brown. Then came David. When he lowered himself on his injured leg, he winced with pain. *Oh, David, how are we going to get out of here?* Even if she could reach the derringer, she was no match for Spectrum.

Yesterday, when she was inside the vault, the fifteen-by-eight size seemed large. Now, with five people, it was crowded.

Cerise whispered instructions. "Brown and Green, empty the cabinets into your bags. Stacey, there's the safe.''

Tasha nodded. It didn't escape her attention that Cerise had called her Stacey. If Cerise believed it, if she were greedy enough to join in partnership, she might kill Green.

Tasha knelt in front of the safe.

Brown squatted directly behind her. In Russian, he said, "Jezebel is a difficult safe. Underwriter's Laboratories rates it TRTL-60X, the most difficult to break through."

"I can open it," she said.

She glanced over her shoulder. Cerise and Green had set their weapons aside. Carefully, they lifted case after case of jewelry into large canvas satchels. Now would be the perfect time to attack, but David sat slumped against the far wall. His eyes were closed.

Still whispering in Russian, Brown continued, "I am an undercover agent. I will help you and your friend to escape. First, we leave the vault. Then I help you."

"Brown! Stop yakking," Cerise snarled. "Load your bag."

"I want to see her open the safe."

Tasha inhaled deeply. She willed the trembling in her hands to stop. Brown was on their side. He would help them. That was why he had no record with Interpol. He was an undercover cop.

She wished she could communicate with David and inform him that they were almost home free. But she needed to concentrate on the safe. When she placed her sensitive fingertips on the cool metal, she felt the secrets of the lock. Though she knew the combination from the numbers that Henning had given her, she approached Jezebel with respect.

The dial twisted stubbornly in her fingers and she turned clockwise, then counter, then clockwise again. When she touched the last number, nineteen, there was no click. It didn't feel right.

She grasped the handle. It wouldn't turn. Something was wrong! Henning had not given her the correct combination. Or perhaps she hadn't remembered the right numbers.

Spinning the dial, she tried the combination again.

"I knew she couldn't do it," Green said. "Get the thermal lance. We'll have to cut through."

"Wait," Tasha said. "Give me one more try."

She closed her eyes. Lightly she turned to the first number Henning had given her. She felt the tiniest resistance. That number was correct. The second, third and fourth were also exact. The problem was the last digit.

Easing past the nineteen, every fiber of her being focused on her sense of touch. Twenty. Twenty-one. Twenty-two. At twenty-nine, she felt the click. In her mind, she could see the lock opening.

She gripped the brass handle and turned. Stiffly, it turned in her hand. The safe was open.

Tension flowed from her, and she reached inside, grasping a black velvet case. She lifted the lid, and her eyes beheld the red fire of rubies. She couldn't resist touching the necklace, holding the priceless treasure that had been stained by the blood of beautiful women.

A familiar voice cut through the silence in the vault. "How very skillful you are, Miss Lancer." A British accent and a Scotsman's burr. "What a remarkable talent!"

Inspector Henning stepped through the opening. He held a sawed-off shotgun in his hands. "Don't reach for your gun, Mr. Green. You'll be dead in an instant. Besides, I believe you'll be most interested in what I have to say."

"I'll never deal with—"

"Shut up, Green." He nodded to the others. "Hello, Cerise. You have done well. It's most gratifying to finally meet you in my true identity."

"What are you saying?" Cerise demanded.

"Come here, luv. Reach inside my outer suit coat pocket."

Cerise did as she was ordered, extracting a passport.

"Now read the name," Inspector Henning ordered.

"Charles Jacob Black." She gasped. "My God, you're Mr. Black."

"Indeed, I am. And you three are privileged to be in attendance at my swan song. This will be my last job as the leader of Spectrum. It's time for me to retire now. But I want the rubies to finance my old age."

"What about my share?" Green snarled.

"I daresay there's plenty to go around with what you have in those satchels. And it will only be a two-way split. Because one of you is a traitor."

He leveled the shotgun at Brown. "You've worked four jobs for me. Twice I've had to directly manipulate the evidence so you wouldn't be caught. I thought you were just sloppy, but it's something more. You want to be caught. You're a cop."

Henning unloaded both barrels of the shotgun. In the enclosed vault, the blast was deafening. Brown flew back against the wall. His blood spattered on Tasha.

"A terrible shame," said Henning. "He was a genius with computers and electronics."

"He got what he deserved," Cerise said coldly. "Will we split the rest?"

"You're not listening, dear. The rubies are mine. You and Green take what you have in the satchel. It's a good haul. Now, get out."

"I want my share of the rubies," Green said.

"Be glad I'm allowing you any portion at all. I shan't alert the police for another two hours. That should be sufficient time to make good your escape."

"But I want—"

"My finger grows tired on this trigger. Don't test me."

Henning stepped aside so they could leave. Then he turned his attention to Tasha. "You really are astonishing, Miss Lancer. I had thought you wouldn't be able to open the safe. That way, Green would have killed you and saved me the trouble."

"You don't want to kill me." Tasha rose from the floor. Playing for time, she fastened the Sheikh's Rubies around her throat, knowing the stones would dazzle him. "You've always been fond of me, Henning. Admit it."

"You know I can't leave witnesses. Are you trying to enchant me?"

"Like Aziza and the sheikh," she purred.

"What a liar you are!"

"I'm the most honest of women. I'm willing to admit that I find wealthy men more attractive than bums. You're rich, Henning. And powerful."

Cruelly, Henning turned the gun on David who had wakened enough to force himself into a standing posture. "And what if I kill him first? Would you be so willing to come with me?"

"David?" Despite her racing heart, she kept her voice calm. "He means nothing to me. I was only using him to get at the rubies."

She sidled up behind David. Her movements were graceful as a dance. "Poor David. He cares for me a lot. Maybe he even loves me."

Peeking around him, she pretended to look up into his face. At the same time, she manipulated the latch on the handcuffs. She fumbled once. "If I really loved him, would I be hiding behind him? Would I let you shoot him first?"

David covered her actions with his own speech. "She's a liar and a thief, Henning."

"Precisely," he murmured. "That is what I find so intriguing about her."

Tasha unfastened the cuffs.

Gracefully, she slipped out from behind David and approached the inspector. "You're a powerful man, Henning. Wealthy as the sheikh. Let me be your best wife. Like Aziza. I promise to make you happy. And if I displease you, you may chop off my head."

"Quite tempting, luv. But I haven't come this far to be tricked by a woman."

Rudely, he pushed her away from him and she fell to the floor.

In the instant Henning took one hand off the shotgun, David reached into his trouser pocket.

Henning sensed the movement. He wheeled around.

But David was quicker. He fired three shots into Henning's face.

As soon as the inspector hit the floor, David shouted to her. "Get his gun."

Tasha moved fast.

From the other side of the wall, she saw Green coming through the small, chiseled entryway. His movements were cramped. He had to duck his head. She fired with the shotgun, and the recoil kicked her back against the wall.

She felt the world fading to darkness. The last thing she saw was David's face.

NINE DAYS LATER, Tasha wakened in her bed. For the past week and a half, since she and David had dismembered the Spectrum gang, her life had been an idyll.

After she'd fallen in the vault, she sustained a slight concussion, enough that she was in the hospital for two days while David dealt with the police and the guards from Pola and Tweed. Every word he said checked out, including the discovery of a multimillion-dollar Swiss bank account that Henning had left to his club in London.

Once she and David were in the clear, Janet Pola had paid for the workmen who repaired the refrigerated unit in Bloom's, and special order sales had been excellent. It seemed that there was nothing like a dose of notoriety to perk up business. Half of the people who ordered from Bloom's wanted to hear the story from her own lips.

Each time Tasha repeated the events, they faded, finally becoming more myth than reality. It was only at night that she occasionally dreamed of Brown, Green and Henning, all dead. They haunted her from the grave. When they crept up upon her, she turned to David in her sleep. His presence comforted her and protected her from the nightmares.

This morning, he sat at the edge of her bed with a mug of coffee. "You're awake," he said.

Lazily, she gazed into his gentle gray eyes. He was already showered and shaved and groomed to perfection in a white shirt and navy blue striped tie.

"Are you really this handsome?" she wondered. "Or is it me?"

"It's you," he said.

Though she wished their time together would never end, Tasha was well aware that today was the final day on his contract. They hadn't spoken about his leaving. Each time David mentioned the time slipping by, she shook her head and refused to listen.

Tasha knew that she loved him. She didn't want to face losing him.

"There's something we need to talk about," he said.

"Hush, David."

"Tasha, we can't avoid it any longer."

"I know what today is," she said. "I know what's going to happen. I just don't want to—"

The telephone on her bedside table rang, and she pounced on it, grateful for the interruption. "Hello?"

"Hi, sis."

Tasha pushed herself up on the bed. "Stacey? Is that you?"

"I'm the one who should be asking all the questions. I can't believe you single-handedly rounded up the most dangerous thieves in the world."

"Not single-handed."

"But it was Spectrum! I can't believe it. What happened to you? You were always the quiet one."

"Even a mouse can roar," Tasha said. "Where are you?"

"Rio," she said lightly. "I've been on a cruise with the most adorable man. That's why it took me so long to call."

"Do you remember when we did the magic act on a cruise ship to pay for our passage to Europe?"

"God, that was a long time ago. Seems like another lifetime."

"Yes," Tasha agreed. "It was."

"But tell me about you. I'd heard that Spectrum was planning a move on the Sheikh's Rubies."

"And, I'll bet, you also heard that they were working with you—the infamous Stacey Lancer."

"I'm sorry," she said without the tiniest hint of contrition. "Maybe I should have come out there to help you. But I just met this guy. Besides, I sent a body-guard."

"*You* hired the bodyguard?" Somehow, Tasha wasn't totally surprised.

"How did he work out?"

"Better than you would believe, Stacey."

"So? Tell me the whole thing."

Tasha sipped her coffee and recited her story while her sister was uncharacteristically silent. "And that's it. Henning was Mr. Black."

"I really and truly am sorry," Stacey said. "You've been through hell. Do you forgive me?"

Indulgently, Tasha replied, "How could I not? You're my twin. We were hatched from the same egg. But, Stacey, I worry about you."

"Don't. I'm having a wonderful life."

"When are you going to be in touch again?"

"It might be soon. I think this gentleman is going to propose marriage. And he's rich enough to support me in the manner to which I am accustomed."

"You're getting married?"

"It's not so hard to believe, is it? Your biological alarm clock must be going off, too."

Tasha looked up at David. It was strange that she and her twin sister had fallen in love at the same moment. Though worlds apart in terms of life-style, they really weren't all that different. "Let me know, Stacey, if you make a decision. I want to dance at your wedding."

"Bye, sis. Take care."

Tasha hung up the telephone. Her happiness for Stacey was bittersweet, tinged with her own sorrow that David was leaving. She took his hand and lifted it to her lips for a light kiss. "All right, David. I guess I can't put this off any longer. We should talk."

"You know that I love you, Tasha."

"Yes, I know." But love wouldn't stop him from leaving. She also knew that.

He dug into his trouser's pocket, wincing as he touched the bandage dressing on his thigh.

"Here," he said, placing a small, black velvet box into her hands.

Tasha gasped.

The three-carat, marquise-cut diamond from Pola and Tweed sparkled in a platinum setting. The gemstone caught and held the morning light, taking on a life of its own. "David, this is beautiful. But it's much too expensive."

"I can afford it. Don't get practical on me."

"All right. I won't." Tasha slipped the ring on her fourth finger, left hand. A perfect fit.

"Tasha, will you marry me?"

"And be your wife? And live with you forever and ever?" She stroked his cheek. The shimmer of her engagement ring paled in comparison to the brilliant love that shone from his eyes.

"Yes, David."

When they kissed, she experienced the most perfect moment of fulfillment. Finally, she'd gotten her just reward.

REBECCA

43 LIGHT STREET

YORK

FACE TO FACE

*Bestselling author Rebecca York returns to "43 Light Street"
for an original story of past secrets, deadly deceptions—and
the most intimate betrayal.*

She woke in a hospital—with amnesia...and with child.
According to her rescuer, whose striking face is the last
image she remembers, she's Justine Hollingsworth. But
nothing about her life seems to fit, except for the baby
inside her and Mike Lancer's arms around her. Consumed
by forbidden passion and racked by nameless fear, she
must discover if she is Justine...or the victim of some mind
game. Her life—and her unborn child's—depends on it....

Don't miss *Face To Face*—Available in October, wherever
Harlequin books are sold.

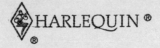

HARLEQUIN ®

®

43FTF

1997
Reader's Engagement Book
A calendar of important dates and anniversaries for readers to use!

Informative and entertaining—with notable dates and trivia highlighted throughout the year.

Handy, convenient, pocketbook size to help you keep track of your own personal important dates.

Added bonus—contains $5.00 worth of coupons for upcoming Harlequin and Silhouette books. This calendar more than pays for itself!

Available beginning in November at your favorite retail outlet.

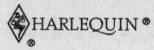

HARLEQUIN ®   **Silhouette**®

HARLEQUIN®

I N T R I G U E®

WANTED

12 SEXY LAWMEN

They're rugged, they're strong and they're WANTED!
Whether sheriff, undercover cop or officer of the court,
these men are trained to keep the peace, to uphold the
law...but what happens when they meet the one woman
who gets to know the real man behind the badge?

Twelve LAWMEN are on the loose—and only
Harlequin Intrigue has them! Meet them every
month for a new adventure.

David Torbel
#393 SWEET REVENGE
by Jenna Ryan
November 1996

LAWMAN:
There's nothing sexier than
the strong arms of the law!

The collection of the year!
NEW YORK TIMES BESTSELLING AUTHORS

Linda Lael Miller
Wild About Harry

Janet Dailey
Sweet Promise

Elizabeth Lowell
Reckless Love

Penny Jordan
Love's Choices

and featuring
Nora Roberts
The Calhoun Women

This special trade-size edition features four of the wildly
popular titles in the Calhoun miniseries together in
one volume—a true collector's item!

Pick up these great authors and a chance to win
a weekend for two in New York City at the
Marriott Marquis Hotel on Broadway! We'll pay
for your flight, your hotel—even a Broadway show!

Available in December at your favorite retail outlet.

NEW YORK
Marriott. ®
MARQUIS

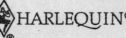

Merry Christmas, Baby!

A romantic collection filled with the magic
of Christmas and the joy of children.

SUSAN WIGGS, Karen Young and
Bobby Hutchinson bring you Christmas wishes,
weddings and romance, in a charming
trio of stories that will warm up your
holiday season.

MERRY CHRISTMAS, BABY! also contains
Harlequin's special gift to you—a set of
FREE GIFT TAGS included in every book.

Brighten up your holiday season with
MERRY CHRISTMAS, BABY!

Available in November at
your favorite retail store.

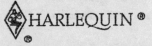

MCB